The Song of Montségur

The Song of Montségur

by
Sylvie Miller & Philippe Ward

translated by
Brian Stableford

A Black Coat Press Book

Visit our website at www.blackcoatpress.com

ISBN 978-1-935558-56-9. First Printing. September 2010. Published by Black Coat Press, an imprint of Hollywood Comics.com, LLC, P.O. Box 17270, Encino, CA 91416. All rights reserved. Except for review purposes, no part of this book may be reproduced or transmitted in any form or by any means, electronic or mechanical, including photocopying, recording or by any information storage and retrieval system, without permission in writing from the publisher. The stories and characters depicted in this book are entirely fictional. Printed in the United States of America.

Introduction

Philippe Ward is the nom-de-plume of Philippe La-guerre, born in 1958 in Bordeaux, who lives in the Ariège region of Southern France, in the foothills of the French Pyre-nees mountains, not far from the Cathar redoubt of Montségur and the medieval citadel of Carcassonne.

After contributing short stories to a number of French genre magazines and building a substantial reputation for his ability to tap into the darkest veins of French folklore, Philippe wrote his first novel, *Artahé*, which was published in 1997 and received considerable critical acclaim. He followed it up with *Ir-rintzina* (1998), a Bas-que horror thriller which won the coveted Graham Masterton Award in 2000 and the Ozone prize.

An expanded ver-sion of *Artahé* incorpo-rating Seabury Quinn's famous occult detective Jules de Grandin was translated into English by David Kirshbaum and published by Black Coat Press in 2004. An updated and expanded version of *Irrintzina* was released in 2009 under the new title of *Mascarades*.

In 2004, Philippe agreed to become the editor of Black Coat Press's French sister imprint, Rivière Blanche, which

SYLVIE MILLER & PHILIPPE WARD

NOIR DUO

RIVIERE BLANCHE

published two more of his genre novels, *La fontaine de jouvence* [The Fountain of Youth] (2004), a modern-day scifi thriller, the macabre *16, Rue du Repos* (2009), as well as an illustrated novella, *Confession d'un Vampire* [Confession of a Vampire] (2009) and *Noir Duo* (2007), a collection of earlier short stories written alone and in collaboration with Sylvie Miller. As the editor of Rivière Blanche, with over 100 titles to his credit, Philippe has won publishing awards for his skillful choice of novels by both older, established talent and young authors. Parallel to that, Philippe has also written two award-winning mystery novels taking place in the world of Occitan rugby, which is his other passion, *Meurtre à Aimé Giral* [Murder at Aimé Giral-Stadium] (2006) and *Dans l'Antre Des Dragons* [Inside the Dragons' Lair] (2008).

Sylvie Miller teaches law and economics in the Paris suburbs, and has a distinguished career writing academic books. She is also known as one of France's top translators, not only of English, but also Spanish-language science fiction and fantasy, for which she has twice won the Grand Prix de l'Imaginaire, in 2003 and 2010. Three of her anthologies, *Dimension Espagne*, *Dimension Latino* and *Interférences* (devoted to Cuban author Yoss) have been published by Rivière Blanche.

PHILIPPE WARD
ADAPTED BY
DAVID KIRSHBAUM

ARTAHE
THE LEGACY OF
JULES DE GRANDIN

INTERFERENCES
science-fiction cubaine

YOSS
traduit par
SYLVIE MILLER

RIVIERE BLANCHE

Sylvie met Philippe in 2000. Together, they have collaborated on several short stories, collected in *Noir Duo*, which have also won several awards, including the Graham Masterton and Merlin prizes.

The Song of Montségur, published in 2001 was their first novel. Montségur is best known today for its mountain-top fortified citadel, which was the last stronghold of the Cathars, a Christian sect considered as heretics by the Roman Catholic Church, and mostly exterminated during the Albigensian Crusade of the 13th century.

The fort of Montségur

In 1243, Montségur was besieged by 10,000 troops, and finally surrendered in March of the following year. Some 200 Cathars were burned at the stake, but legends tell that a few managed to escape before the end, carrying with them a mysterious "treasure." The nature, destination and even very existence of this treasure has never been ascertained, leaving room for much speculation, ranging from Parsifal's Holy Grail (the name Montségur being associated with that Montsalvat) to secret Church documents à la Dan Brown's *Da Vinci Code*.

The Nazis, of course, took great interest in the legends surrounding Montségur. German medievalist Otto Rahn traveled to the Pyrenées in 1931 where, aided by various French mystics and local historians such as Antonin Gadal, Maurice Magre and Déodat Roché, he sought (in vain) for the Grail, which he thought was hidden nearby. Rahn later wrote two books linking Montségur with the Holy Grail: *Kreuzzug gegen den Gral* [Crusade Against the Grail] (1933) and *Luzifers Hofgesind* [Lucifer's Court] (1937). After the publication of the first work, he came to the attention of the occultist Karl Maria Wiligut and Heinrich Himmler, who brought him into the SS and financed further searches. But eventually, Rahm, who was gay, was forced to resign and died in 1939 on a Tyrolean mountain top.

Jean-Marc Lofficier

The Song of Montségur

"My Kingdom is not of this world."
(Cathar treatise)

Chapter 1

Like a sad and spellbinding monastic chant, the music flowed from the guitar to impregnate the confined space of the studio: subtle harmonies, a mixture of folk and Occitan tradition with a slow, almost oppressive tempo.

The musician's fingers fluttered over the strings: three minor chords for the refrain, an arpeggio to conclude the melody, and the instrumental section was done. All of the singer's distress surged forth then in his gravelly voice, which interpreted the refrain one last time before dying in a final sigh as the notes faded away.

The magnetic tape continued to turn without any sound coming out of the quadraphonic speakers placed in the four corners of the room. Peire Aicart remained motionless for a few moments, his head tilted back, eyes closed. Finally, he stretched his arms wide, set his electric guitar—a Stratocaster—on its stand and got up to switch off the tape-recorder. His drawn features reflected the numerous sleepless nights he had spent recently.

He remained silent for a few seconds, his gaze wandering over the apparatus crowding the soundproof recording studio installed on the first floor of his house: mixing desk, echo chamber, effects console, sampler, sequencer, digital voice-recorder, sound-recording equipment and various musical instruments. He rewound the tape and pressed the PLAY button. His deep and hoarse voice immediately filled the room: a voice with a southern accent, accompanied solely by the guitar.

"Shit! It's worthless!" he exclaimed, furiously.

Peire went back to the mixing desk, moved several switches, and then turned down the sound with an ill-tempered gesture. The song was flat, affected, and too ordinary. It did not sound right. The chords did not flow...or perhaps it was the words. Something was awry. He could not contrive to transpose the emotion he had in his head. His talent had served him better in the past.

Three days of his life shut up in his studio, incessantly composing and playing his music; he needed to stand back. Otherwise, his next album would never be finished. It had been more than five years since his last.

He took two steps across the room, took an almost empty bottle of Evian from the top of one of the speakers and finished it off in a single gulp. He held it in his hand for a few seconds before tossing it mechanically into the waste-bin, which was already full of crumpled pieces of paper on which embryonic verses were scribbled. The results of today's session were far from satisfactory. Hours of work were accumulated there.

Peire suddenly felt completely exhausted. A breath of air and a little sleep would do him more good than anything else. The song that would not emerge had emptied him out. Neither the words nor the melodies that he had attempted to compose in the last four months had found favor with his ears. He was too demanding, undoubtedly, but that was his nature: perfection or nothing.

Peire left his studio. He went down the old wooden staircase, went along the hallway and opened the front door of his house. Outside, silence reigned. It was total: the calm of the countryside. Thick grey clouds were accumulating in fleecy masses in the sky. It would soon start to snow.

He had chosen to return to live in the village of Montségur, far from the metropolitan bustle of Toulouse. Even there, his residence was isolated on the edge of the village, lost in the wilderness at the foot of the Pic de Saint-Barthélémy. Montségur loomed up in front of him. Perched on a rocky crag, an immense stone ark set to defy the sky's assaults, the ruined citadel dominated the valley. At this early hour the feeble rays of the rising sun were grazing the mountain peaks, barely touching the heights of the keep. The walls were silhouetted like a dark stain on the deserted mountainsides. The castle defied time, like some strange decadent ship run aground there by chance.

Montségur, sanctuary and sepulcher. A ruin. The remnants of ramparts worn down by time, stones mingled with hectic vegetation, grasses and bushes. Nothing special. An ancient fortress, of which there are hundreds in France.

And yet, this particular ruin exercised a certain influence upon humans, as if the place were inspired. Montségur bore a name that rattled in the wind of History.

Today it was a bare, deserted ruin on the summit of a crag, a skeleton contemplating lands reddened by the blood of martyrs to the Inquisition. But it was also a symbol: the last refuge of the Cathars; a legendary place set above the plain of Languedoc, to which thousands of tourists flocked every year.

Peire sighed. Seeing this landscape every day made him a little less mindful of the castle, but he always experienced a strange sense of admiration and despair when he looked at it: admiration for the men and women whose faith had been tested to the limit in March 1244, going to the stake rather than renouncing their religion; despair for the martyrs pitilessly pursued by the ambition, cruelty and intolerance of crusaders. Seven centuries after the death of 200 Cathars, nothing had changed.

His thoughts abandoned the castle to return to his music. His album.... The idea made him smile. Who was still waiting for a Peire Aicart album? No one any longer—and yet, at 42, he was still considered one of the best guitarists in France to accompany singers or rock bands. He was one of the rare session musicians, always in demand in numerous studios, but no one wanted to give him another chance as a solo performer— no one except Jacques Desplas, his producer and friend.

At the age of 18, Peire had chosen so-called *chanson engagée*–"politically-engaged singing"—proclaiming his rebellious tendencies by singing in Occitan, his mother tongue: that of his ancestors, who had lived in Montségur for more than 700 years.

15

In the late 70s, he had faith in his music and his struggle, which were, for him, coupled together. His songs were in complete contrast to those that occupied the top spots in hit parades.

He had begun as a simple troubadour, in youth clubs and small venues, singing with no accompaniment but his acoustic guitar. Little by little, his fame had grown, leading to the recording of his first 33rpm record, a mixture of rebel songs and love songs. The album, entitled *Revolum,* had circulated in leftist and anarchist milieux. His political commitment had then led Peire into various local Occitan struggles: a wine-growers' strike in Languedoc and a protest against the establishment of a military base in Larzac. There, for the first time in his life, he had sung in front of 30,000 people—one of the highlights of his career.

Then, as the years went by, his political engagement and militarism had been eroded little by little, giving way to his true passion: the guitar. That had translated itself into eight albums with more and more songs in a popular vein, in French, sometimes even in English—and, most of all, by increasing fame.

Today, he spent the greater part of his time in recording studios or on tour through France, but never as the main attraction, merely as a guitarist.

Peire took several deep breaths of glacial air, gazing at the castle without really seeing it. His nascent beard, peppered with grey, emphasized his attitude of defeat.

He stayed outside for a few minutes, letting fresh air into his lungs, and then went back into the house and into the kitchen, where he made a black coffee. Cup in hand, he went into the dining-room. He sat down in his old leather armchair facing the huge regional stone fireplace.

The cup burned his fingers while he was not really paying attention. His gaze was fixed on a framed image situated on the mantelpiece. His wife Hélène, sitting on top of a mountain, smiled at him mischievously from the photograph.

Behind her, the castle of Montségur was visible. Peire's eyes closed.

They had lived together in happy tranquility, sharing one another's passions. He had helped her to discover the world of music; she had initiated him into the skiing circuit, climbing and potholing. It had lasted six short years....

He contemplated the face for several minutes. A few months earlier he would have wept, but time had begun to ameliorate the pain, without suppressing any of the grief that he still felt.

A year ago, almost to the day, Hélène had died. A cave situated a few kilometers from the house, which she knew by heart and was not supposed to be dangerous...a rock had fallen, starting a slide that had crushed the body of the 33-year-old woman as well as her two companions...the search-party had taken more than a week to bring them out: eight long days of anguish, hoping for an impossible miracle.

After the first weeks of despair, he had gone through a period of depression, finding no meaning in life, spending long periods sitting on the doorstep, waiting. Waiting for what? He did not know himself.

The image of Hélène haunted him. Her absence tormented him. He no longer wanted to do anything. His music suffered in consequence, contracts became fewer and further apart. The occasional royalty payments that still came in enabled him to survive. The house was his; his needs, in respect of food and clothing, were simple.

His producer, who had been with him since the beginning, had extracted him from this slow suicide by confronting him with a true challenge: to go back to his former triumphs, remix them and add three or four new tracks to the album. After his initial refusal, Peire had finally launched himself into the enterprise wholeheartedly. Little by little, he had recovered his self-confidence. His music had not deserted him.

He got up from his armchair and climbed the stairs to return to his recording studio. He took up an acoustic guitar, the one that Hélène had given him for his birthday, and started to play. He was in search of inspiration. After ten minutes, during which none came, he decided to abandon the session and resume work later.

He went back to the kitchen, poured himself a glass of Armagnac and drank it in a single draught. For eight months, alcohol had kept him alive, by plunging him into a deceptive sense of wellbeing. Today, the necessity had gone. He put down the glass. After a few moments of reflection he decided that a little sleep would do him good. After 36 hours without sleep, thanks to liters of coffee and his passionate obstinacy, he was exhausted.

Peire went to his bedroom, pausing momentarily at the window to look out at the mountain. The glass returned the image of a pallid face with hollow eyes. He let himself fall on to the bed. The alcohol was beginning to take effect. Sleep immediately overwhelmed him.

A dull sound drew him out of his dreams. Bewildered, he took several seconds to realize that it was coming from the front door. Someone was knocking insistently.

He got up, still half-asleep, passed a hand over his coarse beard, and opened his bedroom window.

"Hey Peire—I need you."

Peire squinted, dazzled by white light. There had been a heavy snowfall. His childhood friend Michel was standing in front of the house. A short, stocky man, beginning to go bald, he was dressed in an orange ski-suit. He was hopping up and down to keep warm. The coldness of the air materialized his breath as a diaphanous vapor. His footfalls had left tracks in the uniform carpet that covered the garden.

"Shit! I can't even sleep in peace!" Peire complained, struggling to open his sleepy eyes.

"When I got up at five this morning, I saw the lights on in your house and knew that you weren't in bed yet…you won't live to a ripe old age keeping those hours!" Michel reprimanded him gently. "Well, are you going to open up or would you rather I froze to death?"

"I'm coming. Give me a minute."

Peire closed the window again, crossed the room, went through the dining-room and opened the door.

"Come in!"

They had grown up together, done the same stupid things, and courted the same girls. Michel had even accompanied him on several of his tours, taking care of all the administrative matters. When Hélène had died, Michel was still there to support him. Having previously worked as a teacher, for the last two years he had kept an antique and curio shop in the village, open in the summer. He supplemented the earnings of his shop by working as a ski instructor at a nearby resort.

Michel came through the door.

"There's no time to rest—I need you. It's urgent. Four youths have gone missing while skiing downhill. There aren't enough gendarmes and rescue workers to mount a search. They're afraid that the kids might fall prey to hypothermia because of the cold. Get a move on." He broke off as he caught sight of Peire's weary face. "If you're too tired to come with me, you don't have to come."

"On the contrary—this changes things. Just give me time to find my skis and snowshoes."

"Don't bother—I've got them. You left them at the house last winter. They're already in my car." Michel went out again, running towards his vehicle. He had left the motor running. Before climbing in he shouted: "I have to warn Jordanne, so she can make us a snack. Then I'll go to the gendarmerie to get the rescue equipment and instructions. You dress up warmly and hurry over to her place. I'll pick you up there. I won't be long, hopefully."

Five minutes later Peire closed the door behind him and set out. He headed for the village, which was about 800 meters away, at a rapid pace. The wind had got up, lifting the snow accumulated on the roofs in white clouds.

Out of breath, Peire stopped in front of the *Leg d'Amor*—the Court of Love—a bookshop-restaurant where he sometimes gave concerts, accompanying himself on the guitar like the troubadours of old, one of whose last descendants he was.

He knocked. The door to the shop opened to reveal Jordanne Sutra, a smiling woman as tall as Peire. Another native of Montségur, she had left once to go to university before coming back to help her father run the family restaurant—a restaurant that she had since completely transformed , making it an eccentric place where culture and regional cuisine mingled. Now quite well-known, the place was popular with the tourists who came to visit the castle every year.

Jordanne's smile broadened when she saw Peire. Her delight was reflected in her eyes, sparkling with life. She had grown up with the "two horrors," as she called them, and time had not weakened their old comradeship. She still felt as much pleasure on seeing them, one as much as the other. "Hello, Peire," she said, kissing him on the cheek.

Peire looked her over appreciatively. For once she had left her long black hair loose to dangle over her shoulders in pliant waves. That rejuvenated her. A few wrinkles in the corners of her eyes were all that betrayed her age, which was the same as Peire's and Michel's. "Hello, Jordanne."

"You've finally come out of your lair! I was beginning to get worried. You don't like my cooking any more, then?"

Peire returned the smile, and a little laugh escaped her mouth. "As if! You know perfectly well that I love eating at your place—but I have to finish my album by the end of March, and it's taking up all my time."

"You still have a month and a half."

"I haven't managed to compose anything, unfortunately. I reworked my old material without any problems, but I'm up against it with the new stuff."

Jordanne touched his arm, sliding her hand over his black anorak in an affectionate gesture.

"Go out for a walk sometimes. You work too hard. You need to escape once in a while."

As usual, Jordanne had hit the nail on the head. Peire nodded. "You're right—I'll start today. Has Michel been? We're on our way to search for four youngsters."

"Yes, he called in. If I didn't have to open the restaurant for a bunch of pensioners, I would have come with you."

The blast of a horn made them turn round. Michel's Landrover drew to a halt beside them.

"Have you made us something to eat?" Michel asked.

"Of course! I wouldn't let you die of hunger." She handed a basket to Peire, then turned to Michel. "Have you any news of the young men?"

"They've just found their car at the start of the skislopes on the Monts d'Olmes. Several groups are going to search the area today.

Jordanne frowned. "Look after yourselves. The weather forecast predicts significant snowfall this afternoon."

"We're only searching," Michel replied. "In fact, when I get back, remind me that I've got some books for you. I've been clearing an old man's house, and I found some old books that might interest you."

Peire climbed in beside his friend. Jordanne waved to them as the four-by-four got under way. Michel drove carefully until he was out of the village, and then accelerated when he reached the main road.

"Will you make your fortune with that?" Peire asked, using his chin to indicate the rear of the car. As he put the basket in the boot he had noticed four large boxes.

"I haven't had time to make an inventory," Michel replied. "I'll take care of it one of these days. I was called out yesterday by a chap who wanted to dispose of the effects of a friend, an eccentric living like a hermit in the Galamus gorges, near the monastery. There were a few items of no obvious value, mostly books. I'll give them to Jordanne. The lot didn't cost much, anyway."

"I didn't know there were any monks still in the place. I thought only tourists went there."

"There haven't been any for ages. According to my contact the fellow's been living in a cave nearby for years, far away from everything, hardly ever seeing anyone. He's an eccentric."

Peire closed his eyes. The Galamus gorges, 50 kilometers from Montségur, were famous in the region. He had not been there since he had explored them as an adolescent. Perhaps he ought to go out there and wander around, to see what he could find. Jordanne had advised him to get out more. Who could tell? It might make a theme for one of his songs....

By the time the four-by-four reached the highway, he had already begun to cast around for words.

Snowshoes grated on the bed of snow and the black ice that covered the downhill ski-slope. Peire was panting, spirals of white vapor escaping his mouth every time he breathed out. Droplets of sweat formed on his brow in spite of the cold. He had been pressing forward for nearly an hour, preceded by Michel and two gendarmes. Unfortunately, the snow that had fallen during the night had covered any tracks.

The search was continuing intensively. The authorities had had no further news of the young men for 48 hours. The families were beginning to worry, especially with the weather conditions being so difficult.

Peire stopped to get his breath back; fatigue was beginning to stiffen his muscles. The drone of the helicopter that was quartering the area resonated in the muffled calmness of the snowbound mountain. It passed over their heads before vanishing into the clouds that were descending further and further, already covering the neighboring summits. It would soon be impossible to survey the region from the air.

"Group eight, are you receiving me?"

The nasal voice, punctuated by static, emerged from the radio receiver suspended from the neck of one of the gendarmes.

"Receiving you, four five."

"The other groups haven't found anything. Continue as far as the shelter. You should get there in an hour."

Pierre resumed the climb. In spite of a stitch in his side he set the snowshoes one in front of the other unthinkingly. Above all, he did not want to fall behind. If he did, he would become a dead weight for the search party.

Five hundred meters further on the first gendarme crouched down. He was looking intently at something in the middle of the trail. Peire accelerated his pace in order to draw level.

The snow formed hollows and hummocks within an area some two meters in diameter. The gendarme extended his gloved hand to brush aside the fresh layer. After 30 seconds, the clear imprints of skis and shoes appeared. He stood up anxiously.

"They took their shoes off here."

"Are those their tracks?" his colleague asked.

"There's a strong probability. We'll clear the snow higher up to see whether they continued in the same direction or turned back."

Peire listened to the two men distractedly. His gaze, surveying the surrounding area, was suddenly caught by a point in the track beside the trail, where a gap opened in the mountain-side. He took a dozen steps, bent down and then drew aside some dead branches. A few of them were broken at the base. In front of him was a small cave.

His stomach clenched, for no apparent reason. He frowned. The musician experienced a strange sensation: a dull anguish, curiously tinged with excitement. Hélène's face appeared in his mind. Although he could not explain it, he knew that the young men had gone this way.

"I've found something!" he called, loudly.

One of the gendarmes came to join him, knelt down, brought a torch from his backpack and shone it into the hole.

The light dwindled away in the darkness.

"It's large enough for a man to go in," murmured the gendarme. He leaned further forwards. "Hey!" he shouted into the darkness.

His voice echoed from the rocks.

"Do you think they took shelter in there?" Michel asked.

"It's possible—one never knows," replied the gendarme.

"Someone will have to go down to make sure," his colleague added. He put down his backpack, took out a long rope and attached it to a tree-stump. He made several knots, and then tugged it several times to test its solidity.

"That's not strictly necessary," Michel said. "The slope's quite gentle; you could go down there without insurance."

"I prefer to take every possible precaution," the gendarme replied. "The rope might be useful if it's necessary to bring someone out."

"Do you want me to come with you?" Peire asked. "I did some potholing a few years ago."

"Wouldn't you prefer it if I went?" Michel put in.

"No," Peire replied, dryly. Since Hélène's death he had abandoned spelunking entirely. He knew, however, deep inside himself, that he must one day overcome his reticence in order to move on—and the gulf that yawned in front of him was attracting him like a magnet. His head was spinning; he felt the icy wind on his skin in spite of the thickness of his clothing.

"Hold the rope for us, Paul," said the gendarme, as he disappeared into the cave.

Peire lowered himself into the hole in his turn. His throat was constricted momentarily. He took a few deep breaths, then crept forwards, closing his eyes.

A bare handful of seconds went by before the tunnel that he had taken broadened out into a larger chamber.

The first thing that struck him was the silence—a silence that he had forgotten. He saw himself with Hélène again, exploring caves and feeling as if he was in another world, hidden from the external one. Then the gendarme shone his torch around them, bringing the musician back to reality.

Their eyes fixed themselves on the macabre spectacle that was offered to them. Two tangled bodies braced against a wall of rock. Peire felt nausea mounting within him while the torch-beam displayed two further bodies lying side by side, holding hands, faces to the ground. The sight caused terrible and painful images to surge forth from his memory.

He took a step back, numb with shock. The chamber began to spin around him, faster and faster, obliging him to lean against the wall.

The gendarme turned the first body over and shone the light on it. His hand was trembling.

Peire could not tear his eyes away. His pulse accelerated. The calm features of the dead man reflected serenity, almost happiness. Peire bit his lower lip until it bled, then turned away, bile rising from his stomach and catching in his throat. His wife's face superimposed itself upon the boy's. She had displayed the same calmness, as if she had waited for death with pleasure. The torch-beam left the ground to climb the wall again, towards the other two corpses.

Again Peire felt himself shiver under the impact of shock. Directly in front of him, engraved in the rock, there was an immense pentagram. An upright man could have placed himself within it without the slightest difficulty. There had been an identical geometrical design in the cave where his wife had died.

Without thinking, Peire moved forward and found himself facing the wall with his right arm extended. Moved by a will of its own, his hand followed the lines engraved in the rock, then placed itself flat in the middle of the design.

A wave of heat struck Peire all over, as if his body were in the middle of a pyre. He smelled the acrid odor of his burning flesh. His heart began beating as fast as it could. Alarmed, struggling to recover his senses, he tried to draw away from the pentagram. It was impossible. His hand seemed to be held by an invisible force. He began to panic.

Calm down!

25

Hélène's voice. The hairs on the back of his neck bristled.

Calm down—nothing will happen to you. Pull yourself together, and you'll be able to take your hand away.

Peire made his mind go blank and slowly withdrew his hand. The fire vanished. The odor faded. He illuminated his right hand and looked at it for a moment; there was no trace of burning. He directed his torch at the pentagram, which seemed unchanged. The voice had died away.

He remained still for a moment, uncomprehending and somewhat bewildered. Contradictory emotions seethed within him. Hélène had spoken to him. It was no illusion; he would have recognized the sound of her voice among 1000. A light, blinding him, dragged him brutally back to reality. The gendarme had shone the beam of his torch in his direction and was speaking to him.

"Go back—this isn't a pleasant sight. Tell my colleague to call for help."

Pierre nodded his head as a sign of acquiescence and obeyed. He soon found himself beck in the open air, where snowflakes were now falling densely. He remained motionless for a few moments. Someone grabbed his shoulder. He turned round abruptly.

"Have you found them?" Michel demanded.

Peire did not reply for several seconds. "They're dead."

The second gendarme took up his radio while Michel put his arms around his friend to comfort him.

"That's the way it goes," Peire murmured.

"I should have stopped you going down."

Michel's voice was friendly and reassuring. Peire did not reply. Drawing aside, he took a few steps in the snow. He was no longer able to think about Hélène. Her face had been replaced by the image of a pentagram.

26

Chapter 2

The weak winter sun illuminated the ramparts of the citadel. From the window of the compartment the man admired the triple rank of walls, bristling with crenellations and towers. A masterpiece of medieval architecture, which has resisted all assaults before yielding to the Catholic Church and the King of France in the 13th century.

The loudspeaker announced the arrival of the high-speed train at Carcassonne station. The man got up, took his suitcase from the luggage-rack and headed towards the carriage door. Clad in a dark blue, he had the appearance of a high-ranking officer. A small silver cross pinned to the left lapel of his coat was the only thing that testified to his clerical status.

He was tall—more than 1.90 meters—and weighed about 130 kilos: a veritable peasant's build. His large and slender hands, without any apparent calluses, did as much as his distinguished manner to dispel the first impression his appearance produced. He had just completed his 61st year, but retained such a cheerful face that he might have been taken for a much younger man. His white hair, cut very short, accentuated the squareness of his face and the firmness of his rough-hewn features. His high-set and pronounced cheekbones, his straight nose and elongated chin gave him an austere appearance, which contrasted with the warm gaze of his clear blue eyes.

As soon as the carriage came to a halt he came down the steps and made for the exit. His eyes made a tour of the concourse, searching for the person who was coming to meet him.

"Monsignor!"

The call came from his right. A man of about 30 came running towards him. He was also wearing a cross on the lapel of his jacket. He came to a halt, out of breath, then bowed down to kiss the cardinal's ring.

"Please excuse my lateness, Eminence. I had difficulty finding a parking spot. Welcome to Carcassonne."

"Bonjour, Brother Jean-Michel. I'm glad to see you again."

Cardinal Anto Sakic allowed the other man to take his luggage. Brother Jean-Michel was a member of the Dominican Order founded in 1206 by Dominic de Guzman—who was later canonized—to combat the Catharist heresy, which had spread throughout the south of France and Northern Italy, threatening the very authority of the Pope. Since then, the Dominican brotherhood had dispersed into all the continents, but the monastery founded in this region, the Order's cradle, was still active.

"If you would like to follow me.... You'll be staying at Fanjeaux, in your usual room in St Dominic's house. Brother Bernard is waiting for you eagerly."

A crease formed in Anto Sakic's forehead but he made no comment. He followed his chauffeur across the parking lot and climbed into Brother Jean-Michel's white Clio. For the duration of the journey he contented himself with observing the vineyards and cultivated fields extending over the 20 kilometers that separated Carcassonne from the village of Fanjeaux.

Born in Dubrovnik, Anto Sakic had spent his childhood in war-torn Yugoslavia. Religious and nationalist in his convictions, his father had chosen the wrong side, that of the pro-Nazi dictatorship of the Ustashi, founders of the independent state of Croatia in 1941. In 1944, after the capture of Belgrade by Tito's partisans, Radovan Sakic had sent his wife and son to Rome, to shelter them from communist reprisals, before dying in front of a Serbian firing-squad, convicted of war crimes. He left behind a widow and a deracinated orphan.

In the Eternal City, the young Anto had embraced the Catholic faith, and was ordained as a priest in the early 60s. In the early years he had been discreet with regard to his origins and, above all, the political convictions of his family, occupying a subordinate post in the Archives. He had taken pleasure in studying the old registers, quickly making himself indispensable. In the course of time he had acquired a thorough knowledge of theology and the heresies combated by Christianity, some of which traced their roots back to his country of origin.

This competence steered him in the direction of diplomacy, more precisely towards relations with the representatives of different religions. He had participated in negotiations with the Russian Orthodox Church. Soon, the Pontifical Biblical Commission had noticed his abilities and had proposed that he should come to work in the Vatican. The institution's mission was to make sure that Catholic writings, particularly university theses engendered by certain archaeological discoveries, did not stray too far from dogma.

After 20 years spent dissecting texts of a religious or historic nature, Anto had then joined the Congregation for the Doctrine of the Faith. Heir to the Holy Inquisition, the organization was dedicated to the elimination of all threats to the unity of the Catholic Church and to protect that unity by all means. The members of the institution were, in fact, officially authorized to employ all possible measures to defend the Faith.

Anto Sakic's secret ambition was to become head of the Congregation, in order to re-establish respect for tradition. The times were moving in his direction. Two years earlier, Jean-Paul II had elevated him to the rank of Cardinal in spite of certain reservations on the part of the reformist faction of the Curia, who considered him a reactionary traditionalist.

Anto mulled over the events that had brought him here. Two days before he had got off the train, he had returned from Bosnia, where he had been helping the Catholic Church recover from years of war, to find a car waiting for him at Rome airport to take him directly to the Vatican. There, the chairman of the Congregation, seated behind a massive desk, had welcomed him. The other was an old man, word down by age, who was finding it increasingly difficult to discharge his obligations. Anto had rejoiced inwardly; he had coveted the man's position for a long time.

"Congratulations on your work in Bosnia," the prelate had commenced. "His Holiness has instructed me to give you his compliments. Now, would you care to acquaint yourself with this document? Brother Bernard had it sent to me yesterday, for your attention."

He had slid an enveloped across the desk, which Anto Sakic had opened delicately. It contained a press cutting from a French newspaper detailing the deaths of four young people in a cave in the South of France, close to an immense pentagram. After deploring the accident, the journalist made reference to a cave used by the Cathars for the initiation of their clergy. That religion had, indeed, possessed no consecrated sites; any farm, château or cave sufficed for taking part in their observances.

Anto had put the article back into the envelope and deposited it on the desk. "Exactly like a year ago," the Croat had murmured, lost in his memories.

The person sitting across from him was not slow to respond. "All that is long past, Anto. You've lost track of time. Don't start again. These matters are anecdotal. It's just another simple accident. I can't let you go—I need you for a delicate mission here in the Vatican."

Anto had paused for reflection before adding: "What if St Dominic was right? You're forgetting the warning in his last letter. Then again, His Holiness belonged to the Dominican Order; he pays particular attention to this problem, as he confided to me last month."

His superior had stared at him intently. Anto had just pronounced an important phrase, which opened all doors in the Vatican. No one contradicted the Pope's decisions, even though his intellectual faculties had been weakened by the illness that was eating him away.

"I see that you won't change your opinion," the discouraged Churchman had said. "Pursue your chimera, then. Bring me a full report when you return."

Anto had not even taken the trouble to unpack his suitcases, not wanting to lose any time. It would undoubtedly be his last chance to solve the mystery that had haunted his thoughts since he had discovered St Dominic's letter, addressed to Pope Innocent III. If the various indications could be trusted, the moment was imminent. Was he mistaken? Deep down, he was impelled by a strong intuition. He wanted to know, to obtain the answers for which he had searched throughout his life, to discover the truth at last and defend his profound convictions.

He had left the Vatican to go to France without delay.

The village of Fanjeaux loomed up before him, sprawling over the summit of a hill. It was a Dominican refuge in the very heart of Cathar country. The car went past the right turn that led to the village, keeping to the main road. A few minutes later it arrived at the monastery.

Brother Jean-Michel took Anto to the cell that had been reserved for him. The room was bare; the simple décor comprised an old wooden floor, a narrow bed, a bedside table on which there was an old Bible, a table and a simple chair. A small uncurtained window overlooked the grounds.

"Brother Bernard will see you this evening before mass, when you've had time to recover from your journey. If you need anything, you know where to find me."

Anto put his suitcase on the bed and opened it. From a black leather satchel he withdrew a piece of parchment, which he carefully unfolded on the wooden table. How many times had he studied it? Countless, no doubt—but the design still fascinated him. He remained standing while he examined it pensively. His fixed stare seemed lost in the distance between the figures traced in ancient ink. He had not yet succeeded in solving the enigma posed by the parchment.

Since his departure from Rome, questions had been gnawing away at him. The answers were doubtless within range, somewhere in the mountains that he could see on the horizon through the window of his room—but the solution still escaped him.

A year earlier, almost to the day, he had thought that his years of searching were at an end. During the last 12 months he had learned more, and had made an important unexpected discovery. There were still many elements missing, though. He hoped to find new indications imminently.

Anto sat down on the room's only chair. His eyes immediately went back to the table. An important part of the puzzle was there.

The map was drawn in black ink. The author had stylized rivers, mountains, caves, lakes, villages and—in the centre—a castle. There were five pentagrams, each centered on a mountain.

There were no names on the map, but Anto could name all the places marked on it. What escaped him, on the other hand, was why the plan had been made. It was important. It contained a secret, but gave nothing away—nothing obvious, at any rate. Anto thought about all the research he had done, all the manuscripts and incunabula he had consulted, by the light of a small lantern, in the immense Vatican library, in the hope of elucidating the mystery.

Anto got up, then lay down on the bed, where he drifted off to sleep.

Someone knocked on the door of his cell, waking him up.

"Come in," he said.

Brother Jean-Michel appeared. "The Superior is waiting for you, Monsignor."

The cardinal followed the Dominican through the corridors of the monastery. The walls bore a succession of portraits of men of austere appearance.

The monk opened a heavy wooden door. Anto went into a room deprived of all ornamentation, with the exception of a silver crucifix hanging on the wall facing the door.

The prior came around an armchair to meet Anto. "Welcome once again, Monsignor," Brother Bernard said, affably, after kissing the ring. "The house of St Dominic is yours. I hope that your researches will reach a conclusion this time."

The cardinal interrupted these pleasantries, coming directly to the subject that preoccupied him. "Thank you for sending the press cutting. Now we know the position of the fourth pentagram."

"Brother Jean-Michel was able to visit the cave. The pentagram is undoubtedly identical to the three preceding ones."

Anto raised an eyebrow. "Have you observed changes in the region? Anything that might indicate that the time foreseen by St Dominic is imminent?"

"None, apart from the four dead men and some strange manifestations around the corpses," the Superior replied. "But that's a matter of the utmost discretion. Do you think that the moment has arrived?"

"I think so. I've obtained new information and discovered allies whose existence we did not suspect." Under the perplexed gaze of his interlocutor, he continued: "We'll have an opportunity to talk about that in the days to come. I want to go see this cave."

"Brother Jean-Michel will take you there. He's at your disposal, as before. You can count on all the brothers of the Order to the same extent. I've made all the preparations; they'll be ready when you require them."

Anto left the prior. In the corridor he suddenly remembered the confession he had received in April 1965 from a former SS officer who had taken refuge in Rome. That testimony had transformed his life as a simple priest into that of a searcher, eventually leading him to St Dominic's letter. Now, scarcely having arrived at Fanjeaux, he thought about it again...there must be a reason for that. Was it a sign from God? Perhaps the hour had come.

A thought sprang into his mind: *On the day when the temporal and the spiritual are reconnected, our Church will dominate the world.*

Perhaps that day was imminent.

Chapter 3

A February cold spell had set in. An icy blast of wind surged through the immense gateway of the castle and whirled around the interior, momentarily imprisoned by the walls, before fleeing over the crenellations and spreading out in the valleys girdling the Pog, the crag that supported Montségur.

On the path, lower down, a silhouette advanced towards the ruins that had not yet been invaded by tourists. Montségur was deserted in the winter months; the ruined citadel did not recover any signs of life until the start of spring—March 16, to be exact, the anniversary of its capitulation.

Occult guardian of that silent world, the solitary shadow passed through the immense gateway to go into the castle, and then headed for the walls. It climbed the stone steps that led to the battlements. There it paused, contemplating the splendor of the landscape offered to its gaze. Its blue eyes, profoundly set in their orbits, were searching for something in the snowy mountains that rose up before it.

The shadow admired the magnificent panorama for some time, and then made a tour of the castle, making a further long pause in the keep, as motionless as the ruins surrounding it.

It looked at the place where Ramon de Perelha had gathered the defenders, then the place where Guilhabert de Castres had preached, with his back to the western wall and his face turned eastwards. It was on that same spot that the Cathar hierarchy had been reorganized to combat the Inquisition.

For the first time in the course of its very long life, the shadow became conscious that things were about to change. Infinitesimal signs testified to that. The wait would soon be over.

Overhead, the sky was darkening. No cloud troubled the transparency of the air. Night fell; the first stars appeared. In the midst of the emptiness, the silhouette sensed the presence of a force that it had not felt for a long time—a very long time.

Its eyes closed; it was envelope by obscurity. It was certain then that a new piece had appeared or the chessboard: a piece that had been awaiting its moment for centuries.

It turned round, went carefully down the steps, and then left the castle, taking the route taken by 200 Cathars centuries before, to a pyre built at the foot of the citadel.

The laurel would soon flower again.

Chapter 4

Peire left the subterranean garage where he had parked his car and went out into the main square, facing the Mairie of Toulouse. He walked over the immense Occitan cross that ornamented the square, surrounded by the signs of the zodiac. He bought a copy of the *Dépêche du Midi*. A week after the drama there was no longer the slightest mention of the four dead men in the newspaper. The affair was no longer page one news: a simple accident due to the imprudence or ignorance of young people, who had underestimated the mountain's dangers even though the weather conditions were deplorable. Peire, however, was still mindful of the calm faces of those mummies, of the pentagram engraved in the rock and, most of all, of his wife's voice—a voice that continued to haunt him.

He folded the newspaper, went into one of the busy shopping-streets and idled there for a while. He stopped in front of a record shop, hesitating over the most recent Carlos Santana album, but postponed the purchase until later. There was not enough time. The impending event was very important to the continuation of his career. He was to be given an award—a worthwhile one—not for his achievements as a guitarist, but as an Occitan singer.

After walking for ten minutes, Peire came to a splendid building illuminated by the fading light of late afternoon. Constructed in a harmonious assembly of brick and stone, the façade was sustained by simple columns. He arrived before the immense wooden door, whose two battens stood open. Ahead of him, a dozen people were going in.

The building, built as a town house by a famous citizen of Toulouse in the 16th century, housed several cultural associations, including the one that had invited him today: the Société del Gai Saber.

Every winter, for more than 600 years, the Société del Gai Saber awarded gold and silver Laurels. Today, Peire was

36

to receive the silver Laurel, for having dared to sing in the Occitan language in an era when most musicians swore by none but English.

Peire went into the interior of the building, slightly intimidated by the calm and dignified ambience of the place. He went through a hallway, where the lights were reflected in mirrors hanging on the paneled walls, and arrived in the reception-room. A fairly numerous crowd had already gathered there. He stopped, searching for a familiar face. After scanning the unknown visages for a few moments, he perceived Jacques Desplas, the director of his record company, who was hastening towards him.

"Ah, Peire! I thought you'd never arrive. We've been waiting for you for more than a quarter of an hour. I was beginning to lose patience."

"Even though I detest this kind of reception," the musician replied, laughing, "I wouldn't have missed this one for the world. For once, my talent is being recognized."

"Come on, I'll introduce you to the president of the Société. He's asked me when you were coming several times."

They crossed the room and stopped in front of a man who was about 70, but still alert. Tall and thin, he was wearing a formal black velvet suit. His short white hair emphasized his angular features and jaundiced complexion, but his lively chestnut-brown eyes looked at Peire interestedly.

Desplas made the introductions. "Monsieur Jean Rudel, may I present Peire Aicart, to whom you are about to award a silver Laurel."

In spite of his height, Jean Rudel seemed small and thin beside Peire. His lively gaze studied his visitor. A smile accentuated the numerous wrinkles engraved on his face. "Very happy to make your acquaintance," he said, retaining the musician's hand in his own for several seconds. "Some ten years ago I attended several of your concerts, always with pleasure. I mean those in which you sang in Occitan. Your presentation is fully merited. I regret that you have abandoned that kind of singing for music of a more international stripe."

"It's an honor for me to receive the award," Peire replied, trying to put as much conviction as possible into his voice. "But it's necessary to move on, even in music, in order not to become stuck."

"You would have had a great career as a modern troubadour, though. Our Société has always helped them since its foundation 700 years ago."

"I certainly don't disapprove of what you do on a cultural level," the musician opined, "but aren't you anxious about defending the values of the past? I've recently come back in the direction of my former struggles, you know." In a slightly provocative tone, he continued: "I don't want to be disobliging this evening, when you're honoring me with an award, but I've always considered the Société del Gai Saber as a group of old men in love with a poetry that's a little too verbose for me. That's why I'm surprised to be here."

The old man was content to smile. "Perhaps you're right. I recognize yet again the free speech that has always been typical of you—but don't forget that, without us, the Occitan language would have disappeared. We're its last defenders."

Peire nodded his head, knowing that any dispute would be in vain.

"I knew your grandfather very well, you know," Jean Rudel said. "We were close friends at one time."

The president of the Société pronounced the final phrase as if it had some significance to Peire, who looked at him interestedly. Peire's grandfather, who had died more than six years before, had never told him that he knew a member of the Société del Gai Saber.

"He never mentioned you to me...or perhaps I wasn't paying attention."

"That's understandable. Our last meeting was a long time ago, in 1944—March 16, to be precise."

Peire could not hide his surprise. His interlocutor took advantage of it by continuing: "The date must be familiar to you. You wrote a magnificent song about the pyre of Montségur."

"The 700th anniversary of the castle's surrender."

"Exactly! Seven of us braved the German prohibition to celebrate the occasion."

"I didn't know my grandfather was part of that group."

Jean Rudel looked at him intently. "I can assure you that he was definitely with us. He even recited several poems. I still remember quite well the last one that he declaimed before we left Montségur, written by a troubadour whose name I've forgotten: *Al cap de set cents ans, verdeja lo laurel.*"

Peire tried to remember the poem: *After 700 years, the laurel will flower again.* He could not remember the name of the poet either. It had been composed 700 years earlier by a troubadour who had not accepted the dominion of the Catholic Church over the Cathar church, his *dame.*

Jean Rudel continued, as if he could still see himself climbing the Pog to Montségur: "To be present on that day was the most important thing in the world to us," he said, shaking his head with a resigned smile. "We risked being deported for daring to resist the SS; Montségur was in a forbidden area."

Peire made no reply, intrigued by the unexpected direction the conversation had taken. He expected more, but the other changed the subject again. "Come on, I'll introduce you to some other members of the Société." Jean Rudel took him by the arm and led him into the crowd to introduce him to several men and women who were in discussion in front of the rostrum. After ten minutes, Peire was only following the conversation distractedly. The word *laurel* had continued to resonate in his head, without his knowing why. Then his thoughts returned to his grandfather. He felt disorientated. Why had the old man—who was so proud of telling his grandson all the legends of the region and took pleasure in talking about his adventures—concealed this veritable feat of arms from him?

The conversations died away. Someone had just rapped on the microphone to demand silence.

"Mesdames, messieurs, please take your places. The award of the gold and silver Laurels is beginning.

A man in a black coat came up to Peire to ask him to sit in the first row, in company with the other nominees, and then guided him to his seat, between a novelist and a painter. Before sitting down, Peire turned round, without any particular reason. Two rows behind him, Jean Rudel was staring at him intently.

The orator began speaking again to open the ceremony, which proceeded straightforwardly. It was a specific matter of encouraging the development of the Occitan language across the spectrum of the arts, and there was no prevarication about the event.

Half an hour later it was Peire's turn to go up on stage, amid the applause, to receive his Laurel. He was presented with a stylized silver leaf mounted on a backcloth of black velvet in a boxwood frame: a small gem of the silversmith's art. He gave a short speech, thanking his producer, the members of the Société and the public.

As he set off back to his seat the master of ceremonies asked him, in a whisper, to sing. Peire smiled; he expected that kind of request. A young boy appeared to his right, carrying a plain guitar, which he held out. Peire accepted it and installed himself in front of the microphone. He had chosen the song that he would sing in advance—one of his earliest....

Suddenly, his fingers found other chords than those of the original song. To his great astonishment, words followed of their own accord: *Al cap de set cents ans, verdeja lo laurel.* The song had never figured in his repertoire. Peire met Jean Rudel's eyes then. His grandfather's friend nodded his head in acquiescence.

The troubadour sang for nearly four minutes, not knowing when he had learned the words or how he knew the music. His performance was perfect, though. He finished by repeating the first words, but this time in French: *Au bout de sept cents ans refleurira le laurier.*

He set down his guitar, thanked his public once again, got down from the stage amid the applause and went back to his seat.

Three quarters of an hour later the ceremony ended with the traditional group photograph of all the laureates. Several people came to congratulate Peire, who answered their questions politely.

After saying goodbye to his last admirers, he went to look for his producer to tell him that he was about to leave. He felt tired, and wanted to escape from the cocktail party that was to follow. He saw him at the back of the room, in conversation with a veritable model.

Having arrived next to the couple, Peire looked the young blonde slowly up and down. He was so absorbed that he was incapable of following the conversation. She was tall—as tall as him—and slender. She was wearing a black silk ankle-length sheath dress, very low cut at the back. He studied her in fascination, finding her extraordinarily graceful. He watched her talking without hearing the words she spoke. Her vivid red lips, her immense deep blue eyes, the fluffy curls of her blonde hair and her pale complexion were reminiscent of a porcelain doll.

Finally turning round, the young woman noticed Peire's admiring gaze. She pouted slightly—an enigmatic expression that the musician was incapable of interpreting. There was something attractive and disquieting about her strange attitude that he could not quite define.

Jacques Desplas finally became aware of his presence. "Ah, Peire, may I introduce Elke Ströder. She runs a record company in Munich and wants to produce a CD of Medieval music, including songs in Occitan."

The young woman held out her hand to Peire. He shook it delicately. She delayed releasing her grip for a few seconds, looking him straight in the eye, while their fingers brushed one another imperceptibly.

"Do you think that Occitan singing has a future?" Peire asked, ironically.

"I'm quite convinced of it," the German woman replied, in perfect French with a slight guttural accent. "You only have to look around us to realize that there's an audience for that kind of music. Everyone has been won over by your performance—me most of all."

"Perhaps you're right," Peire said, "but I'm not seeking glory or immortality. I love my music, and that's enough for me."

The producer made haste to intervene. "You might let her listen to your latest recordings, Peire. You've been working very hard, I know. The tape you sent me is superb."

The singer dampened Desplas' enthusiasm. "I haven't finished all the mixes. Besides I'm having problems with the three original songs that I have to write."

"I'd very much like to hear what you've composed, even if it's only a rough draft of the work," the German woman put in, enthusiastically. "Your style interests me greatly."

"Peire records at home in Montségur," Jacques Desplas said, stepping up the pressure as he scented a commercial opportunity. "He has a veritable studio—but I'll give you two or three of his CDs. I brought a few of them with me; they're in my car. Wait for me a minute—I'll go fetch them."

Elke did not let the opportunity pass. She watched the producer draw away, and then turned back to Peire.

"I expect to be staying in your part of the country for a few days," she said, with a broad smile, still wearing that indefinable expression. "If you'll permit me, I'll come to see you."

"Gladly," Peire replied, politely, in spite of his reservations about letting the world invade his privacy.

A waiter offered them a glass of champagne. Elke raised her glass. They made a toast to music. Several people joined in with them before leaving them to their tête-à-tête.

They chatted for several minutes. The German woman told him about her production company and the albums that she had edited. The most recent was an *hommage* to Woman in European lyrics, with works from the 12th and 13th centuries.

Desplas finally came back, out of breath, and offered Elke three CDs. "These are for you. Here's my business card too, as well as directions to get you to Peire's house."

"Thank you," said the young woman amicably, putting all the items into her handbag. "I'll listen to them and tell you honestly what I think of them. I hope we'll be able to work together."

The musician took the opportunity to announce that he was leaving. Desplas tried to retain him in order to introduce him to other people, but without success.

Peire put down his glass and said *au revoir* to the young woman, who confirmed that she would come to see him within the week. He left the reception-room, walking rapidly. His footsteps echoed in the vast empty hallway.

A shrill sound suddenly attracted his attention: a sort of whistle at the limit of audibility. Peire paused to look about him in every direction, without seeing anything strange. Then, mechanically he lowered his eyes. It took him several seconds to recognize the mosaic figure in the middle of which he was standing: a large pentagram.

His feet were nailed to the ground. His heart leapt within his breast. He had not noticed the decorations in the ancient parquet on his arrival.

He felt a sudden shock behind him. It seemed to him that hands, emerging from nowhere, grabbed him by the hair and pulled his head violently backwards. He felt as if his body was on fire. His lungs emptied with a single exhalation.

Abruptly, the ground opened up between his feet and he had the impression of being precipitated into a bottomless black pit. An intense pain shot through his head, followed by a dazzling flash of lighting and a red glare. His entire body was seized by a shudder.

All at once, he felt himself become light. He had the impression of taking flight. At the other end of the room he saw Jean Rudel, standing upright, silently, staring at him in a satisfied manner. Then he realized that the old man was not looking in his direction. Turning round, he shivered; he looked down from above at his own body, laid out on its back, arms and legs splayed, perfectly slotted into the interior of the pentagram designed in the 16th century. Then came darkness.

Chapter 5

The voice came from a great distance. It was deep and slow, like a tape-recording that had been slowed down. Peire concentrated, without being able to understand a single word. Then he transferred his attention to another of his senses: sight. Everything around him seemed dark. Were his eyelids open? They seemed to be.

He was not experiencing any pain. An invisible cocoon enveloped him, isolating him from the external world. The darkness was gradually illuminated. He was in a tunnel, which was giving off a soft orange-yellow light.

An invisible force was bearing him along the tunnel. Now he was plunged into a pale mist populated with unreal shadows, which approached him to brush his flesh. Among these moving and imprecise silhouettes were, it seemed to him, some that were smiling. They resembled people he had known.

It took him a few seconds to realize that all the people in question were dead—but he was not afraid. On the contrary, he experienced a sensation of serenity: these dead people were benevolent. They were coming to welcome him, to help him cross the threshold. Suddenly, Hélène appeared in front of him—*his* Hélène: peaceful; happy; marvelous. She extended her hand to him.

Peire took it without hesitation, trustingly.

The brightness increased to become dazzling and white. A shadow detached itself from the light: a man of austere appearance, dressed in a long black monastic robe. He walked towards Peire and spoke to him, but his lips did not move.

You cannot stay with us, he said. *The Laurel has not yet become verdant again. But you are certainly the one for whom we have been waiting. Let your mind relax; I shall accompany you back. You have nothing to fear from the pentagram now.*

Peire went stiff. He felt good in this world, next to his wife. He certainly did not want to go back again. His life no longer interested him. His dearest wish was to stay here, with all these beings who loved him—but he understood that he did not have a choice.

The shadow advanced until it enveloped him completely. Immediately, he felt his body move backwards, going through the tunnel in the opposite direction, to plunge back into darkness.

The voice continued speaking to him, but it was no longer anything more than an indistinct murmur. Waves of pain were unfurling now, uninterruptedly, throughout his body. Light replaced the darkness, gently at first, before exploding behind his closed eyes.

The musician tried to raise his eyelids, but perceived nothing but a luminous haze, accompanied by a stabbing pain in his head. He instructed his right arm to raise itself up. To his great astonishment, it obeyed.

"Relax," said a female voice. "Don't make needless efforts. Let yourself go."

Little by little his vision cleared. He was able to make out a nurse in a white uniform bending over him. Then memories returned in a rush, all together: the pentagram, Hélène, his enforced return....

"The pain will soon go away; I've increased the dose of analgesics."

Peire took a deep breath, resuming contact with reality. He tried to get up, but the pain made him wince.

"Don't try to move," the nurse continued. "I'll tell the intern that you've recovered consciousness."

"If I knew what had happened to me," Peire articulated painfully, "that would help me." His mouth was so dry that the mere fact of pronouncing the words made his tongue feel as if it were on fire.

He fell back into semi-consciousness, from which he was extracted by a hand placed on his arm.

"Bonjour, Monsieur Aicart. I'm Doctor Lilan." The speaker paused deliberately, giving Peire a few seconds to react and open his eyes. "Ah, I see that you've finally woken up," the doctor continued, pronouncing his words clearly. "You've been unconscious for two days. Now we can conduct an examination to determine the precise cause of your trouble."

"It seems to me that I can no longer feel my body," Peire murmured, feebly.

"That's the effect of the analgesics that you've been given. Tomorrow we'll see if you're in a fit state to undergo a scan."

"What am I doing here, Doctor?" the musician asked, in a fragile voice.

"You were brought in unconscious. We thought at first that you'd suffered a stroke, but all the clinical signs contradicted that hypothesis. You seemed to be suffering the aftermath of some kind of cerebral disturbance, like the effects of a violent blow to the head. I admit that your case puzzles me. Your symptoms are atypical. There was no witness to your 'accident'. Do you remember falling over? Bumping your head?"

"No," Peire replied, preferring to remain evasive.

"I can't eliminate the risk of a small cerebral hemorrhage or a residual clot," the doctor went on. "The scanner will tell us tomorrow. On the other hand, you're in a state of significant asthenia."

"Asthenia?"

"Fatigue. Your constitution seems exhausted. What sort of life have you been leading recently, Monsieur Aicart?"

"Not brilliant," Peire mumbled, looking away.

"That's what I thought. I'll give you a full health-check and put you in a warm bath. We'll soon have you back on your feet."

"Will I be able to leave soon?"

47

"That's what they all want to know," sighed the physician, with a smile. "I'm not a magician. We'll see how the test-results turn out."

The doctor headed for the door. "Be patient," he advised, as he put his hand on the doorknob. "Get some rest. If you're uncomfortable, don't hesitate to call a nurse. I'll come to check up on you at regular intervals."

For several days, Peire was obliged to submit to a battery of medical tests. He passed through the hands of several specialists. He was given warm baths and presented with numerous medications to take. Every time Doctor Lilan visited him, he asked when he could leave. The latter invariably answered *soon*. One more examination was always necessary.

Little by little, Peire's health improved. He felt better. He was continually haunted by a dream—always the same one, which returned every night. He emerged from a tunnel; his wife kissed him on the cheek before fading to a blur, to be replaced by an old man who spoke to him, without his being able to understand a single word, before disappearing in his turn. Then a pentagram appeared and began to twist around him, assuming different geometric forms, which closed in on him before contracting to choke the life out of him. Every morning, when he woke up, he was unable to erase the nightmare from his thoughts.

Jordanne, Michel and Jacques Desplas came to visit him several times. They brought him books, a Walkman and cassettes. The young woman wanted to bring him his studio tapes, but Peire refused; he felt no urge to work.

One afternoon, Peire was surprised to see Elke come in.

"Am I disturbing you?" she asked, as she entered the room.

"Not at all," he replied, taking off his earphones. "Sit down. The chair's not very comfortable, but I've nothing else to offer you."

The German woman took off her coat. She was wearing an orange muslin dress. The simply-cut garment clung to her tall figure, widening out like the soft petals of a flower at the hemline, just above the knee. Her movements had an almost feline grace.

She sat down beside him, opened her handbag and handed him a small package, saying: "I hope that will help to while away the time. When will you be able to leave?"

Peire unwrapped the gift before replying sadly: "Always *soon*! That's the only reply I ever get."

He put the crumpled paper on the bedside table, next to the telephone and looked at the title of the book. It was a biography of Richard Wagner.

"I hope you like it. Wagner was much influenced by the symbolism of Occitan troubadours. Legend has it that he installed himself at the foot of Montségur to compose one of his operas."

"I must listen to his music some day. I humbly confess that my musical culture began with the 60s—1960, that is."

"Choose a suitable armchair when the day comes," she retorted, seemingly amused. "Believe me, you need to be a masochist to attend a performance. At Bayreuth they last for several hours, and they put you on horribly uncomfortable seats."

Peire smiled. He riffled through the pages for a few moments before falling upon the flyleaf, where a dedication was inscribed in neat handwriting: *To Peire Aicart, this life of a great musician who would doubtless have loved to hear the songs of the modern troubadour*. It was followed by an illegible signature.

He went back to the cover. He had not paid the slightest attention to the author's name.

"I hadn't made the connection," he stammered.

She burst out laughing. "Don't worry—I'm not only interested in dead artists. This biography represents a part of my life. Now I prefer to dedicate myself to living artists. To be fair, though, it was Wagner who led me to you."

Peire closed the book again, holding it tenderly in his hands. "I'm sorry I can't offer you a drink, but hospitals rarely have rooms with minibars...."

"Patience. Take care of yourself first. We'll have the opportunity to meet again in a more amenable place. I've listened to the three CDs your producer gave me. I like what you've done very much."

Peire sighed. "You're saying that because I'm lying in a hospital bed and you want to boost my morale."

"Not at all. To be frank, I prefer your early records—when you sang in Occitan. I find your detour into rock music more perplexing. It lacks originality, in the music and lyrics alike. In the beginning, you knew how to find the right words."

Peire did not contradict her. "One has to live. Occitan song doesn't feed a man. I did enough in that vein to obtain a *succès d'estime*. Anyway, it's necessary to move on in one's career, change one's style...."

A warm smile lit up Elke's lovely face. She re-crossed her legs, opening a narrow space for one brief instant that allowed Peire to see the white skin of her upper thighs. Slightly discomfited, he turned away, and went on: "I thought it best to change when the time seemed ripe, even though I had to set aside the career of a politically engaged singer. I've never sought success. For me, the essential thing is to write and play songs that please me."

"Even so, you're reworking the most beautiful of your early songs for your most recent album—the most poignant—and practically none of your later ones."

Peire could not help nodding his head. "Because I find myself at a turning-point in my life, not only in my career. For three years I've been playing for the studio sharks without composing anything personal. At present I'd love to start afresh from new foundations." He paused before continuing. "Especially after the year I've just lived through."

His voice broke.

"Monsieur Desplas told me about your wife's death," Elke said, softly, after a brief silence.

50

"And the other day, Death didn't want me. From now on, it's necessary for me to live. I'll need my music to get through it."

The German woman smiled at him, as if she understood. "What happened to you, exactly? Everyone feared the worst when you were discovered unconscious in the hall!"

"I have no idea," Peire lied. "I don't remember anything. I simply lost consciousness. If the doctors were explain to what's wrong with me, at least...but there's no detectable sign of any anomaly. I'm much better today."

"I have a personal question to ask you," Elke said, changing the subject. "Is Peire Aicart your real name or a pseudonym?"

"My name is Patrick Aicart. Peire was the first name of a famous Medieval troubadour. I've always used it, even in my English period. Aicart is a surname typical of the Montségur region. My grandfather even worked out the genealogy of our family. He succeeded in tracing it back to the 14th century, thanks to the Church archives."

"That's interesting," Elke murmured. She was looking at him attentively.

"It was one of his hobbies," the singer went on. "he dedicated several years to the work. He was lucky—our family has always lived in Montségur, and that made the task easier. He even thought that one of our ancestors might have been in the castle during the siege."

At that precise moment Jordanne came into the room, after having knocked. On seeing the visitor sitting beside Peire she stiffened. She darted an interrogative glance at Elke, who favored her with an ambiguous smile without offering to shake her hand.

The musician introduced them. The two women greeted one another reservedly. Jordanne remained standing on the other side of the bed. She asked Peire for news as if she were alone with him, deliberately ignoring the other woman.

From time to time, Elke looked at Jordanne attentively, without intervening in their conversation. Then her eyes settled on Peire. They shone with a peculiar brightness.

After five minutes, Jordanne stopped speaking. A pregnant silence fell within the room. Peire no longer knew what to say. He had asked Jordanne several questions about her own activities but she had replied evasively. As the awkwardness persisted, Elke got up, smoothed her dress with a graceful gesture, and drew closer to Peire.

"I'll come to see you when you're home. Be sure not to forget my proposition."

Peire took note of the fact that she had addressed him as *tu* for the first time since they had met. Elke leaned over and kissed him on both cheeks before leaving the room.

"Who's that?" asked Jordanne, in a sharp tone, when the door closed behind her.

"Elke Ströder. She runs a record company in Germany. Jacques Desplas introduced me to her during the awards ceremony."

"And what is her proposition?" She pronounced the sentence in a challenging manner, but seemed to regret the words immediately.

"To produce a CD of Medieval songs, in which she wants to include one of my works," Peire replied, more harshly than he would have wished.

"Excuse me…I'm meddling in things that don't concern me."

Peire took her hand and squeezed it for a few seconds before letting go.

"I fear that her project is doomed to fail. No one's interested in the troubadours any longer. It's necessary to turn the page, live in one's own time."

"Don't be such a pessimist, Peire. For myself, I believe the opposite is the case, that there'll be a revival. A lot of my customers ask me for CDs or cassettes in Occitan. Look how many people are desperate enough to revive Breton folksongs. Besides, when you're on your feet again, I'll have a proper contract drawn up for you to give two or three recitals in my restaurant."

"That'll certainly scare your customers away!" he said, teasing her gently.

It was her who took his hand now, and kept it in her own. "Why don't you come and stay with me while you convalesce?"

"I have to finish my album. I don't work regular hours—I'd disturb you by coming and going Heaven knows when…anyway, I need to work in my studio."

"Come to eat every evening, then…someone has to take care of you."

"Okay," he conceded. "I'd like that."

His friend got to her feet, took a package out of her handbag and handed it to him. "There—I hope you like it."

Peire unwrapped the paper, which enclosed a water-color about 20 square centimeters. It depicted the castle of Montségur perched on its eagle's nest.

"It's an original Maillant. You can put it in your studio."

Peire's gaze scanned the picture. At the base of the Pog the artist had painted a pyre, from which red and yellow flames rose up, topped by black smoke. The charred corpse of a man was within it. Above the inferno a dove was flying skywards.

"Do you like it?"

"Thank you, Jordanne. It's magnificent. I'll hang it up when I get back."

The young woman smiled, looking at her friend affectionately. "Michel will come this evening to keep you company. Let us know when you're getting out and one of us will come to fetch you."

"Believe me, I shan't stay here a minute longer than necessary."

They discussed music and gastronomy for another ten minutes. After Jordanne had gone, Peire took up the painting again and looked at it for a long time.

53

His gaze was continually drawn back to the silhouette in the pyre. He studied the pale face in the midst of the flames.

It was the face of the man who had accompanied him back along the tunnel, who had brought him back to life.

Chapter 6

Reflexively, the man checked the rear-view mirror: no vehicles. For several minutes he had kept track of a Fiat Panda, but it had turned off after five kilometers. Since then, nothing. To his right, his companion was checking the contents of a knapsack without concerning himself with the surveillance that the driver was carrying out. He trusted him.

The passenger lifted his head. He closed the bag—which contained, among other things, a pair of binoculars, a camera with a powerful telephoto lens, a mobile phone and a revolver—then turned to his companion.

"Pay attention, we'll be arriving soon. Take the first sideroad to the right after the next junction."

"You're a genuinely talented co-pilot, Philippe—you ought to go rallying," the driver, laughing.

With a single twist of the steering-wheel he turned and the four-by-four Toyota took a flat dirt road into the Joucla woods, as the map indicated. Four hundred meters further on the terrain became more uneven and gave way to sandy soil covered with large pebbles. In spite of the four-wheel drive, the Toyota had difficulty making headway among the ruts and scattered stones.

The vehicle finally arrived at the foot of a knoll where the woodland road gave way to a pedestrian path.

"Back into the trees and park, Sylvain," Philippe said, slipping the knapsack over his shoulders. "It will be quicker if we have to make a rapid getaway."

They got out of the car, stretched their limbs for a few moments, and set off along the winding path, which went through a meadow at first, then through a little wood. Ten minutes later they arrived at the top of a small hill.

A little valley extended in front of them, pinched between two steep slopes, where the snow that had settled on the mountainside still lingered. A narrow path led to an old farmhouse that had recently been refurbished.

The two men knelt down behind a hedge, set up their equipment and began their surveillance. The silence was scarcely troubled by the distant sound of the stream that ran through the bottom of the gorge.

"No one home," said Philippe, lowering his binoculars.

Sylvain took another photograph of the farmhouse before replying. "As expected. We're half an hour ahead of them."

They remained nestled in the shelter of the trees, always watching the house. Suddenly, Philippe made a slight sign to alert his companion. The sound of a motor resonated on the mountain. Two Mercedes cars came around a hairpin bend and eased on to the road leading to the farm.

"There they are. That's odd—there are two cars. The other crew only saw one vehicle before losing sight of them."

Sylvain steadied the photographic apparatus on a rock, put his eye to the viewfinder, focused the telephoto lens and took several pictures. Any item of information, even the most trivial, might prove vital.

The two cars parked in front of the farm. Four men got out of the first. All of them had the same large build blond hair and stern black suits. The rear door of the other Mercedes opened. A man got out and leaned over, reaching into the interior. An old man clambered out, with some difficulty. The first man helped him out, and then supported him while he walked to the front door of the farmhouse.

The camera's motor purred while the telephoto lens zoomed in on the old man. Sylvain took several pictures of him, then some of his entourage.

Philippe had aimed his binoculars at the old man, who was making slow progress. He saw the old man's body tremble, agitated by nervous tics. Finally, a woman got out of the second car and joined the group as they disappeared into the house.

"Did you recognize anyone?" Sylvain asked.

"The woman was at the ceremory in Toulouse. I remember her very well. I think I might have seen one of the men that same day."

"There's no need to stay any lorger. We have all the information Rudel asked for."

"I'll stay to continue the surveillance. One never knows what might happen. Take the film to be developed—that's the most important thing right now. Ther come back to find me and we'll decide what to do."

Philippe got up and extracted the film, which he put into his coat pocket. He put a new roll into the camera and held it out to his companion, who took it without complaint. Philippe turned on his heel and marched off towards the bushes.

"Make sure you memorize the route," Sylvain added, finally. "I've no desire to spend the night here—it's not warm at this time of year."

"Mind you don't shoot me when I come back!" joked the other, without turning round, as he drew away.

Sylvain resumed his sentry-post, his eyes glued to the binoculars, but no one came out again. He waited patiently for two hours, stretching his legs from time to time, until the sun disappeared behind the mountain, giving way to semi-darkness. The lights went on in the farmhouse.

Another half-hour went by while he saw nothing. In front of him, everything was tranquil. A plume of black smoke rose from the chimney. For a moment, he was tempted to approach the farmhouse to try to overhear the conversation within, but Jean Rudel's orders had been categorical: they must not take any risks, just observe, take photographs, make notes and compile a report of their mission.

A violent gust of wind suddenly swept down into the valley. It lifted the snow, which formed a white cloud all around the house before evaporating. As if carried by the winter breeze, a fetid odor filled the air.

Sylvain raised his head slightly, sniffing to identify the origin of the stink. He looked around without discovering anything. *Probably a dead sheep or some wild animal rotting in its den*, he thought, resuming his observation, his mind alert.

A sound reverberated: a diffuse noise like a stifled cry. It lasted scarcely a second; then silence took possession of the bushes again. Sylvain looked around again, anxiously, but he did not switch on his torch for fear of being spotted. The solitude was beginning to get on his nerves. He darted a glance at his wristwatch; Philippe would be back soon.

He got up and walked back and forth for a while to stretch his legs. He dared not got back towards the road, however, in case something happened at the farm. While waiting for his comrade he had to continue the surveillance at all costs.

He yawned, causing his jaw to click, and decided to call Philippe to find out where he was. He took out his mobile phone and lit up the screen: no signal. The valley must be in a shadow zone, where it was impossible to send or receive a message. Sylvain put the phone into the knapsack, cursing inwardly.

As he turned back to resume his observation, an immense form sprang out of the bushes. It hurled itself upon him before he had time to attempt the slightest defensive gesture. He perceived nothing but the supernatural gleam of its green eyes; then icy skin pressed down on his body, cutting off his respiration.

At every movement he made to escape that grip, it seemed to Sylvain that blades were cutting into his flesh, severing his every nerve. Successive waves of pain irradiated his body, with increasing violence.

The howl of a wounded animal formed within his throat. The beast cut his vocal cords with a single thrust. Convulsive tremors shook his limbs. Claws were digging deep into his flesh now.

The thing clasped him firmly against itself, crushing him, transpiercing him and tearing him apart from the inside. His bones, compressed by a colossal force, broke one by one.

He opened his eyes wide, in a vain attempt to see the sky for one last time. Then the darkness overwhelmed him, like a tomb sealing itself.

The creature cast the disarticulated corpse to the ground. It stared for some time at the farmhouse, which was still as calm as ever, and then vanished into the night.

Chapter 7

"How are you?"

Sitting in an armchair facing the fireplace, Peire had been dreaming. Surprised by the voice that had just resonated in the room, he dropped the book he was holding. He turned round. Jordanne was standing in the doorway holding a plate covered by a napkin.

"I knocked several times," she said, depositing the plate on the table. "As you didn't answer, I let myself in."

"That's all right. I was asleep."

Peire bent down to recover the book.

Jordanne removed the napkin and folded it carefully, looking at her friend all the while. "What are you reading?"

"A biography of a German who made excavations in the region before the war. He was searching for the Holy Grail. It's written by a local author, Christian Bernardac."

"Is it about Otto Rahn?"

"Yes. I found the book by chance among 20 others that I didn't even know I had. As I had no desire to compose, I thought a little reading might give me some ideas."

He had left the hospital two days before to return home. On a physical level he had recovered his strength, but he still felt listless. Mentally, on the other hand, he was simply unready to demand anything of himself.

"I've brought you something to eat: *foie gras*, a magret and apple tart, all home-made."

"You're spoiling me," Peire said, getting up. Setting the book down on the chair, he went on: "Stay and eat with me. I should have a bottle of Sauterne in the fridge."

A broad smile lit up Jordanne's face. "If you really want me to, I will. I've closed the restaurant today—it's the dead season. Tomorrow I've got a party booked in at noon."

Peire walked unsteadily to an old dresser and opened the door. He brought out two plates, which he handed to the young woman.

"Leave it," she said, in a firm tone. "I'll do it. You're still too weak. Sit down." She took the plates from his hands and put them back on the shelf. Then she took him gently by the shoulders and pushed him to a chair, where she sat him down. Her hands remained there for a moment, exerting a light pressure, and then she withdrew them furtively.

She turned her back on him to go back to the dresser. "You aren't working on your CD, then?"

"No—I can't muster the enthusiasm. But I've got time. I've finished remixing all my old songs, plus two new ones, and I think I'll finish the third before the chopper comes down."

His friend chided him gently. "Don't be such a pessimist, Peire. I'm sure that it'll do well—your CD. Then again, your silver Laurel might open doors to new media."

"We'll see," Peire replied, fatalistically.

They conversed for five minutes before Jordanne gave in, tired of beating around the bush. "And your German woman?"

Her voice had trembled slightly as it posed the question. Peire made no reply. His face suddenly took on the expression of someone caught out. He got up, went into the kitchen and came back with the Sauterne. Jordanne looked at him anxiously.

Still mute, Peire uncorked the bottle, poured himself a little wine and drank it. The amber liquid was cool and sweet—just enough sugar to mask the strength of the alcohol. "She had to come to the studio to listen to my songs," he said, finally, setting his glass down in front of him. "She's rented a place locally so that she can stay here for a few days."

Jordanne simply said "Ah!" The flash of sadness in her eyes did not escape Peire.

They stopped talking in order to begin eating. They exchanged occasional glances. Peire filled Jordanne's wineglass. She seemed glad to be there; Peire felt well and relaxed. Talking to her had restored his energy. He had not eaten his daily bread with a woman since Hélène.

"Your Sauterne is excellent—I must eat with you more often," Jordanne said, having emptied her glass.

"I don't know if I have any more bottles left. I haven't thought about restocking my cellar recently."

Jordanne changed the subject. "It's funny—Montségur has always attracted Germans. They've even been accused of stealing stones from the castle. Your grandfather must have told you about Otto Rahn."

"Perhaps, when I was a child—but it didn't make any impression on me. The biography I'm reading is interesting, though. According to the author, he was a fantasist who invented everything, even engraving symbols in caves to corroborate his theories."

"I'll lend you the two books he wrote, and you can make up your own mind. They're always much in demand at the bookshop, especially with tourists. I always keep both the French and German editions."

Peire accepted the offer enthusiastically. "I think I'll come and plunder your bookshop. I don't know why, but I have a yen to know more about Catharism."

"You were never interested before, that's true—but you've written one of the most beautiful songs about Montségur."

"Living underneath the castle I could hardly do otherwise than pay homage to it—but so far as I'm concerned, all the stories are folklore for tourists or victims of facile esotericism. Don't forget my revolutionary period: we must make a *tabula rasa* of the past."

"Why this sudden interest, then?"

"The pentagram. Do you know anything about pentagrams?" The words had slipped out without his being aware of it.

She paused for reflection before nodding her head. "I knew you'd ask me that question—I've known you too well for a long time—so I've been researching it."

Peire contented himself with a smile, without interrogating her.

"It's a symbol used since antiquity," Jordanne continued. "For the Egyptians it represented the god Horus. All civilizations have used it. It's particularly associated with humankind, because a man can fit into the figure perfectly. The five points represent the head, the two extended arms, and the legs held apart."

"I fell down in the middle of a pentagram inscribed in the hall of the Société del Gai Saber. That's the position in which I saw myself, from above."

"There are numerous pentagrams that are attributed to the Cathars, you know. One of them is in the Château de Pieusse, where a Cathar congress was held. Another is in the cave at Lombrives which, according to legend, served as their last refuge. Four hundred dead Cathars were discovered there; the corpses were formed into a circle, holding one another's hands. You saw yourself...from above?"

"I know where there are two more: in the cave that Hélène was exploring and in the one where I found the four young men—not to mention the third, which very nearly took me to the other side. Have you got any books on the subject?"

Jordanne noted that Peire had avoided her question. "No, not on pentagrams—but I can try to find some if you want to order them. While you wait, perhaps you can find some information in works on the Cathar religion."

Peire leaned back against the back of his chair, pensively.

"Peire, you haven't told me what you experienced before recovering consciousness," Jordanne reminded him, gently. "You say you saw yourself from above? Unless you don't want to talk about it...."

Peire hesitated for a while, then took the plunge and told her about his ascension in the hall, the tunnel, Hélène, the light, the faces and the old man who had brought him back to life. The images were still incredibly sharp, as clear as the moment when he had first seen them. When he finished speaking, he drank the last of his Sauterne, relieved by his confession.

Jordanne reached across the table and took his hand. "You've been through a traumatic experience. Don't be afraid, you're not alone. Others before you have talked about the tunnel, the meeting with the people they loved and the subsequent return to life. I'll bring you a book tomorrow—but we can talk about it now if you want. It might do you good."

"I don't know. Everything's still so confused in my mind."

Peire had pronounced these words sadly. Jordanne squeezed his hand. "Why don't you come to the restaurant one evening to sing?" she asked, gently. "For a change of scene."

Peire hesitated, still feeling weak. It had been more than six months since he had played in public. He felt the lack of a stage, though; the proposition was tempting. In Jordanne's place, the little restaurant he knew so well, he might feel safe going back on the boards.

"Okay," he said, with a sigh. "When?"

"Why not next week? We can celebrate your silver Laurel at the same time."

"Good idea...."

Peire did not finish his sentence. He was already making mental preparations for the impending concert.

They finished eating, and then Jordanne cleared the table while Peire relit the fire in the hearth. He put a CD in the player and sat down in his armchair. Jordanne stretched herself out on the sofa facing him, with her arms folded behind her head. Suddenly, she leaned forwards, ruffled her hair teasingly, and smiled at him. For a moment, Peire thought he saw a little flame in her eyes, which disappeared immediately.

Looking down at the book that he had recovered from his seat, he said: "Do you believe that Otto Rahn was a charlatan?"

"I've read both his books and everything written about him. It's not easy to form an impression of his character. All that I can say for sure is that he was far from ordinary." She paused deliberately before continuing. "If it interests you, I know someone who's met Otto Rahn: the Comtesse de Mariel. She lives about 50 kilometers away, in the village of Léran. She provided Rahn with lodgings during his two sojourns in France."

"You don't say! I didn't know that you had aristocratic connections."

"Oh no! The Comtesse is just an old lady. She sold me the contents of her library two years ago. She had numerous works on Catharism. I found some information on pentagrams in one of them. We got on, and I go to see her from time to time. She gave me two signed books by Otto Rahn—I cherish them dearly."

"Could I talk to her, do you think?"

"I'm sure of it. I think she might even have known your grandfather."

Peire could not help raising his eyebrows. After Jean Rudel, here was Jordanne also talking to him about his paternal grandfather. Peire regretted not having sat down with him more often to ask him questions.

"Why this interest in Otto Rahn?" Jordanne asked.

He hesitated momentarily, searching for an answer that he did not have.

"Pure chance, no doubt. I found this book and got absorbed in it. The subject's exciting, and tonight you've told me that there are Cathar pentagrams. Perhaps I'll compose a song on that theme."

"Are you really certain that it's pure chance?"

"No," Peire replied, releasing a sigh. "I wanted to know, to understand what's happening to me. I had the vague impression that it's linked to the history of the Cathars, so I read the first book that came to hand which dealt with that subject. I hoped that Otto Rahn might help me."

"I'd be astonished if he could. Although no one knows exactly when and how he died, he'd be more than 100 years old today."

Peire chewed his lower lip nervously.

"Jean Rudel spoke to me about that song I sang, and I remained convinced that I didn't know it. Then I learned that my grandfather was at Montségur for the anniversary in 1944."

"You must have heard someone in your family humming the tune—when you were a child, presumably."

"No, never. I'm certain of it. The words and the music came to me on their own."

"Even your grandfather would never have sung the song?"

Peire got to his feet and deposited some logs in the fireplace before grabbing the poker to stir up the flames.

"I don't know any more. By sheer force of thinking I end up doubting...."

As he went back to his armchair he suddenly felt ill. He went weak at the knees. His head slumped forwards. Jordanne threw herself forward to sustain him. She took him by the arm and sat him down, propping him up against the back of the large chair. Then she caught hold of his shoulders firmly, helping him to remain upright. Little by little the stupefaction cleared. Jordanne did not release her grip.

Peire's head was at the height of Jordanne's bosom. He lifted his gaze to meet her eyes. They were overflowing with affection.

She stroked his cheek. Suddenly, she lowered her head towards him and kissed him. It was a simple kiss, soft and tender, but Peire felt a sudden desire for her. He opened her blouse. His hand slid over the silky skin. Beneath the palm of his hand Jordanne's heartbeat accelerated. She shivered imperceptibly.

Guided by desire, Peire let himself go. He watched himself act, passively. He did not want to think about what was happening, just to take advantage of the moment. His right hand advanced beneath her skirt. At that contact, he felt Jordanne tense up. Peire suspended the gesture. Immediately, she relaxed. He undressed her.

Peire drew back in order to look at her. Emotion constricted his throat. It was the first time he had held a woman in his arms since Hélène's death. He realized then how much he had missed the touch of a feminine body. He took off his clothes and drew closer to her. For a long moment he was content to hold her in his arms. Suddenly, he laid her down on the sofa and knelt down beside her. Her opulent black hair spread out like the petals of a flower on the yielding cushion. He passed his hand over her naked curves, slowly.

Jordanne emitted little gasps. She put her head back and began to tremble.

Peire positioned himself above her and penetrated her. With hands clasped behind Peire's back, Jordanne arched her hips, better to offer herself. Finally, she reared up, her fingernails digging into her partner's flesh, leaving red marks there.

For a fraction of a second, Peire was submerged by pleasure. He fainted. When he returned to his senses, Jordanne was sitting beside him, still naked, slowly recovering her breath. He took her in his arms and hugged her to him, holding on to her.

Peire was slightly bewildered. He had just made love to Jordanne. He could not explain his weakness. He had let himself go like an adolescent, betrayed by his own flesh. The image of Hélène formed in his mind. He felt vaguely guilty—and yet, he had felt pleasure. His wife was dead, but he had chosen to live. He passed his hand through Jordanne's hair in a timid caress.

"I've waited such a long time for that!" Jordanne murmured. "If you knew...since long before Hélène...."

Jordanne planted a kiss on his mouth and remained snuggled up against him for a long time, without moving. He let her do it. The woman was tender, sweet and reassuring. He had known her since childhood. He trusted her.

She suddenly detached herself. "I have to go. I'm getting up early tomorrow to go to the market. It's imperative that my customers should be satisfied with the restaurant."

For the first time in a long while, Peire smiled: a true smile that was reflected in his eyes. "You'll call the Comtesse de Mariel? I'd very much like to meet her."

"I'll telephone her tomorrow. I'll call in and tell you if she can see you. Then I'll take you there."

They got dressed in silence, and Peire accompanied her to the door. Jordanne kissed him one last time on the lips before hurrying away into the cold and the darkness. He remained on the doorstep for several seconds watching her draw away. He went back into the drawing-room, put on a CD and let himself fall into the armchair.

The moment that he had just spent with Jordanne unwound again before his eyes. He did not feel any remorse. He knew that Hélène's presence was bound to fade some say, even if his memories remained sharp. Making love to Jordanne had given him back his lust for life.

He was allowing himself to be gently lulled by the music when vertigo took hold of him again. His head began to loll forwards. He felt sick. He tried to get up to go to the telephone but a kind of paralysis had overtaken him. His muscles refused to obey him.

Abruptly, he saw himself in the pentagram again. Fear flooded through him. Prey to panic, he grimaced before swallowing saliva. His throat was dry. He was no longer conscious of his familiar surroundings.

At first, there was only a diffuse sensation of movement. Then he realized that he was no longer sitting down but upright, floating towards the fireplace. In front of him, he saw his own body slumped in the armchair: a body that no longer gave any evidence of breathing, which resembled that of a dead man.

Chapter 8

Peire approached his body. His fear diminished. He experienced a bizarre sense of curiosity in the face of this new adventure. He observed himself in a detached manner: his face had the pallor and fixity of death, the eyes closed and the mouth half-open. Time seemed to congeal, the seconds dissolving into a motionless wave outside reality.

Around him, the room seemed more luminous. Everything was still in its place, but a yellow halo surrounded all the objects. A log in the fireplace completed its self-consumption. The music still reached him, muffled, as if he were wearing ear-plugs. He darted another glance at his corporeal envelope and noticed that his chest was still swelling slightly. Good news.

His gaze came back to his new self: the ethereal form contemplating its former self. He examined his hands, touched his arms, shoulders and face, but experienced no sensation. His fingers passed through without encountering any resistance. He spent a few moments experiencing the strange sensation of non-existence.

A phantom, that's what I've become, Peire thought.

He left the room. The house was plunged in darkness. He was about to switch on the light when he realized that it was not worth the trouble; his astral body had begun to radiate a bright light, which now illuminated the entrance hall.

He lifted his head. At the top of the stairs, a man beckoned to him before melting into the wall. Peire did not have time to distinguish his features, but the silhouette seemed familiar, without his being able to put a name to it.

A woman appeared in the same place, clad in a long white dress. Her ageless face was redolent with plenitude. Her lips were opening and closing as if she were singing. Flames suddenly sprang from the ground to surround her and her body writhed in the fire.

She vanished in her turn. A child took her place in the fire, howling as the flames began to devour him. Then everything evaporated. Peire found himself in the bathroom, looking into the mirror.

He looked at himself attentively. It was certainly his own reflection that he was looking at, but the glass was showing him the image of an adolescent. He recognized the features of the young man he had once been, in spite of a few differences: the color of the eyes, brown when his own were green; the paler skin, as if hewn from marble. Peire also remarked that he was wearing clothes from another era: some sort of capacious black tunic, not his sea-blue sweatshirt.

He remained there, bewildered, not knowing what to do. Irrational as it might seem, the events that he had lived through in recent days must be connected with one another. The thing was to find the connecting thread, the common focus.

He left the bathroom, surprised by the facility of the displacement. He felt as free as the air, floating instead of walking. He went along the hallway again, and then headed for the studio upstairs.

Just as he reached the top of the stairs a vaporous form appeared in front of him. Only the eyes were clearly visible: two tiny fires mounted in an indistinct face. Little by little, the outline became more precise: an old man with skin like parchment, who suddenly extended his arm, threatening Peire with an aggressive index-finger.

"Where are you going?"

The voice struck him violently. It had transpierced him, resonating in the interior of his skull, penetrating his thoughts.

Peire recognized the man who had spoken to him at the exit of the tunnel of light—the one who had brought him back to life. In his left hand he held a dove, which he caressed gently. The bird cooed, its eyes closed.

"Who are you?" Peire asked.

"I'm Bertrand d'En Marti, your guide." The answer was flung back as if it were obvious.

"My guide? What do you want from me?"

"That you should return to your body. You cannot join us yet. The Laurel has need of you."

Peire did not understand. "Where's Hélène? She must be expecting me. Let me pass."

"There's no time for questions. Obey!"

The dove took flight amid a flutter of feathers. The guide waved his hand in front of Peire's face, pointing to the ground floor. His voice hardened. "Return to your body!"

The order was irresistible. Peire was constrained to obey without further discussion. Against his will, he turned on his heel without saying anything, went down the stairs and went back into the sitting-room where his body still lay, just as he had left it a few minutes before.

He made as if to draw back. He had no desire to go back, but the imperious will of the Cathar patriarch admitted no contradiction. He had to resume the course of his life, in spite of the disgust that it inspired in him. Within a fraction of a second he was reintegrated into his carnal envelope.

Peire woke up with a start, utterly distraught, as if he were emerging from a long nightmare. He checked the time. His dream had lasted no longer than 30 seconds—but the face of the old man, like those of the Cathar martyrs in the fire, remained imprinted in his mind.

He spent long minutes trying to make sense of what had happened to him. He could swear that it had not been a dream. First he had had that cerebral attack, followed by that strange journey through the tunnel. Then he had quit his body and met a man burned alive 700 years before. Stories that would have made him laugh a month earlier, but marked him profoundly today.

He had to talk to Jordanne. She had already helped him analyze the earlier events; perhaps she would have some ideas regarding what had just happened. It was entirely natural that Peire should think of her, who had always been there since childhood and who was supporting him now in his ordeal.

He remembered what she had said. She had murmured: *I've waited such a long time for that...since before Hélène....* Did that have something to do with it? In the end, he could not hold on to the train of thought. He was afraid of divining the significance of the words.

His gaze fell on the book that he had been reading before Jordanne had arrived. He picked it up and plunged back into it. Perhaps he would find answers there. His sudden interest in that part of the history of his native land was causing him to neglect his music—something that had rarely happened to him, apart from the days immediately following Hélène's death.

He read for more than three hours, resisting the urge to go to sleep. He finished the book and remained pensive for a few moments before slipping into a restless semi-consciousness from which he emerged several times without knowing what had woken him.

In his dreams, he thought he could hear the wing beats of a dove.

Chapter 9

The hairpin bend took Brother Jean-Michel by surprise; he braked sharply as he changed direction. The right front wheel came within a few centimeters of the ditch. Sitting in the rear seat, Anto did not flinch. He raised his eyes from the document he had been examining since they had left Fanjeaux and looked out of the window of the Mégane.

High above, the castle of Montségur seemed to be looming over him from the height of the Pog. The wind had just blown the clouds away and a ray of sunlight illuminated the walls. Seven centuries earlier, Blanche de Castille, the Queen of France and mother of Saint Louis had ordered her troops to cut off that head of the Cathar hydra—the most important head, the one that dared to resist the temporal and spiritual power of the Holy Church. It had sent messengers to ask for the help of the Emperor of Germany: help that never came.

After the citadel's fall, the heresy had survived for about a century before disappearing under the heavy hand of the Inquisition. And yet, more than 700 years later, the head still stood, proud and indomitable. Even though their religion had disappeared, the Cathars had not been forgotten. By an irony of fate, their imprint could still be found in the village he had just left. As one entered Fanjeaux, a billboard proclaimed: *Cathar village*—even though the place had provided shelter to the Dominicans for centuries, the first of whom had fought against the heresy! They were still keeping watch on the region—because, as St Dominic had written, it was not finished.

Anto recalled the exact words written by the first of the inquisitors on the Cathar religion in his letter to Pope Innocent III, particularly the final sentence. Dominic had urged the necessity of the Holy Father organizing a crusade against Catharism. Although he had not been able to penetrate the mystery surrounding the Perfecti, Dominic had come very close. He had recommended that the region be kept under surveillance, in order to be there when *it reawakened*. "It" was evil in its pure state. "It" must be destroyed when it "reawakened". If not, it would be too late.

Anto had searched for the significance of that *it*. He had gone through the entire life and correspondence of St Dominic with a fine-toothed comb without finding anything conclusive. Then he had studied the Cathar religion. Today, his research was reaching its terminus and he still had not discovered what it was that Dominic dreaded. He did not know what it was, or—most important of all—how to destroy it.

Brother Jean-Michel slowed down on a bend before parking the car in the lot, as Anto Sakic had asked when they left the monastery. He switched off the engine and looked into the rear-view mirror. His passenger seemed lost in thought, his eyes closed.

After a minute, the prelate got out and crossed the road. He headed for the stele that stood at the foot of the pathway leading up to the castle. He paused momentarily to read the inscription: *Als Catar, Als martyrs, del pur amor crestian.*

Anto made a gesture of annoyance. They had made the Cathars "martyrs to a pure Christian love," although they had not believed in two of the essential fundamentals of the Catholic faith: the uniqueness of a good and merciful God, and paradise after death, for those who deserved it. They had been dualists who believed in the existence of two divine principles, one Good and one Evil, with equal power. The Earth belonged to the evil one and the Heavens to the good. Human beings remained prisoners of the Evil God so long as they were impure. They would be raised progressively nearer to Heaven by washing away their sins. Now, that might require more than one life. To arrive at the original state of purity, the Cathars believed that successive reincarnations were necessary: a notion that Catholics rejected forcefully.

Anto recalled St Dominic's earliest sermons, his debates with the deacons of the Cathar church, here in this region. He was the first to have understood the heretical and satanic nature of the sect. The inquisition had been born in these mountains, in these villages delivered to the heresy that gained more and more ground from the Catholic Church. The first inquisitors, the Hounds of God, had reacted promptly and efficaciously to extirpate these heretical ideas from the souls of men and women, by fire and bloodshed when necessary. Since then, the Inquisition had been officially dissolved, but Anto was still a Hound of God, an inquisitor

He heard the sound of an engine. He turned round; a Mercedes parked right beside the Mégane. Tourists were scarce at this time of year; it could only be his contact.

Anto tried to make out the shadowy figure seated in the rear but the smoked glass made it impossible. He had never met his correspondent; their exchanges had always taken place by telephone or email. He knew what awaited him, though; sometimes a Hound of God had to ally himself with his oldest enemy, the wolf.

Anto came back down the narrow path, crossed the road, paused in front of Brother Jean-Michel to signify to him that all was well, and then marched over to the car that had just arrived.

The rear door opened, inviting him to sit down on the black leather seat. He recoiled slightly on discovering an elegant woman smiling at him.

"Bonjour, Monsignor," she said, with a hint of irony. "I'm Elke Ströder. We've had dealings with one another. Have you brought the two documents that you reed to give me?"

"No."

Anto wedged himself into his seat, disconcerted by that feminine presence beside him. He had never imagined that his correspondent might be a woman, much less a woman of this sort.

Elke's left hand clenched on the elbow-rest. She resumed, in a firm tone: "That poses a problem. Without those documents, our exchange is invalid. You know that perfectly well—my conditions were unequivocal. Why have you kept our rendezvous? You've made me waste my time."

Anto mentally revised the plan on which he had reflected for a long time. He had to proceed very prudently with this kind of interlocutor. He needed the German woman, but he would not surrender St Dominic's letter under any circumstances. It was too important for him to let it out of his possession. In any case, he had never mentioned it. Perhaps, as a last recourse, he might give her a copy, but only if there was no alternative.

"I have an item of information in my possession that will interest you more than the parchment: an important element of the puzzle, of which I doubt that you have heard mention, and which will permit us to conclude our exchange."

"I'm listening," the German woman replied, suddenly intrigued. "It's in your interest to be convincing—you know the value that we attach to the letter."

"Do you know the story of the massacre of Avignonet?"

"Of course—but I don't see that it has anything to do with our business...."

"You're mistaken," Anto cut in. "You recall that, in May 1242, eleven inquisitors, headed by the Dominican Guillaume Arnaud, purified the town of Lavaur of its heretics?"

"By burning them!"

Anto paid no heed to the sarcasm and continued his narrative. "Their mission accomplished, they established themselves in the town of Avignonet, expecting to go to Rome to carry the document entrusted to them by St Dominic. Unfortunately, they chose a house belonging to an associate of the Cathars. That person immediately warned the garrison at Montségur—which, without losing a minute, sent a small contingent of soldiers. They arrived by night, broke down the doors of the house where the inquisitors were sleeping, and massacred them. As they returned to Montségur, one of them publicly expressed his regret at not having brought the skull of one of the priests from which to drink."

"Did they have the document with them?"

"I am convinced of it."

"Have you been lying to us from the beginning? The Vatican doesn't have it—the Cathars recovered it."

"I fear so," Anto replied, calmly.

There was a silence in the vehicle's interior which the German woman broke, contemptuously. "It's definitely lost, then. Given its importance, the Cathars must have put it in a safe place—and it must have been destroyed since then."

"If you will permit me one question, I don't understand the value that you place on this document. According to the texts transmitted by the Inquisition, it's merely a simple list of names of Cathar Perfecti."

"Are they not important?"

"Explain why."

Elke pouted before replying, dryly: "Why? Since you're obviously not in possession of the object of our trade, I shan't give you any information without obtaining anything in exchange. It's the very basis of our arrangement. It seems to me that we have nothing more to say to one another."

"That's a great pity," Anto said, simply. "Truly unfortunate. A collaboration that promised to be so fruitful...."

"What do you mean?"

"In the course of my various researches, I found a very interesting trail which might lead us to it."

"Which is?"

Anto remained impassive for a few seconds before flaunting an air of satisfaction. His strategy was working.

"Fair exchange is no robbery," he replied, joining his hands across his stomach, signifying that he was waiting.

After a pause charged with tension, Elke brought a book out from under the seat. After holding it in her hands for a moment, she opened it and studied a few pages before closing it again and holding it out to him.

"All right. This is Otto Rahn's notebook—but you can only have the location of the cave with the pentagram when I'm in possession of the parchment, not before."

Anto took possession of the object that he had coveted for more than 50 years, ever since the epoch-making confession of the SS officer, who had told him about Otto Rahn and all the Nazi research on religions in exchange for a passage to Argentina—especially the excavations around Montségur, in which he had participated. The man had told him practically nothing, except for the locations of the various excavation sites; he did not know if the savants had discovered anything. He knew that two boxes had been repatriated to Berlin in 1944, but he did not know what had become of them or what they contained.

After leaving a message regarding Otto Rahn on an Internet discussion forum, Anto had commenced a dialogue with a surfer—an individual he had taken at first for the representative of a group of Third Reich antiquarians in search of information on the Nazis' occult researches. As the exchanges progressed, however, he realized that his correspondent did not care at all about Hitler, but knew as much as he did about history, religion and the Cathar mysteries.

Anto had asked several questions about the boxes. His contact had replied that they merely contained books and objects of no great interest. Even so, the cardinal had been persuaded that Otto Rahn held the key to the puzzle.

Otto Rahn….

Anto was intrigued by the enigmatic individual who had spent two years in this region, in 1936 and 1937, before disappearing mysteriously. Had he ended his days on an Alpine glacier, as certain biographers claimed? Had the Nazis killed him during the war? No one knew exactly when or how he had died. Was he really dead? There was a photograph showing him in Lebanon in the 50s, although no one had been able to provide a formal identification.

Over the years, the legend had overtaken the man. Numerous authors had speculated about Rahn's disappearance in order to sell their books. Some claimed to have seen him prowling around the environs of Montségur.

Anto sighed. Finally, after all these years, he had succeeded in recovering Otto Rahn's notes. He moved his fingers delicately over the cracked and worn maroon leather binding.

He opened the notebook, written in a tortuous hand, and turned the yellowing pages, rapidly scanning the first chapter before closing it again. He turned to the German woman, who was looking at him fixedly, her eyes narrowed, awaiting his response.

"Are you familiar with the Société del Gai Saber?"

Elke could not conceal her astonishment. She lowered her eyelids, nodding her head. "Interesting," she murmured. "Very interesting. According to you, then, they're in possession of the document? Have you any proof?"

"Certainly not! I stumbled on the group by accident, while studying the resurgences of Catharism. It was created in 1323 by seven pseudo-troubadours, in order—according to their charter—to develop and preserve the Occitan language." He paused, satisfied that he had made a telling point. "I've long grown accustomed to analyzing historical facts in the light of the documents we have obtained. The Occitan language was only a cover. The Cathar church knew that its end was nigh. Its only chance of survival lay in semi-clandestinity. It founded a society that might continue to defend its values without the knowledge of our Holy Church and, what's more, with the support of the papacy...."

"Your theory is fascinating. I've never looked at the facts from that perspective. As it happens, I was at a ceremony held on their premises last week, at which something curious occurred."

Elke gave a detailed account of Peire Aicart's accident. Anto listened attentively. He analyzed the implications of the story, which supported his theories. He concluded, in a loud voice: "The pentagram...always the pentagram. If you could rummage through the archives of the Société del Gai Saber you might perhaps discover interesting items. And why not other documents? I've heard mention of a particularly important book, without ascertaining any further details...except that it contains a list. That might be what you're looking for."

Elke reacted instantaneously. "I've also gathered vague information tending in the same direction—but that's your problem, not mine. You need to get hold of that list if you want any more information."

Anto made a face; he had just lost ground. He tried a new approach, changing the subject.

"Getting back to this list, what does it represent?"

"Don't forget our bargain. You'll have to find out on your own. It's no ordinary list. I don't know its contents, but, according to my sources, it's capable of unsettling the strongest faith."

"My faith is in Our Lord alone, and it's far from being under threat. I shall prove the justice of St Dominic's affirmations."

"Amen," Elke mocked. "But you really don't know what you risk discovering in this region. You've been warned."

"Have no fear," Anto reaffirmed, forcefully. "The Catholic religion is still in step with the progress of History. Even the Dead Sea scrolls gave comfort to our Faith. We have no fear of archaeological discoveries. The Holy Church always triumphs over obscurantism."

Anto opened the door and began to climb out. Elke called him back from the depths of the vehicle.

"Don't forget—fair exchange is no robbery. I'm waiting for the document now."

The Cardinal went back to his car, in which Brother Jean-Michel was waiting.

"We're going to Toulouse, to the house that harbors the Société del Gai Saber. I have a fondness for visit such places."

The Dominican drove off, leaving the castle of Montségur behind to rejoin the main road at Pamiers, the headquarters of the bishopric that had accommodated the Inquisition during the Crusade. From there he headed for Toulouse.

Comfortably ensconced in the back seat, Anto opened the file to which he had consigned all the information transmitted by his agents. Patiently, he reread the information he had concerning the so-called cultural society. He concentrated on every word. The part he was about to play was vitally important to his future; he would not get another chance—and this learned society was a new element to study, taking account of what he had just learned. He re-immersed himself in the perusal of his documents.

It had all begun on All Saints' Day in 1323. Seven troubadours had come together to found the *Companhia dels mantenedors dou gai saber*. Their aim was to defend and codify the Occitan language, which the church described as "the language of heresy".

The Vatican archives had not told him much about the founders: two bankers, two merchants, a notary, a bourgeois and a young idler. The most peculiar thing was that he had not found any trace of poems or songs written by six of the seven troubadours, although he had gone through all the anthologies, collections and books on the Cathars. There was no trace of the six names, which were unknown to all specialists. There was, in consequence, only one definite versifier: Bernard de Panassac, a scarcely commendable fellow. To be sure, he had written one song dedicated to the Virgin, but he was also the author of lewd songs, had been implicated in several thefts, and even suspected of murder. Moreover, none of the seven had had any connection with the Cathar church.

The creation of the Société had been conducted with the strictest legality, so as not to offend the King of France or the Bishop of Toulouse, who had seen nothing suspicious in it. Two jurists had formally drawn up the rules of its constitution and function, under the title of the *Leg d'Amor*. Anto knew that all this was merely to throw dust in the eyes of the Inquisition, in order to obtain its blessing and thus be able to operate in the open.

Once the last heretics were dead, the Church had nothing more to dread. The heresy was vanquished, the last Cathars committed to the fire. Even the Comte de Toulouse had abandoned all thought of sedition. He no longer posed a threat to the Pope or the King of France. Only the troubadours carried the seeds of revolt within them, and the Société del Gai Saber encouraged them. Their songs were moral and political satires, which they hawked around every layer of Occitan society, mounting a passive resistance to the Catholics throughout the South of France—but their influence had dwindled away, diminished by the passage of the years.

Why, then, more than 600 years after its creation, did this brotherhood founded by individuals devoid of influence still exist? That question intrigued Anto deeply. The widest possible research was required to lead him to evidence of its ties to the Cathar church.

Anto had obtained one of the Gai Saber's brochures. He opened it. On the first page was a classical portrait of the Virgin with the infant Jesus, bowing down to a troubadour. A second woman was represented on the same page: blonde-haired, clad in a green dress and a purple cloak, with her right arm upraised. The caption beneath the picture named her as *Dame Science*.

A historian had put forward the suggestion that this mysterious Dame must be Clémence Isaure, the society's patroness. Even her existence was unproven. For his part, Anto had his own hypothesis. The woman had to represent the Egeria of the Cathars, Esclarmonde de Foix. At the age of 12, she had sworn to dedicate her life to the Spirit, and had become an ardent propagandist of heresy throughout the southern regions of France. She had even received, at Fanjeaux, from the hand of Bishop Guilhabert de Castres, the greatest Cathar sacrament: the Consolamentum. She had become the principal adversary of Foulque, the Bishop of Toulouse. Finally, it was her who had offered the castle of Montségur to the Cathars. In the work presented by the Société del Gai Saber, however, the hierarchy of the Catholic Church had only seen the Virgin.

Anto closed the file again. One particular indication confirmed him in his certainty regarding this Société. Whence came its financial resources, seemingly inexhaustible for six centuries? Undoubtedly the treasure of the Cathar church, the gold and silver it had possessed—for it was a historically recognized fact that the Cathar church had been rich.

They reached Toulouse after an hour. Having left the by-pass they arrived in the main square, where they lingered, caught in a traffic jam. The car finally made its way into the side-streets of the town centre. The chauffeur succeeded in finding a place to park not far from the building in which the Société's premises were located.

"Would you like me to accompany you, Monsignor?"

"No, just watch the door."

Anto Sakic idled for a few minutes on the pavement, looking up at the façade, and then decided to go into the building. He walked round the courtyard before finding an open door. He went in and walked along a hallway, studying a collection of paintings hung on the walls.

"Are you looking for someone?"

Anto started with surprise. He turned round. A young man, whose approach he had not heard, was looking at him interestedly.

"I'd like to meet one of the members of the Société del Gai Saber," Anto said. "I'm sorry, but I haven't made an appointment."

"I think one of the directors is here. If you'd like to follow me, I'll find out whether he can see you."

Anto agreed. They walked together to an imposing door of solid wood, beside which a copper plate advertised the list of associations lodged in the building.

"I must ask you to wait here."

His guide disappeared; Anto waited patiently for a few minutes until the door opened again.

"Monsieur Jean Rudel will see you. Please come in."

The cardinal went into the room. Woodwork wrought from valuable species covered the walls. Three blown glass lamps diffused a soft light. Seated in a black leather armchair behind a massive desk covered with papers, Jean Rudel raised his head to look at his visitor. On the wall behind the officer of the Société was a picture representing a blonde woman with a troubadour at her feet.

Jean Rudel got up and came towards Anto, extending his hand.

"What can I do for you?"

"I'm Cardinal Anto Sakic. I'm interested in everything concerning the religion and art of the Middle Ages. As I was passing through your city, I wanted to visit your premises."

"I'm surprised that the Catholic Church should pay us a visit. Are we so famous, then?"

The astonishment that his interlocutor had manifested, for a brief moment, was not lost on Anto. He let nothing show, though, and continued in the same tone: "Don't be so modest. Was it not created, originally, to honor the Virgin Mary. The engraving behind you testifies to that, I think."

Jean Rudel had a slight smile at the corners of his mouth. He indicated a leather armchair in which Anto Sakic sat down.

"Unfortunately, the works that we reward at the present time have become somewhat distanced from religion," the President said, returning to his own seat. "Our aim is to see that the Occitan language does not fall into disuse—a language that the Church considered heretical at one time, I seem to recall."

"That was a long time ago. Having said that, what interest me about your society is its relationship with Catharism—but from a historical point of view rather than a polemical one."

"That's reassuring," Rudel could not help replying, in an ironic tone. "For a moment I thought the Inquisition had returned to our lands to build more pyres."

Anto controlled himself, so as not to let his annoyance show. "I assure you that my interest is purely academic. I'm doing some research of a personal nature."

"I don't want to mislead you; the relationship to which you refer does not exist. Oh, I'm not saying that the members of the Société don't include a few who are sympathetic to the Perfecti—but who is not, nowadays, in this region, when one considers the Inquisition's tortures?"

"I have made a close study of the Société's origins," the cardinal persisted. "I find it strange that it was founded a few years after the fall of Montségur."

"A few years after?" Jean Rudel replied, determined not to yield an inch of territory to his adversary. "It was almost a century."

They locked stares for a long interval. Anto finally sighed, aggravated by his recalcitrant interlocutor. "I don't share your opinion," he said. "In my view, the connection exists. The Dame your troubadours venerated was not the Virgin Mary but the Cathar Church."

"Your interpretation is not based on any specific historical fact. The founding members only had the simple artistic ambitions that we still pursue today. The proof of that, I think, is that none of them was troubled by your Inquisition, although it was very powerful and sent people to the stake for much less."

"How do you explain that no trace exists of the works of six of the seven founders?" Anto asked, directing a frosty stare at him.

"They have been lost in the course of centuries. Many historic relics of the Middle Ages have disappeared, especially with regard to popular traditions."

"Even though the songs of other troubadours have survived into the present and we know them in detail? That's convenient."

"I see that no objective argument will find favor in your eyes. What is it that you want?"

"I'm spending a few days in the vicinity, and I'd like to take advantage of the opportunity to study your archives...." Anto fixed his host with an intense stare, and then added, in a soft voice: "Unless you have something to hide."

Jean Rudel got up from his seat, came around the desk and came closer to his guest, who remained seated. He examined him with undisguised scorn. "All our documents are at the disposal of the public, and you will not be the first to consult them. Numerous researchers have already studied them."

He paused for a moment before continuing: "One simple question: do you speak Occitan?"

Seeing that the conversation was reaching its conclusion, Anto got up in his turn. "Of course. It's always necessary to understand an enemy's language in order to fight him effectively, isn't it?"

Jean Rudel chose not to respond to the prelate's provocation. "I must take my leave of you," he said, simply, while extending his hand. "Duty calls."

Anto took the hand and shook it while they challenged one another with their eyes.

The director went to the door and opened it, adding as he showed his guest out: "You may spend the day here whenever it suits you. Come directly to me. I'll take you to the room where our archives are held. You'll be able to establish that we have nothing to hide."

They went their separate ways outside the office. As he went out, Anto paused for a few moments inside the pentagram inscribed on the floor. He examined it minutely. Then he closed his eyes and remained motionless. He was calm, but his mind was alert. Nothing happened. He left the figure and took a dozen steps forward, then turned round to look at it again. He went back to place himself upon it.

Suddenly, he shivered. He experienced a vision, as rapid as a lightning-flash. He pronounced a single word in a loud voice: "*DRAC*."

Chapter 10

The cold wind shook the branches of the plane-trees bordering the village's single street. A slightly stronger gust lifted a few dead leaves from the deserted pavement. Dinner time was approaching; the people were at home.

Hand in hand, Peire and Jordanne strolled past the old houses before stopping in front of one, nestled in the depths of an unkempt garden. Night was beginning to fall and the streetlights were coming on.

"You're very nervous this evening," Jordanne murmured, as she opened the garden gate. "What's wrong?"

"I don't know. I'm afraid of learning something about my grandfather or Hélène's death."

She stopped to look him in the face. "You're sure that's it? Or do you regret that you made love to me? We can leave it at that, if you want...."

Peire looked her in the eyes for a moment, then drew her to him and kissed her tenderly, without passion. "Will you stay with me tonight, Jordanne?"

"If that's what you want, yes. But you have to meet the Comtesse...or would you prefer to go back?"

"No, I want to see her. I don't know why, but if this meeting doesn't happen, I'll regret it all my life."

Jordanne knocked on the door. After a few seconds, it swung inwards and a little old lady peered at them suspiciously through thick spectacles.

"Bonjour Madame la Comtesse. I'm Jordanne Sutra. I telephoned you yesterday to say that we'd come to see you this evening."

"Come in, come in—I didn't recognize you in the dim light." She let them pass before closing the door behind them. "Go into the sitting-room. You know the way."

Darkness reigned within the room. Only a little lamp and the meager fire burning in the grate diffused a feeble light.

The shutters were closed, preventing the light of the street-lamps from penetrating into the house.

Leaning on her walking-stick, the old lady followed them at a slow pace. She invited them to sit in two Empire arm-chairs, which had known better days, then sat down in a digni-fied manner on an old green velvet settee.

"Would you like something to drink?" she asked them. "I can only offer you tea or port."

Peire and Jordanne refused politely.

"What can I do for you?" the Comtesse asked, looking curiously at Peire.

"My name is Peire Aicart. Jordanne told me that you might perhaps have known my grandfather, Camille Aicart."

The old lady closed her eyes; the lines in her face seemed to smooth themselves out into a more relaxed appearance il-luminated by an inner joy. She shook her head knowingly.

"Camille...yes, I remember him very well. A very close friend. He sat on the armchair you're sitting in more times than I can count. Now I understand why I had the impression that I recognized your face when I saw you. I've seen you with him, when you were little."

"You saw one another often?"

"Before the war he came every week. I had a sort of sa-lon, you know, where Occitan was spoken. We put the world to rights, we wrote about the Cathars...I was never alone, as I am today...."

"And afterwards, he continued to come?"

"No, the war had broken out. Our circle was shattered by events. Everyone went his own way afterwards."

"What events?" asked Peire, with a knot in his stomach.

The Comtesse concentrated, furrowing her brow. As if to herself, she murmured: "It was a long time ago, I'm afraid I don't remember...and what good does it do to rake up the past?"

"Because it's come back to the surface, and most of all because I need to...." Peire told her about his illness at the Société del Gai Saber, the song that had come from nowhere, the death of his wife and the four young men, and the pentagrams.

The Comtesse studied him attentively, tapping the armrest of her settee. When Peire had finished his story, she said: "Come here."

Peire was lost amid the images of his recent past. He did not realize immediately that the request was addressed to him. The Comtesse renewed the invitation: "Come here, Peire."

He finally got up, and came around the table to lean over her. She took his hand and nodded her head thoughtfully. She took a deep breath.

"Very well, I'll tell you what I know. You'll be the judge of whether it's any use to you....."

There was a moment of silence while they looked at one another. Eventually, she released him, and Peire sat down at her feet to listen.

The Comtesse de Mariel began to speak in a firm voice. "It all began in 1936, when Otto Rahn arrived in Montségur. He was a young German student infatuated with Wolfram von Eschenbach's *Parsifal*. He made contact with erudite men who shared his ideas. Afterwards, he wrote *Crusade Against the Grail*. For him, Parsifal was quite simply Trencavel, the Vicomte de Carcassonne. He believed that that Inquisition had come to the region to combat heresy, but also to recover the Holy Grail."

Peire nodded. "I've just finished his biography. He was considered to be a fraud, who often mingled truth and falsehood. Some people thought he was a spy."

"It's more complicated than that," the Comtesse went on. "Hidden behind Rahn were the Polarians, people who had revived the legend of Ultima Thule."

"The Nazis?"

"No. They came later. Don't forget that Rahn's expeditions began in 1930—in France, at that time, no one had heard of Hitler."

"Who were this Thule group, then?"

"German savants associated with occultists, who transformed their research group into a secret society."

"Why did they come to Montségur?"

"The Cathar philosophy attracted them, because it ran counter to Catholicism—and the legends associated with Montségur, as well. From the time of his arrival, Rahn was surrounded by a veritable court, to which your grandfather became attached. I became a sort of Egeria to it. Well, he succeeded in convincing me...." She nodded in confirmation in the face of Peire's astonishment. "At that time, I believed in Otto Rahn's ideas, in the crusade against the Grail, in Montségur as the Temple of the Cup. We spent hours in this room inciting one another to erect ever-crazier hypotheses. But we didn't just talk. We followed Rahn in his researches in the field, around Montségur and all the caves in the region."

"You've seen the famous fakes that he tried to pass off...."

"Certainly—but they were a mask for his real discoveries."

Peire and Jordanne could not hide their surprise. "You really found something?"

"We discovered four caves, each containing a geometrical figure—four pentagrams, in all. You bear their mark, Peire. You've escaped from one of them. That's why I decided to talk to you this evening."

Peire allowed his surprise to show; he could not help exclaiming: "Like the one where my wife was found dead?"

"According to Rahn, there were five caves containing pentagrams."

"They served as places of initiation for the Perfecti," Jordanne said, speaking for the first time.

"That's what everyone believed, but Otto Rahn thought that it was mistaken. He claimed to have discovered their true significance." After a brief pause, the Comtesse de Mariel went on: "According to him, they marked the place where the Cathars' treasure was."

Jordanne and Peire exchanged a swift glance. "Did Otto Rahn find it?" Jordanne asked.

"No. He only found four pentagrams. He was never able to discover the last one, although we scoured the entire region. One day, he had to leave...a matter of a bankrupt business. The French legal authorities were after him—but I've always had doubts about the lawsuit. In my opinion, his research disturbed certain people."

"Who?" Peire asked.

"I never succeeded in finding out. There had been articles in the newspapers claiming that Rahn was a spy. I think someone was trying to prevent him from achieving his goal. It's just an impression, without any proof."

Jordanne nodded her head, and then asked: "And you didn't continue the search on your own?"

"No, Rahn was the soul of our group. After his departure, we ended up forgetting the story of the treasure. Each of us had his own ideas regarding Otto Rahn's theories. Then the war broke out."

"What do you think about the treasure?" Peire asked.

The Comtesse re-immersed herself in her memories before replying. She took advantage of the pause to take up a carafe placed on a side-table near the settee and pour herself a glass of water.

"In the beginning, I was excited by Rahn's hypothesis and his famous crusade against the Grail. Then I realized that it didn't stand up, that it was too idealized, that there was no historical evidence for it." She paused, took time to drink, and then continued: "The Cathars would never have worshipped an object that had belonged to Christ. The Grail isn't a Cathar object but a Catholic one. All of that depends on a fantasy. The treasure must consist of gold and silver coins, perhaps jewels...on the other hand, I remember that your grandfather had an interesting theory concerning the pentagrams."

"What was it?"

The old lady hesitated for a few moments before replying. "For him, they were the true guardians of the treasure.

They protected it from intruders, like the Inquisitors or the troops of the King of France."

Memories of the four young men, then of Hélène, imposed themselves on Peire. He stiffened. Beside him, Jordanne took hold of his hand and squeezed it hard. Finally, he was able to speak. "My grandfather believed that the pentagrams killed people who risked entering certain caves…?"

The Comtesse had perceived the distress in Peire's voice. She replied as prudently as possible. "That was Camille's idea, not mine. He was serious. At the time, though, we said all sorts of things, constructing 1000 hypotheses. I'm not sure one can believe in any of them…."

"It's impossible!" Peire exclaimed. "The four young men who took refuge in the cave couldn't have known anything about the treasure. Hélène was a simple potholer. Hundreds of people must have gone into those caves without anything happening to them."

"Your grandfather believed in the power of the pentagrams, though. That's the reason he never helped Otto Rahn in his search for the fifth cave."

"Rahn didn't find it, then?"

"I can't swear to it, but he never told us that he had. Something in his attitude though, when he said goodbye to us, made me think that he knew where the fifth pentagram was, or at least that he knew exactly where to look. Afterwards, in Germany, he wrote his two books. Some of our group, including me, were shocked by his discourse, which didn't correspond to the Rahn we had known."

"His second book, *The Court of Lucifer*, was influenced by the Nazis," Jordanne put in.

"At the time, we didn't know that. Sometime later, we heard that Rahn was dead. Our lives had moved on. The treasure of the Cathars was no longer on the agenda."

"There's one thing I wonder about," Peire said. "When did he really die? I've read several theories on that subject. He could have come back with the German savants who rooted around Montségur during the war, for example."

"I don't know any more than you do. The last letter I received from Otto Rahn was in 1937. After that, the Spanish Civil War monopolized our attention, with the influx of refugees into the region, then the Second World War. Our group remained together until 1943."

"And then?"

"In 1943 a company of Germans established themselves in the vicinity of Montségur, comprising historians, geologists and military men, who were joined by a militia consisting of local youths. For their part, the Nazis put the area under interdiction; only people who lived there had passes to go in and out. Their commandant was named Dietrich Ströder. He came to chat with me several times."

Peire could not hide his stupefaction. Ströder: the same surname as Elke. That could not be a coincidence. A new piece had just been added to his puzzle.

"He knew the history of our region better than we did," the Comtesse continued.

"Had he met Rahn, perhaps?"

"We asked him that question several times, but he always avoided it. The Germans' excavations lasted until November 1943, and two members of our group participated in them."

"Who?"

"Etienne Dupré and Pierre Cadoul."

Peire reflected for a few minutes, but the names did not ring a bell.

"Where was the research carried out?"

"All around Montségur, but also in the gorges of the Frau. Especially, according to the information I was able to obtain, around the village of Ussat."

"That's right!" Jordanne put in. "It seems that the caves of Ussat harbored numerous Perfecti for a long time."

The Comtesse nodded. "Not far from Ussat the Germans had established a workshop for repairing their aircraft, in the Bédeilhac cavern. At the end of 1943 they left, before returning in the spring of 1944 to celebrate the 700th anniversary of the fall of Montségur."

"What happened on that day, exactly?" Peire asked.

"To commemorate the anniversary, our group decided to undertake a pilgrimage to Montségur, in the forbidden zone. We had to go to Foix to ask for authorization from the Kommandantur, the German general staff. There, Dietrich Ströder welcomed us into his office with a broad smile. We explained what we wanted to do but he refused point blank, without any explanation. He merely added that Montségur would be nobly honored after the victory of the Reich; the Berlin Philharmonic would come to perform Wagner's *Parsifal* there."

A fit of coughing interrupted the old lady for several seconds. She resumed in a slightly tremulous voice: "We had decided to go ahead. In spite of the risks we were running, we met up at Montségur and we climbed the Pog. I no longer remember which of us made the speech affirming Cathar independence against all oppression. The others read a poem."

The Comtesse stopped again, prey to a new coughing-fit. She had to pour herself another glass of water. When she felt better she went on: "At that moment a small aircraft flew over the castle, circled several times, then traced a Celtic cross in white smoke—two perpendicular branches inside a circle."

"That's true, then?" Jordanne put in. "Some authors attribute that event to popular legend."

"Oh, the facts are quite real. We were unable to make out who was piloting the plane, though, or who his passenger was."

"No one ever knew that for sure. The story has become one of the myths of Montségur. There's a book in my shop that mentions it."

There was a brief silence. Each of them seemed to be lost in thought. Then the Comtesse said, in a firm voice: "Yes, someone did know."

"Who?" Peire exclaimed.

"Pierre Cadoul. He was waiting for us at the foot of the Pog. He allowed us to leave without any fuss. He worked for the Germans. He joined the Waffen SS afterwards and fought against the Red Army in the siege of Berlin."

"Did he tell you who piloted the plane?"

"No, but shortly afterwards, I overheard a conversation between him and Jean Rudel. Cadoul mentioned the passenger. When they saw me, they went away."

"What became of Cadoul?" Peire asked.

"After the liberation he was seen abroad in the region for a few days, and then he shut himself away in a cave in the Galamus gorges."

Peire turned to Jordanne and said: "He might be the hermit whose belongings were sold. I'll ask Michel when I see him tomorrow." He turned back to the old lady. "Did you ever see him again?"

"I went to visit him at the beginning of the 50s, but he didn't want to see anyone. He lived in total isolation. He consented to receive me, for old times' sake, but on condition that it would be the only time. We talked all afternoon, but never mentioned Rahn or the group. Cadoul had become an authentic mystic. He only talked about God, and evil, and no longer read anything but the Bible. When I got up to go he said something bizarre—*I am the guardian*—and he read me a passage from one of the gospels. After that, I didn't try to make contact with him again, respecting his wishes."

In a hesitant tone, Peire risked posing the question that he was itching to ask: "Guardian of what?"

"I don't know. As I left he told me that the laurel would flower again one day, and that I ought to be on the lookout."

Peire could not prevent himself singing: "*Al cap de set cents ans, verdeja lo laurel*. It's the song I performed just before I fell ill."

"I've researched it," Jordanne said. "I couldn't find the name of the troubadour, but the song dates from the 13th century."

"What do you think it means?" Peire asked the old lady.

"All that I can tell you is that nothing happened on March 16, 1944. We all went home. After the war, I was no

95

longer interested in such questions. I replied to queries from various authors regarding my relationship with Rahn. Others wanted me to write my memoirs, but I preferred to keep my memories to myself."

The Comtesse stopped speaking, visibly exhausted. She was having increasing difficulty breathing. Peire darted a glance at Jordanne. They got up together to take their leave.

"Wait!" said Madame de Mariel. "I want to give you something."

The Comtesse crossed the room with difficulty, leaning on her stick, and opened a writing-desk. She took out a package wrapped in yellowed newspaper, which she gave to Peire.

"That accompanied the last letter that Otto Rahn sent me. They're notes made during his sojourn in Ariège. They're in German. I tried to read them but I gave up—too complicated for me. If they're of any use to you, I'll make you a gift of them."

Peire took the packet delicately, turned it over in his fingers several times, and then slid it into his jacket pocket. "Thank you. Unfortunately, I don't speak the language, but I'll try to find a translator." He had thought automatically of Elke.

"Don't bother," Jordanne put in, a trifle dryly. "I can read German fairly well. I'll translate them for you."

"Come to see me again whenever you wish," murmured the Comtesse de Mariel, as they went out into the darkness. "You're nice young people...."

Outside, the cold enveloped them, chasing away the gentle warmth of the hearth. Just as they got back to the car the church bell chimed eight. Peire leaned over to open the door, but the gesture was cut short. He sensed that he was being watched. He turned round. An unknown man was walking towards them.

The darkness prevented Peire from distinguishing the man's features, but he was sure that he did not know him. The shadow came to a halt two meters away from the couple. It was an old man, whose pale blue, almost transparent, eyes stood out above the dark skin of his wrinkled cheeks. He stared insistently at Peire.

"*Adissiatz!*" said Peire, seized by an abrupt desire to bid the man good evening in Occitan, for the pleasure of speaking that language.

"Bonsoir Peire, bonsoir Jordanne," the man replied, in French, in a deep voice devoid of any accent.

Peire was surprised to be addressed by his first name, for the face was completely unfamiliar to him. He tried to recall whether he had ever met the man, without result. Perhaps in Montségur? No—he would have remembered. He told himself that the man might possibly have been present at the award ceremony at the Société del Gai Saber.

"Can I help you?" he asked.

He was surprised when the old man's hand seized his arm violently, with incredible force.

"I'm the one who will help you, one day, Monsieur Aicart."

Stupefied, Peire was unable to make any reply. Without adding anything more, the man released him, drew away rapidly and disappeared behind the church.

"Do you know him?" Jordanne asked.

"His face told me absolutely nothing...."

Peire was perplexed. He also felt an intense frustration. Since coming out of the hospital, he had had the impression that had neglected some small thing, without being able to figure out what. There was something he could not put his finger on.

As he drove off, he tried to rid himself of the anxiety that gripped him. Anxiety about what? He did not know. Since his accident, he seemed to be living in a world in which anything was possible.

Peire went rapidly through the village of Montségur without encountering a living soul and went into a shop where utter chaos reigned. Michel was arranging books, plates, glasses and little Chinese statuettes in a small display-case.

"Hello, Peire. When will the CD be out, then?"

"It's coming along—just one more song to write and it'll be finished. I have a question to put to you. What was the name of the man who lived in that cave at Galamus?"

"Pierre Cadoul, I think," the second-hand dealer said. "At least, that's the name I was given."

Peire felt a tingle in his spine. It was definitely his grandfather's friend, the member of the group who had collaborated with the Germans. "Did you meet him?" he asked.

"No, I dealt with an intermediary. The man had given him all his effects, because he no longer wanted to keep any of them. A strange person, according to what his friend told me. He made a vow in 1946 and has lived in that cave ever since."

"He didn't say exactly where?"

"Not far from the monastery. There's a path leading down to it from the parking lot. Why all these questions?"

"I need to see him as soon as possible. He can help me with my research. Can you tell me the way? I've never been into the gorges."

Michel sighed and shook his head.

"You're truly hopeless, Peire! You were born here, but you're unfamiliar with half the region. I'll come with you. You're quite capable of getting lost."

Peire only hesitated for a moment.

"All right, I'd like that." In his conscience, he told himself that perhaps it might be as well if there were two of them to confront what they might find. Some presentiment told him that a part of the answer was to be found at Galamus.

Chapter 11

Galamus: the beauty of the place struck Peire immediately. In the heart of the Corbières region, in the most precipitous part of that mountainous area, the river of eagles, the Agly, had carved out one of the deepest and most beautiful gorges in France, nearly 300 meters deep in places.

Here, Nature's laws ruled supreme. The arid terrain was as grandiose as it was wild. In the winter cold, a few rickety bushes extended their branches in the midst of impassible rocks. The tops of the gorges were lost in the white mist that flowed over the vertiginous peaks.

In ancient times, this region had attracted men of faith, for Galamus, distant from human beings, was close to God— or, rather, the Gods, as attested by numerous caves in which pagan rites had been practiced before they received the first hermits to take refuge there in the 7th century.

Michel drew up in a deserted parking lot. Few people visited the site outside the tourist season. Peire got out of the car and walked to the belvedere. He studied the landscape, fascinated. Inexplicably, the place attracted him. A vibration climbed up from the cliffs to grip and penetrate his soul, like a summons from some distant past.

"The hermitage is down below." Michel's voice tore him from his reverie. His friend had joined him at the balustrade and was also contemplating the panorama. "It seems that it was German prisoners who built these flights of steps and the bridge, immediately after the war," Michel went on, pointing to a road that wound towards the Agly.

Peire could not help raising his eyebrows on hearing the word *German*, which immediately made him think of Elke. A chill ran down his spine. He leaned forward to look over the wall and observed the river running torrentially through the bottom of the canyon, a few hundred meters below. He turned to his friend.

"Where's the cave?"

"If I remember what the vendor told me correctly, the path starts on the other side of the road."

They discovered a narrow pathway which clung to the side of the mountain. They walked for more than half an hour, stopping several times to get their breath back. They finally emerged at a cave masked by several bushes. Peire parted the branches. A palisade of arbitrarily-assembled planks served as a barrier against the intemperate. A narrow opening between the laths provided access to the interior. Peire rapped on the planks and called out in a loud voice: "Monsieur Cadoul!"

He waited some ten seconds before repeating his call. There was no response. He pushed one of the planks, which almost came away in his hands, and went in.

The cave was very dark. A strong odor of mould emerged from the depths of the cavity. An intense cold accentuated the impression of dampness. Peire waited for a minute to give his eyes time to adapt to the gloom.

The interior was furnished in Spartan fashion: a wooden chair and a round table in the centre, a simple iron bed set against the wall. Peire made a rapid tour of the one and only room comprising Pierre Cadoul's domicile. On the table there was a plate, a glass and a jug. There was not the least trace of food or human presence.

"Perhaps he's in hospital," said Michel, who had remained at the entrance. "It wouldn't be surprising, given his age and the place he lived in."

"Can we make go to see the man who sold you his effects? Perhaps he can tell us."

"If you wish. He lives in Saint Paul de Fenouillet, a few kilometers away from here. But what are you going to ask him? I don't understand your determination to meet a hermit who hasn't left this place for decades."

Peire told him about his discussion with the Comtesse de Mariel. He explained that he was trying to trace the connections between the protagonists in the story into which he felt that he had been drawn. He was counting on Pierre Cadoul to give him more details. The solution turned on the pentagrams. Every night he dreamed about them: frightful nightmares, in which he fell into a bottomless well or wandered through tunnels with no end. He relived the shock he had felt in the hallway of the Société del Gai Saber. Contact with such pentagrams had killed Hélène and the four young men. One question remained unanswered: why them, and not others? They were not the only ones to have gone into those caves over the years. That element of the enigma still eluded him.

Michel saw an expression on Peire's face that he did not recognize: an intensity that transformed his friend's features, a visionary gaze.

"I need to know what really happened on March 16, 1944 and afterwards," Peire murmured. "There are now only two survivors. I want to know the reasons why he group broke up, and also to find out why Pierre Cadoul shut himself up here for such a long time."

"It's the distant past, Peire. The story's more than 50 years old. It's no longer of any concern to you...."

"On the contrary, I'm in it up to my neck. How do you explain that I sang a song that I didn't know, and almost died thereafter? At the ultimate moment, I was obliged to return to life...." He told him about his passage through the tunnel before continuing, in a less assured voice: "Something's pursuing me, haunting me, and I have to find out what it is."

Michel looked at his friend for several seconds, then put a hand on his shoulder and smiled. "I understand, old man. We'll go to see the man who sold me Cadoul's effects."

I'd like to look around here first, to see how he lives," Peire added, turning towards the depths of the cave.

"All right—I'll wait outside."

Peire walked around the room. Every trace of Pierre Cadoul's residence had disappeared, but the man had lived there for decades; he must have left some imprint. Peire was examining the place one last time, attentively, when a foul odor invaded his nostrils—a stink emerging from the depths of the cave. It was probably a dead animal in the process of decomposition—or perhaps Cadoul's corpse? Peire forced himself to take a look, but found nothing but the granite wall.

The atmosphere became truly unbreathable. Seized by a feeling of sickness, Peire quit the place after darting one last backward glance, reluctant to search the room thoroughly out of respect for the person who had lived there. He could no longer stay there; in any case, he would not have found anything. Pushing the branches aside, he found himself back in the fresh air. Michel was pacing back and forth a short distance away.

"What did Cadoul's effects amount to?" Peire asked, watching his step because the foot of the cliff was covered with small pebbles which rolled under his feet.

"Nothing of any great interest. About 20 books, plates, bowls, a lamp…I only glanced at them. The price seemed low enough for me not to have to examine them in detail."

"Could you take a closer look and tell me what there is? I'd very much like to buy the books."

"I'll make an inventory this evening, but don't expect any sensational revelations. As for the books, I've already promised them to Jordanne. See her about them."

They went back to the parking lot. Before leaving, Peire turned towards the cave one last time. He looked at the mountain, asking himself what secret Pierre Cadoul had kept for more than 50 years, then got into the car, where Michel had already gripped the steering-wheel."

From the shade of the bushes, two green eyes watched them draw away.

After driving along a winding road for about ten minutes they arrived at Saint Paul de Fenouillet. Michel parked outside his vendor's house, a building in the traditional style. They got out, and the second-hand dealer knocked at the door. A man opened it almost immediately.

"Bonjour," Michel said. "Do you remember me? I came to collect several boxes a fortnight ago. We'd like to talk to you about their owner, if it's not too much trouble."

"Not at all—but he has nothing more to sell, you know."

"I'd just like you to tell us about Pierre Cadoul," Peire said. "He was a friend of my grandfather's."

"Come in," said the man, standing aside. "But I don't know if I can tell you anything interesting."

The interior of the house had been entirely renovated. The décor was surprisingly modern, in such an old building. The walls had been knocked through to create a large space on the ground floor, which was subdivided into several zones by sober utilitarian furniture. Their host invited them to sit down in the reception-room corner and offered them a drink. Then he began his story.

"I've known Pierre Cadoul for about 20 years. At that time the village curé asked me if I would take him his food, and I agreed. Every week, therefore, I delivered bread, cheese and fruit to him. He never wanted anything else. About three weeks ago, he wanted to get rid of all his effects."

"We've just been to the cave. It's empty."

"I know. I went there last week. Pierre wasn't there. I alerted the gendarmes right away. They organized a search, without success. Even the dogs couldn't pick up his trail."

"You don't know where he might have taken refuge?"

The man reflected for a few seconds before replying. "In my opinion, He must have gone to die in another cave, some distance away. At Galamus the mountain is full of them."

Peire and Michel showed their astonishment. "Gone to die?" said Peire "But why?"

"He no longer had any desire to live. He knew that he was ill. Worn down by the burden that he had carried too long, presumably. He'd passed the point at which the spirit gives up all resistance. He must have preferred a discreet departure, so as not to owe anything to anyone."

"And the gendarmerie found nothing? Not a single clue?"

"The search revealed nothing. The area is packed with excavations, you know."

Peire was silent for a moment. "Cadoul never told you why he installed himself there after the war? It's a strange thing to do, though…."

"I asked him the question at the beginning of our acquaintance. He didn't answer, and I didn't press him thereafter. Besides, we hardly exchanged a word when I went to see him. Often, I got nothing but a simple thank you as I left."

"He never talked to you about going up to Montségur for the 700th anniversary in 1944? He was in company with my grandfather, Camille Aicart, and five other people."

"No, the rare discussions we had concerned the Bible. He didn't tell me anything about his past."

"And no one in the village knew him?"

"Stories about him went around. According to one of the elders of Saint-Paul, Pierre Cadoul was a member of the Waffen SS, and must have been one of the last combatants in Berlin. After his return, in order not to fall victim to the reprisals of the purge, he installed himself in that cave where he lived apart. That's all I can tell you."

"Thank you," said Pierre, in taking leave of their host. "Excuse us for disturbing you."

They went through the garden to return to Michel's Toyota.

"Did he tell you anything of interest?" Michel asked, as he took the keys out of his pocket.

"Not really. A few suggestive items, nothing concrete. Perhaps, when Jordanne's finished translating Rahn's journal I'll find some information there. I hope so."

"You'll have to tell me about it—your stories are beginning to intrigue me."

The sound of wings caused them to turn their heads. A dove had just perched on the garden gate, immediately in front of them, scarcely a meter away. Not at all timid, it looked at them, making little movements with its head. Peire had the impression that it was staring at them intently, curious as that might seem. Immediately, the image of the pentagram surfaced in his memory. The dove cooed, then took flight. Peire,

104

intrigued, watched it fly away at a rapid pace. He was almost tempted to follow it, to see where it was going....

Chapter 12

His vitreous eyes had ceased craving. Utterly passive, he had withdrawn into himself. For him, extreme suffering was no longer of any importance. He knew that his end was nigh, at last.

The old man's face was altered beyond recognition: lips bloodied, cheeks puffy, eyelids swollen, skin reddened by blows. A trickle of sweat and blood had stained his shirt. His entire body was trembling. His respiration was no more than a painful rasp. Head slumped forwards, he waited, half-conscious, for someone to put an end to his torment, one way or another.

His torturer seized his hair and pulled his head violently backwards. Elke Ströder leaned over him.

"Monsieur Cadoul, I know that you can hear me. I only want one item of information from you: the location of the fifth pentagram. Afterwards, we'll take you back to your cave, where you can end your days in peace."

The old man opened his mouth, and articulated, in a hoarse voice: "*Le Drac.*"

"Where is Le Drac?" Elke demanded, drawing closer.

"Everywhere."

The reply had emerged in a sigh. Cadoul's head fell back on to his chest, which was rising with increasing difficulty.

Elke stood up straight and turned her head towards Wolfgang, who was standing beside her. She gave an order in German: "Open up the map. Look for a place named Le Drac."

She walked to the window and glanced out. Then she addressed Kurt, who still had the old man's hair in his hand. "Go check the grounds. I don't want any problems. The other day's incident must not be repeated."

The discovery of the atrociously-mutilated corpse, with a camera beside it, remained an enigma. The man had undoub-

106

tedly been watching them; the development of the film proved it. Among the prints were two photographs of the farmhouse, obviously taken the day before, after the arrival of the cars— just the two. Either the individual had been killed shortly after his arrival or he had changed the film and the earlier one had not been recovered.

Who could have been watching them? Anto? It seemed quite probable that the priest had followed them; that was entirely typical of his methods. But another question preoccupied Elke: who had killed the man so savagely? After the discovery of the man, she had posted a sentry, but the surveillance had produced no result.

She would find answers to her own questions later. The essential thing, for the present, was to extract the maximum amount of information from Pierre Cadoul.

She came back to kneel in front of him and considered what she would do with him was the place was discovered. His life was only hanging by a thread; he would die soon enough. He might still be useful, though. He must possess a great deal of information. Was he not one of those rare Frenchmen who had accompanied Otto Rahn during his two sojourns at the German university in Ariège? He had also been part of the group of seven that had gone up to Montségur on March 16, 1944: one of two survivors, along with Jean Rudel. Rudel was untouchable—too well-protected.

Elke had got on Cadoul's track by chance, during a previous journey through the region. She had learned that a hermit had been living alone in a cave for more than 50 years, and had eventually been given the name of that eccentric. The conclusion seemed obvious: if Pierre Cadoul had quit the world to shut himself up in solitude, it was because he knew something. She had, at all costs, to obtain as much information as possible from him before he died.

She drew closer and murmured in the old man's ear: "What happened on March 16, 1944?"

"*Le Drac*," Cadoul repeated, mechanically, his voice increasingly feeble.

Elke persisted. "You've already said that. Talk! What did Rahn discover?"

The old man raised his head again. The German woman found herself paralyzed by the gaze of Cadoul's bulging eyes. He had the air of a madman. In the depths of his eyes there was a bright flash of supernatural golden light, incredibly violent. Then he began to recite a prayer.

Elke took several seconds to realize that it was in Latin, but eventually recognized a Cathar prayer: the Consolamentum. She listened, with an uneasy feeling, until the old man had finished. He ended in a murmur and fell back into semi-consciousness.

Just as Elke was about to ask a question, Pierre Cadoul abruptly stood up. Wolfgang tried to sit him down, but the old man turned round to push him away forcefully. He knocked his chair away. Elke took a step back. Kurt came in precipitately, alerted by the noise. He aimed his pistol, but the young woman stopped him with a gesture.

Pierre took a step forward. He reached out his arm and set his hand on Elke's forehead. She remained motionless. He hesitated momentarily, then articulated, weakly: "The laurel will flower again."

Then he collapsed, dead.

Elke stared at the corpse. Pierre Cadoul's last words had reminded her of Peire's song: "After 700 years, the laurel will flower again." She turned to her bodyguards and said to them: "Get rid of him. Do it in such a way that no one will find him."

She left the farmhouse and got into the Mercedes. The time had come to get back in touch with Peire, as she had promised him.

Elke parked the car in front of Peire's house. One of the villagers had shown her which way to go. She got out slowly, her gaze drawn to the somber castle emerging from a fog-bank at the summit of thee Pog.

108

She knocked on the door and waited. Peire finally opened it. His face was drawn.

Elke smiled. "Bonjour. I hope I'm not disturbing you."

She was wearing a sheepskin flying-jacket, and had wound a thick scarf negligently around her neck. A woolen bonnet hid her blonde hair; only a few stray wisps hung down over her eyes.

"Not at all," said Peire, standing aside. "Come in."

She brushed past him as she went into the house. A discreet hint of perfume lingered around her. He studied the young woman's sensuous curves, softened by the black leather of her miniskirt, which clung like a second skin. He felt a sudden desire to fondle her buttocks as she went forward, provocatively. She took off her bonnet and shook her head, letting her hair descend in a golden cascade over her shoulders.

He helped her take off her jacket and scarf, which he hung up on the coat-rack, then opened the sitting-room door and offered her an armchair.

"Do you want something to drink? I was just about to make some coffee."

She looked around the room before replying. "I'd like that very much."

While Peire was busy in the kitchen, Elke picked up the biography of Otto Rahn that was on a side-table in front of the fireplace. When he came back, carrying a tray with two cups and the coffee-pot, the German woman was sitting down, legs crossed, exposing her silk-clad slender thighs to the firelight.

She showed him the book and asked: "Have you read it?"

"Yes, I've just finished it. I realized that I've been living in the heart of Cathar country for 30 years and have never really taken an interest in its history."

"I'm quite familiar with Otto Rahn, you know," she said. Without waiting for Peire's response, she continued: "When I was doing my research on the works of Richard Wagner, I happened on Otto Rahn's book *Crusade Against the Grail*. It suggests that Wagner obtained the inspiration for his opera,

Parsifal, from the Vicomte de Carcassonne, Trencavel. Montségur is none other than the famous Montsalvage where the legendary Grail is lodged."

"You told me that Wagner never came to Montségur."

"We have all his correspondence. I combed through his life to write his biography and never found the slightest evidence of his presence in this region, but some authors have continued to propagate the hypothesis, with is quite romantic in the eyes of the public. Imagine Wagner sitting at the foot of the Pog, contemplating the castle and composing his most successful opera."

"Another beautiful legend debunked," Peire replied. "All the same, Otto Rahn still seems to be a fantastic individual. He combed the entire region searching for the Grail, and might even have found it...."

He hesitated for a few seconds over mentioning the notes that Jordanne had translated, but decided to keep the secret.

"Is your recording studio installed here?" Elke asked, getting up from her seat.

"Yes, on the first floor. Would you like to see it?"

"What I'd like most of all it to listen to your songs."

Peire led her to the room in which he had shut himself up for several weeks.

"So this is where you compose," Elke said, sitting down in front of the computer. "May I listen to your most recent song?"

"I've just finished writing it; it still lacks musical accompaniment. I made it up while I was walking in the Galamus gorges recently. The place inspired me. It's so magnificent...it's as if the stones spoke to me."

"The Galamus gorges."

"Do you know them?"

"Only by reputation," Elke replied, looking away. "The song, then?"

Peire noticed her reaction, but made no comment. He took a cassette, inserted it into the recorder and pressed the PLAY button. He installed himself in a chair to observe Elke.

110

She frowned momentarily, and then became impassive again until the end of the song. She crossed her legs again.

"I don't quite understand the significance of the word *Drac*...."

"The Devil, for the inhabitants of the region," Peire replied, deliberately sitting down facing her. "I preferred the word to Satan or some other synonym, because it seems more expressive. The Drac is part of our land and our traditions."

The musician could not help allowing his gaze to drift to the young woman's stockings. She found his embarrassment amusing.

"I had the impression that it was a place-name."

"I don't think so. There's certainly a Devil's pool, with a legend attached into it, but I don't know of any other in the region."

"Tell me the legend."

"It's nothing special. My grandfather told it to me once when we went fishing there. He told me that I mustn't on any account throw stones into it, because that would bring misfortune to the region."

"Where is this pool?"

"At an altitude of 2000 meters, between the Pic du Soularac and the Pic de Saint-Barthélémy."

Near a cave with a pentagram, Elke thought.

"According to the legend, there was once a village beside the pool. The villagers were famous metal-workers, because they'd discovered a vein of gold in a deep cave. They hid the extracted ore there. One day, when the men were at work, the women fishing and the old men guarding the flocks of sheep, a cloth-merchant arrived. As the children were the only ones still in the village, he took advantage of the opportunity to try to discover the gold. He found the hiding-place. At the sight of the treasure the merchant's body was transformed into that of a horned devil with a long tail. His odor stank out the entire village."

Peire got up to take the tape out of the recorder, and then continued: "He plunged his hand into the gold and grabbed it.

Then he went up on to a rock overhanging the pool and harangued the villagers: *Here is the weapon with which I shall light fires, sow hatred, fabricate ruins and make blood flow. With this I shall destroy that which is good in the hearts of men, and I will steal their souls from God!"*

Peire put the cassette back into its case. Looking directly at him, Elke was listening attentively.

"Bearing the treasure with him, he dived into the icy water, which began to boil and hiss. An enormous dragon appeared, which became the guardian of the pool. The men tried to kill the beast, in order to recover their gold, but without success. Three days later, the sky became covered in thick black clouds, a chilly wind stirred the waters of the pool and lightning flashes streaked the sky, accompanied by detonations that shook the mountain. The waters expanded to inundate the village, devastating everything in their course. Sometimes, when the weather allows, one can see a shape in the depths of the pool; people say that it's the dragon. Since then, no one has dared to profane the place."

"Like all legends, that one must have a basis in reality. Have you never tried to find out more?"

"No, I've never been interested in all that folklore. I only know that all the people of the region tell the story, nothing more."

"That's mistake. Do you think the pool is accessible at this time of year?"

"I'd be very surprised, with all the snow that has fallen recently, even with snowshoes. If I were you I wouldn't try to go there. Anyway, the water must be frozen."

"That's a pity...I would have been very interested to see it."

Peire remained silent for a moment, thinking about the vague malaise he had felt in response to mention of the Drac. The aftermath of recounting the legend left him slightly nauseous in the pit of his stomach.

"What are you thinking about?" Elke had drawn closer to him.

"The Devil," he replied, distantly.

"Why?"

"I don't know. I'd completely forgotten the tale of the pool...but it's sent a chill down my spine."

"Did you know that the Cathars believed that the Earth was the Devil's domain? It's logical that people should have given the name to certain geographical locations, no?"

"I've never made the connection."

"It's a trail worth following," Elke concluded. Abruptly, she changed the subject. "Wouldn't you like to give me a cassette of your new CD?"

Peire took a few seconds to react. His mind had begun to enumerate all the places in the region dedicated to the Devil.

"Certainly. I copied one this morning, but the sound quality isn't perfect and I wanted to work on it."

"That doesn't matter. It will give me an idea of what you can compose."

Peire took a cassette from a second recorder. He rummaged in a drawer, found an empty case, inserted the recording in it and gave it to Elke. Then they went back down to the ground floor. As they reached the door she said: "Will you come with me?"

On the pathway, Elke placed her hand gently on Peire's arm.

When they reached the Mercedes, the German woman suddenly turned to him and put her lips to his mouth. Without more ado, she got into her car and drove off. Peire watched her go anxiously.

Chapter 13

Jean Rudel stared at the photograph for at least five minutes. The scene was so intense that it made him feel ill at ease. The old man, held by two young blond men, seemed to be staring at him, as if appealing for help. The man was familiar—quite familiar, in fact; 50 years had not altered his features. Their last conversation had been on that sad January day in 1946, when he had found him in a cell in Carcassonne prison.

The encounter had been cartoonish: on one side Jean Rudel, hero of the resistance; on the other, Pierre Cadoul, traitor and collaborator. Jean had struck a bargain with his old friend at that time: silence regarding his release from prison and no judiciary pursuit. Their paths had not crossed since. On several occasions Jean Rudel had been on the point of visiting the man they called the Hermit of Galamus, but he had put off the interview every time. Now it was too late. He would never see Pierre Cadoul again.

He put the photograph into a filing cabinet, which he closed before raising his eyes to look at Philippe, who was sitting in silence, facing him.

"What have you done with Sylvain's body?" Rudel asked.

Philippe started. He remembered the discovery of his friend's body—a horrible vision that never left him. "It's still out there. I didn't touch anything; that was the best solution. Either it'll soon be discovered by a rambler, or the Germans will take charge of its disposal to avoid an inquest. They must have left it in place to give us a warning."

Jean Rudel hesitated momentarily before replying. The photograph of Sylvain's mutilated body was still on his desk.

"If they really were responsible...."

"There was no one else near the place. I made sure—but the Germans could have seen us shadowing them. The first crew must have been spotted."

Jean Rudel shook his head skeptically. "We have many enemies. It's not so much a matter of finding out who killed Sylvain as of taking a lesson from it. From now on we must be much more careful."

"We failed in our mission. We should both have left after taking the photos. Who knows whether they might not have followed us back here?"

"Oh, our existence is no secret. Elke Ströder's presence at the ceremony was no coincidence. I don't believe that her interest was professional—and the cardinal's visit can't be a matter of historical research. They've all come for one sole purpose."

"Who could have given us away?"

"Otto Rahn."

"But he's been dead for a long time!"

"Since 1944—March 20, to be exact. He knew a great deal about us, and about the treasure."

"He probably left documents, which are now in the possession of the Germans."

"The book in which he made his notes, for certain."

"And the old man the Germans kidnapped. He might have talked."

"No. He swore me a solemn oath never to reveal anything."

"Do I have to continue the surveillance at the farmhouse?"

Jean Rudel reflected, weighing the pros and cons before replying. "No, it's of no interest. They're bound to remain in the vicinity. One more month remains to us, in which we must simply remain vigilant. We have an advantage over the Germans and the Vatican: we've been ready for 700 years. Let them stew."

Philippe was appalled. "Aren't you going to avenge Sylvain? They slaughtered him! I've never seen such butchery!"

Nazis, Catholics or whatever, they haven't changed. Always this mindless violence…it's the way things are." Rudel understood from Philippe's rebellious attitude that his response was unsatisfactory. He looked at the photograph of the corpse resting on his desk, to face up to its horror: the face disfigured by blows, reduced to a mess of flesh and bone; the body lacerated, covered with deep cuts.

Rudel sighed; he was unable to confess that the murderer was not a man. That was his secret. "Be assured, Philippe, Sylvain will be avenged in due course. I promise you that."

The young man nodded his head as a gesture of acquiescence, then asked: "Who's the man we photographed?"

"An old friend," Rudel replied. He paused, drew breath and continued: "We were friends until 1944. After that, he chose the losing side, and I the victorious one."

"Now I understand how he ended up with the Germans. He must have maintained contacts."

"You're mistaken. They came looking for him because he's a survivor of a group which lived through certain events during the war. In consequence, they thought he could tell them certain things." He allowed himself to gather the thread of his memories before continuing. "And they were right. He knew one part of our secret."

"Why wasn't he eliminated before he fell into their hands, if he was in the Nazi camp?"

"Because I trusted him. He was also my best friend."

Philippe made a face. "You're very sure of him."

"He gave me his word, and I know that he's kept it."

"With modern means, anyone can talk. Under torture, a promise no longer counts for anything."

Rudel raised a hand to interrupt his interlocutor. "Don't worry. He's undoubtedly dead by now. He won't say any more. He's probably given them some items of information, but not others. He was much stronger than you think, and he had errors to redeem."

"I'm sorry. I didn't know…."

"When you've lived as long as I have, you'll learn that death is sometimes a necessary evil...the only thing that matters is our mission. We must continue the work."

"What do you want me to do?"

"The Cardinal has surely posted his Hounds of God outside the Academy. The Church has always kept an eye on Montségur by placing its soldiers at Fanjeaux. He doesn't know everything, or he wouldn't have come to see me. Let's let him search. On the other hand, we must protect Peire. You must go to Montségur to watch over him. Nothing must happen to him."

"You can count on me."

"I know that, and I appreciate your devotion. There aren't many young ones like you and Simon to keep things going...one day, when all this is over, you'll take my place. I've been preparing you for that since childhood."

Philippe squirmed in his seat, embarrassed. "You still have years ahead of you. In any case, Simon's much better qualified than me."

"On the contrary, I have little time left—scarcely enough to complete your apprenticeship and to finish transmitting all our ancient knowledge to you. You know full well that death signifies nothing to a true Cathar. I don't fear it."

They remained silent for a moment, each weighing the import of that sentence privately. Jean Rudel passed his wrinkled hand over his forehead, signaling his tiredness.

"Aren't you afraid that the Dominicans might follow me to Montségur and thus locate the musician?" Philippe asked, eventually.

"I gave his name to the Cardinal voluntarily. He would have made the connection one day or another. For the moment, no one has yet understood his role. That gives us a start on them—and Peire has nothing to fear from our rivals."

"Why protect him, then?"

"Because we have another adversary much more worrying. He can't touch Peire yet, but he possesses certain means of applying pressure that we mustn't neglect."

"Who is he?"

"I prefer not to tell you for the moment. Watch everyone."

"When should I leave?"

Rudel drummed his fingers on the table, wondering what the best solution might be. He seemed to have very little choice. He could only trust fully in three men and he was reluctant to put them in danger, but the mission was demanding, especially so close to its goal. He took a sheet of paper, wrote an address and handed it to Philippe.

"Leave for Montségur right away. The man whose name I have written down will put you up without asking questions. You can trust him, but he mustn't know anything. Be discreet. Keep me informed of everything that happens in Peire's house, down to the last detail.

Philippe read the address rapidly before withdrawing.

Rudel watched him leave the room, then got up and went to the bookshelves that filled one wall. He hesitated before selecting a book: *La Croisade contre les Albigeois.* It was a rare edition, one of the earliest printed versions, in which one of his predecessors had inserted eight pages. They had hastened the fall of Catharism and condemned numerous Perfecti to the flames, but Bernard d'En Marti had judged that they must never belong to Rome. The Inquisitors had take possession of them in France, following an unfortunate combination of circumstances, but none of them had grasped the importance of the document. In Rome, on the other hand, scholars would have been able to establish a connection between those pages and the letters of Saint Dominic. The Cathar patriarch had sent his knights to recover them at Avignonet, thus definitively sealing the fate of Montségur. He knew for sure that the Pope would not leave such a crime unpunished.

Jean Rudel set the book down on his desk, studying it for a few seconds before opening it. He riffled through it rapidly to get to the end, where the pages unique to this exemplum had been appended to the original text. He reread them for the 1000th time, proud of the responsibility that his predecessor had entrusted to him—for these words had never been seen by any other person than the director of the Academy. Only one man outside the Brotherhood was destined to read them, and he, Jean, would be the one who would have the immense joy of giving them to him.

He arrived at the end of the incunabulum, where a long list had been inserted: always the same surname, followed by a forename, a date of birth and of death, traced in different handwritings. Jean had had the responsibility of making the last inscription: a surname, forename and a date of birth, which represented the future. After him, another would come, for the list must never end.

One day, perhaps, the last name would be written, but centuries would pass—millennia, even—before that moment of grace arrived.

Chapter 14

"No reply—but where can she be?" Peire muttered, replacing the telephone receiver in its cradle.

He remained immobile for ten seconds, not knowing what to do. Since early afternoon he must have telephoned the Comtesse de Mariel ten times, but had received no reply. He had called Jordanne; she too had had no news of the old lady since their recent visit.

Peire let himself fall into an armchair and took up Otto Rahn's notebook again. Jordanne had begun to translate it, but she had not wanted to read him anything until she had finished. He had so many questions in his head that he had wanted to see the Comtesse again. In particular, he wanted to ask about the relationship between Dietrich Ströder and the group that had accompanied Rahn during his journey around the Ariège region. More generally, he wanted to know more about the German.

Certain details of his first conversation with the Comtesse led him to believe that she had not told him everything, that she was concealing one essential element. Peire wanted to obtain a number of clarifications.

He got up, put on his anorak, and left the house. The afternoon would soon be over. The answers to his questions could not wait one more day. He would hazard an unexpected visit.

Outside, he hastened his steps, heading for Jordanne's bookshop-restaurant in the hope that she might be able to get away and go with him. He recalled the memory of their evening together. The connection established between them had brought a hint of warmth back to his life, breaking his solitude—and Jordanne seemed happy too….

He went into the bookshop. Two customers were standing in front of the shelves with books in hand. Behind a table, Jordanne was making up a small package. When she saw him, she made a hand signal. Peire waited patiently for a few moments, to give the tourist couple time to leave, and then he went to Jordanne and kissed her on the mouth.

"I can't get hold of the Comtesse," he said. "I'm going back to see her to ask her some questions. Do you want to go with me?"

Jordanne moved a stray wisp of hair. "If you'll give me time to close the shop. I won't get any more customers today. I'm not opening the restaurant—it's closed today. Look behind the counter—there are four books for you. On the other hand, I haven't finished the translation. I still have about ten pages to do. I hope to finish this evening."

"Well? Is it interesting?"

"You can judge for yourself. I don't want to influence you."

While Jordanne put things in order, Peire took the four volumes from behind the counter. Three were devoted to the history of the Cathar religion, the fourth dealt with experiences of life after death."

Five minutes later, Jordanne closed the Leg d'Amor. During the journey she summarized the books for him.

They soon arrived in front of the Comtesse's house. Peire notice that the door was ajar. For politeness' sake he rang the bell and waited for ten seconds before trying again. There was no response. He turned to Jordanne to seek her approval before opening the door. She nodded her head and gestured to him to go in.

A current of cold air escaped the moment they entered the house. They went through the hallway to the sitting-room where they had talked to the old lady before. They pushed the door. A dazzling light shone in short pulses. It came from the chandelier, where seven light-bulbs were blinking on and off like a stroboscope. Peire and Jordanne remained in the doorway momentarily, nonplussed, until a groan attracted their attention.

The Comtesse was crouching in front of her armchair, her hands clapped to her eyes as if to protect them from the light. They hurried towards her.

"Are you are right, Madame de Mariel?" asked Jordanne, in a placatory voice, before putting a hand on her shoulder.

The old lady parted her fingers. She looked at Peire and Jordanne but did not seem to recognize them. The she screamed hysterically for several seconds before collapsing again.

At that moment, there was a strange noise: a sound that resembled nothing familiar, as if someone were breathing heavily—very heavily—while laughing simultaneously. Then the laughing grew louder and more sibilant. It seemed to be coming from the foundations of the house.

Finally, silence resumed.

Jordanne leaned over the old lady and took her hands. She spoke to her calmly, asking her what was wrong. The Comtesse did not react. She lay there unmoving, stupefied. Her respiration was feeble. Jordanne tried then to lift her up in order to sit her in the armchair but she could not do it.

"Help me," she murmured, grimacing.

Peire crouched down on the other side and tried in his turn to move the Comtesse, without result. The body seemed to be too rigid.

"What if we stretched her out?" he said. "We have to call a doctor—I think she's just had a fit."

The Comtesse suddenly fixed her gaze on a point behind them. A hideous grimace distorted her features, and then her lips articulated a few words which she repeated mechanically several times: "The Drac! Rahn was right."

The lights in the room became blinding, then all the lamps went out simultaneously. The room remained in darkness for 20 seconds before a greenish light appeared in the doorway.

At first, it was only a mere glow floating a meter above the ground. Then, by degrees, it intensified, acquiring form, until a visage was discernible, facing them. A nauseating odor invaded the sitting-room.

Peire recognized the stink that he had smelled in the cave. He stared at the luminous phenomenon, his mouth dry. He was surprised by his calmness. He should have been terrified, but he did not experience any dread. It was as if he had lived through such moments before, as if he recognized the creature. It emerged from a very remote past, lurking in the utmost depths of his memory.

The green glow concluded by taking shape completely. The beast stood in the doorway of the room, motionless. Its putrid breath emerged from a mouth equipped with pointed teeth. It had a hooked nose, hollow cheeks, shaggy hair, horns and a beard: the face of the Devil, as the popular imagination had the habit of representing him.

The body was more imprecise, as if it had not completely materialized. Huge and massive, it was humanoid in form. Its squamous hide was covered in scales, animated by a vibration of its own, which ran over it in iridescent waves. It had long hook-like fingers terminating in claws. Its feet terminated in cloven hooves.

The beast's piercing eyes studied the three occupants of the house, and then fixed themselves on Peire. The pupils contracted and the creature whistled. It stared intently at the musician.

Peire walked toward the creature, irresistibly attracted to it. He did not want to move, but he advanced in spite of himself. Behind him, Jordanne was paralyzed. She watched Peire's inexorable progress anxiously.

An intense cold permeated the room. Peire shivered and his teeth chattered. He heard Jordanne sobbing behind him. He had the sensation of watching himself move, as if he were external to the scene. And the creature continued to draw him forward, to command his movements. Then, when he was less than a meter away, The Comtesse's clear voice rang out, resonating within the room.

"*I saw the Spirit descending from Heaven like a dove, and it abode upon him.* That is written. You may take me, but him you shall never have!"

She had quoted a sentence from the Gospel according to St John, the sacred text of the Cathars. At those words, the beast snarled. It turned its gaze to the Comtesse, extended a finger in her direction, and whistled again. The old lady was thrust violently backwards. An invisible grip pinned her to the wall and compressed her rib-cage. She groaned.

Peire watched the performance, incapable of intervention. He was completely paralyzed—and yet he refused to be a powerless witness to the murder. The Comtesse's choking sounds tore at his heart. He tried desperately to move without being able to do so.

Suddenly, he had a vision of the pentagram. The geometrical figure vibrated, giving off a blue light.

The creature immediately began to lose consistency. The green light grew fainter, then exploded with a sharp hiss. An intense pain shot through Peire's brain.

When he reopened his eyes, the room had resumed its normal appearance. The lamps in the ceiling fitment were shining now with their usual intensity.

Peire turned round. Jordanne was standing still, facing him, her fists clenched. He took her by the shoulders and shook her gently before embracing her. She put her arms around him and snuggled against his torso, pressing herself against his body forcefully.

Peire understood, confusedly, that the events of the preceding days had only been the beginning of a much more sinister drama. His stomach felt knotted. Stroking Jordanne's hair, he spoke to her softly. "How are you? Can you hold it together? We must see to the Comtesse."

Jordanne nodded. She drew away and set her clothing to rights.

Peire turned to the Comtesse, whose body was collapsed, doubled up at the foot of the wall with the head slumped forwards. He bent down and tried to find a pulse, but understood very quickly that the woman was dead. He got up and picked up the telephone receiver to call the police.

Two hours later, Peire and Jordanne left the village after answering the gendarmes' questions. To avoid difficulties, they had decided unanimously to say nothing about the supernatural events that had taken place and to say that on arrival at the Comtesse's house they had found her inanimate. The duty physician had diagnosed a natural death, and had issued a permit for burial after a rapid examination.

They drove for ten minutes in silence.

"What did we see?" asked Jordanne, letting herself relax into the back of the seat.

"I don't know anything. I've never been so afraid in all my life! It was as if I were exhausted and my body refused to obey."

"Could that have anything to do with your illness? It's all so bizarre…you're no longer the same person."

"I don't know, Jordanne. So many strange things have happened to me recently. Listen—I didn't invent that song! I've come back from the dead! And where did that old man who came to speak to us spring from?"

Jordanne remained pensive.

"I haven't been dreaming Jordanne," Peire went on. "It's all quite real. You definitely saw all of that just now, no?"

Jordanne turned her head away and remained silent for a long time, looking out of the window at the passing countryside.

Peire resumed, in a supplicatory voice: "Please, Jordanne…don't let me down. Not now. I need you…."

He took her hand and squeezed it. She let her head fall back and released a long sigh. Finally, she turned towards him and replied: "It'll be all right. I've had a shock. Don't worry."

The road was interrupted by a series of bends. Peire let go of her hand in order to steer. With his eyes on the road, he asked: "What did the Comtesse say before she died? I was too absorbed to pay attention."

"She mentioned the Drac—the Devil."

Peire remained thoughtful for a few seconds. "Why did it want me?" he murmured, as if to himself.

"It's all to do with the Cathars. The man you saw at the end of the tunnel, according to your description, seems to have been Bernard d'En Marti, the last patriarch burned at Montségur—but I don't know what he was trying to tell you."

Peire thought hard. "The pentagrams!" he said, suddenly. "I'm sure they're important. Don't forget what the Comtesse said: according to my grandfather, they were the key. That explains why I became ill at the Société del Gai Saber. And just now, when I was facing the Drac, I had a vision of a pentagram. One way or another, I'm linked to those figures...."

"What are you going to do?"

"Go to one of the caves that has a pentagram. That's where the solution lies. I should have done that at the start."

"When will you go?"

"Right away! I still have time before nightfall—but the cave where the four young men died is inaccessible without skis. Do you know where the others are?"

Jordanne reflected for a few moments.

"With regard to the other three, I only know one that can be reached without difficulty, but I don't know if that one will be any use to you...." She paused conspicuously before resuming in a hesitant voice: "The Buffarnière grotto."

Peire braked abruptly and the car went into a skid, swerving and then stopping on the edge of the road. He clutched the steering-wheel tightly. He could not draw breath. A flood of memories overwhelmed him. The place where Hélène had died....

He hesitated momentarily, but an imperious need was pushing him towards the pentagrams.

"I have to go there, Jordanne. I don't know why, but it's necessary. I'll call in at Michel's to pick up equipment."

"I'll come with you, then. Ask him to come too. I'll feel more confident if he's with you in the cave.

126

"All right. We'll take him with us. I don't think he'll refuse."

Peire pressed down on the accelerator. Now that the decision was made, he felt almost joyful. He went on with his mind clear and his heart impatient; the proof was waiting for him.

Chapter 15

Anto paced back and forth in his little cell. He paused at the narrow window to admire the church of Fanjeaux, which stood on a hill overlooking the entire plain of Carcassonne. He suddenly felt the need to renew his resources in the presence of his patron saint, Dominic.

He had been incessantly mulling over recent events, especially his meeting with the German woman. He was certain that she was hiding something important from him. He was convinced of it.

He left the monastery, after informing Brother Bernard where he was going, and indicated that he would prefer to be alone. Solitude was necessary when he needed to reflect.

The cardinal took the road that led to the village and went to the chapel. He took a place in the first row, knelt in front of the altar and began to pray. He meditated for a few minutes before directing his attention to the famous relic—a partly-burned beam—that was proof of the verity of the gospels and the message of Christ.

The fragment of wood suspended on the wall, which was about three meters long, was the last witness of the theological debate between the Perfectus Guilhabert de Castres and Saint Dominic in 1207. The beam bore the traces of the fire started by Dominic's burning parchment, which had not been consumed, thus affirming the superiority of Catholic ideology to the Cathar heresy. The beam had been an object of pilgrimage ever since.

Anto approached and kissed it. He imagined the flames whirling around the piece of wood, and then leaping up towards Heaven. They called to him: a fire triumphant over Evil, which purified the hearts of sinners. In his imagination, he felt the heat of the fire upon his hands and his body. He must act now.

He left the church.

Jean Rudel would not give him any clue. On the contrary, he would put him on a false track. On the other hand, Elke Ströder had much more to tell. A little conversation with the Hounds of God would make her much more loquacious.

He went back along the road that St Dominic had taken 700 years before. On returning to the monastery he went directly to the Father Prior's office and revealed his plan. Five minutes later, two cars left the location.

Elke took off the earphones and set the cassette-player down on the dining-room table. Peire's last song had just finished. She found herself humming the refrain. The musician delighted her more and more. To begin with, she had come up with the idea merely as a pretext to meet him, but now she really wanted to produce his record when this was all over. Besides there was another thing about him that intrigued her: his name, the same as that of the man who had brought the treasure to Montségur. She wanted to investigate that; there must surely be a connection.

One of her men came into the room and spoke to her in German.

"Speak French!" she said, dryly.

"Two cars are coming towards the house," Kurt repeated.

"Do you have any idea who is inside them?"

"None. They'll be here in ten minutes."

"Ah. Our dear cardinal is probably coming in search of news. I was beginning to find it curious that he abandoned us so quickly...."

"What shall we do?"

"Let him come. Treat his men with respect, but be careful. These fanatics aren't coming to preach the good word. They're dangerous."

"Don't you want me to remain by your side, in case things turn ugly?"

"No. I want to maintain the impression he's gained, that I'm afraid of him."

129

The man immediately left the room, while Elke went into her bedroom to change. She took off her jeans, bulky sweater and underwear, and put on the dress she had worn during the ceremony. She went back into the dining-room, turned the armchair towards the fireplace, with its back to the door, and picked up the cassette-player, rewinding the tape. She made herself comfortable, with the earphones in place.

The first song had just ended when she heard the door open. She did not move.

Anto crossed the room and planted himself in front of the fireplace. She slowly raised her eyes. She waited for a few seconds before stopping the tape and taking off the earphones.

"You might have knocked before coming in!" she said, remaining seated.

"Don't play games with me, Miss Ströder. Your hirelings informed you that we were coming. Be aware that they didn't put up any resistance—my men came via the mountain. Let's not embarrass ourselves with vain formalities, if you please."

Elke acknowledged the coup. She had underestimated her adversary's strength. She was at his mercy. It would be necessary to play a tight game. She got up and made a tour of the armchair before coming back to confront Anto.

He met her gaze. The staring-match lasted for some ten seconds.

"Who was the man that you brought here?" the prelate asked, in a dry tone. "What became of him? What connection does he have with Montségur?"

"Three questions. The price to be paid goes up accordingly. I don't think you have the means to acquire the answers, my dear Cardinal."

"On the contrary, it seems to me that you're not in a strong position. I have *all* the means necessary to obtain the answers."

"Do you think I'm defeated?" Elke asked, suavely, drawing closer to him.

The German woman assumed a provocative attitude and slowly unhooked the two buttons which secured the shoulder-straps of her dress. Undulating her body in a lascivious fashion, she slid out of the garment, which fell to the floor. She stood before him, obscenely nude.

Anto looked at her disdainfully. "Temptation! Haven't you found anything better? Perhaps you imagine that I'll violate you on the spot? Or whip out a crucifix, crying *Vade retro Satanas*? It's grotesque!"

"I'd prefer the former alternative." She passed her hands over her hips, caressing them languorously. Then her hand slid across her abdomen.

"Who was the man you brought with you?"

"Elke's only reply was: "Hmmm...."

At first she had only sought to shock and challenge the priest to distract him. Now, the game amused her—excited her, even. Never before would she have dared to behave in this manner, especially before a man of the church, and she would never have believed that she could take any pleasure in it. Her own perversity disgusted her and excited her beyond the limits of the imaginable. The silence was filled by Elke's sighs.

Anto remained stoical. He was totally unmoved by the temptress's body. All that mattered was his faith and his mission. Abruptly, his right hand shot out, slapping Elke violently across the face. She reeled under the shock of the blow.

"Get dressed—you're obscene!" the cardinal snarled, picking up the crumpled dress and hurling it at her face. "You're wasting your time. Answer my questions and you can return to your turpitude."

"I've nothing to tell you!" Elke spat, putting her dress on. "We've completed our bargain. I fulfilled my part even though you had nothing to tell me. Now it's every man for himself."

She went around the armchair, crossed the room and opened the door. Two priests blocked the doorway.

Anto rejoined her, took her by the arm and squeezed very hard, until Elke released a little cry of pain.

"Who is that man?"

"Go to Hell, Anto Sakic! Go practice your perversions on the Serbs or the Bosnians instead!"

Her reply was followed by another cry, as the cardinal tightened his grip on the tender flesh of her arm.

"I want a name and an explanation, and I'll get them, by consent or by force."

"Perhaps you intend to torture me?"

"Oh, that wouldn't bother me in the least. I can also occupy myself with your men, while you watch. Do you really want a bloodbath? Or we could *have a quiet chat*, like two friends, in front of the fire, like two good friends. You see— I'm giving you the choice."

Elke licked her lips. The game was over. She had thought that she could manipulate the cardinal, but she had been sadly mistaken. She admitted that she was beaten, but this would not be the end of the matter. She would make him pay very dearly.

"Pierre Cadoul," she said, with a sigh. "He was part of a group of seven Occitans who climbed the Pog to Montségur on March 16, 1944."

"Good," said Anto, relaxing the pressure on her arm. "You see, that wasn't so difficult. Why did you abduct him?"

Elke got her breath back. "After the event, he shut himself up in a cave, not far from here, where he lived as a hermit for more than 40 years. I thought that if Cadoul had taken refuge in solitude, it must be because the group had discovered something important that day."

"Did he talk?"

"He told me that he had joined the Waffen SS and that when he returned he wanted to expiate his sins. Nothing more."

Anto stared at her momentarily, not knowing whether to believe her or not. He had heard rumor of this story but he had not paid much attention to the anecdote. What he had just heard changed his view of events.

"Where is he?"

"Buried behind the house."

"You killed him?"

"Not at all. His heart gave out."

"Did he say anything else?"

Elke hesitated deliberately. She had to release some significant information if Anto were to believe her.

"He gave me a name."

"What name?"

"*Le Drac*. I think it must be the name of a place."

"Do you know where it is?"

"I haven't yet succeeded in finding that out—presumably in the region."

Anto narrowed his eyes. "You haven't told me everything."

"That's what happens when one doesn't trust people and uses force to obtain information. One can't help oneself doubting."

"I can still make you talk, if you're stubborn."

"Yes, you're perfectly capable of that. But you won't know whether I'm telling the truth. Even if you torture me you'll always be asking yourself the question. I might lie to you, Anto Sakic. Go on, make me talk…."

An angry expression passed across Anto's features. He understood that he would get nothing more from the German woman. Elke made an ironic face at him. She wanted to trap him.

"All right," he concluded, dryly. "From now on, it's every man for himself. One piece of advice: don't cross my path again."

Making a sign to the two priests who were waiting at the door, he turned on his heel and left the room. He had obtained a new piece of the puzzle, which he needed to follow up.

Outside, he studied the landscape while taking a deep breath. Now he had to find *Le Drac*. He got into his car, without noticing the green glow that was pulsating at the edge of the trees clustered behind the house. Nor did he hear the creature snigger, satisfied because it had just witnessed a very instructive confrontation.

Chapter 16

At the foot of a wall of rock was the opening of a dark hole, just wide enough to let a man through. Peire crouched down at the edge of the opening, while Michel knelt down beside him. Behind them, Jordanne waited.

"You're sure you want to go in there?" Michel asked shining a torch into the cave entrance.

"Yes. I've made my decision."

"Then I'll go with you. Don't forget that I'm now part of the rescue service. I know how to take care of myself in there."

"I wasn't expecting to go in on my own, in any case."

Michel got up, put a helmet on his head and adjusted his shoulder-band. He put the rope through the ventral snap-buckle and tapped Peire on the shoulder. "Get ready, we'll set off now. We don't have much time." He turned to Jordanne. "We ought to get to the chamber in less than an hour, if there aren't any hitches. If we haven't returned in three and a half hours, you'd better alert the gendarmes."

"All right. You can count on me."

Michel nodded and disappeared into the cavity. Just as Peire was about to disappear into the hole, Jordanne took him by the sleeve and said, in a soft voice: "Take care of yourself."

"I promise."

At the first progress was easy. The tunnel was high enough to go forward simply by bending one's back. Peire stopped for a moment to get his breath back.

"How are you doing?" Michel asked.

"I'm just out of condition."

"Hold on—it gets complicated further on. We'll get to a passage that's partly obstructed by a rock-fall. It'll be necessary to abseil down for 30 meters or so. Afterwards, there's a damp section with a ford, then a long walk through exceedingly slippery *gours*. Finally, we have to get through three roof-vents to reach the chamber. Shall we carry on regardless?"

Peire signaled his acquiescence with a nod of the head. They resumed their progress. After some ten minutes in a difficult section, Michel stopped. He wound the rope around a massive column and tugged several times to test its resistance. When he was sure of it he passed it through the bracket attached to his shoulder-band. Then he turned to his friend.

"I'll go down first, to make sure there are no problems. The passage is usually clear. I'll call up to you from down below, then you take hold of the rope. If you feel two tugs, pull me back up; if you feel three, you can come down. Okay?"

"Yes. Don't worry."

Michel tested the rope one last time before beginning the descent. Peire watched him draw away by the light of his helmet-lamp before losing sight of him in the darkness.

Peire waited for several minutes. A muffled shout finally rang out. He grabbed the rope, which tightened three times. He breathed deeply, in preparation for the descent, and then plunged into empty space.

Peire was rusty, not having done any physical exercise for too long an interval. Moreover, he had never been entirely at ease abseiling. He had difficulty balancing his weight and controlling the pulley that let out the rope. His body continually bumped into the wall. Nevertheless, he made progress. Finally, he felt two arms grip his legs. A harsh light dazzled him.

"Not too hard?" Michel murmured.

"I must have bruises everywhere. Dangling on a rope isn't my forte."

"Can we go on? We're not making good time. Jordanne will start to worry."

They resumed their long march through a sector with abundant clay and moisture, and then turned into a secondary gallery, dry now although it had once accommodated a river. The passage of water had left certain characteristic concretions in the ground, in the form of little smooth-sided hollows with swollen rims, known as *gours*.

Michel finally came to a halt in order to illuminate a narrow gap that opened in front of them. He went into it, crawling. Peire followed him, leaving a gap of about a meter. He was having difficulty breathing and his helmet kept bumping into the excessively low ceiling. He detested his uncomfortable posture. The mass of rock above him seemed oppressive.

After 50 meters or so, they climbed through the three roof-vents, and then emerged into a chamber that was about five meters high. When Peire stood up he experienced a mixture of fear and sadness.

The walls seemed to be impregnated with the drama that had unfolded there a year before. Peire remained rooted to the spot for several seconds.

"Is this it?" he asked, already knowing the answer.

Michel did not reply. He directed the beam of his lamp toward the wall immediately behind them. It took Peire several seconds to make out the pentagram.

The man who had inscribed it had been content to engrave five more-or-less straight lines in the stone, to a depth of about half a centimeter. The whole figure measured about 1.80 meters.

Peire took several steps back in order to study the pentagram in its entirety. He change the angle of illumination several times, then drew closer to see whether there were any further inscriptions—but the stone bore only the simple design.

"What now?" Michel asked, content to illuminate the geometrical figure without intervening.

"How much time do we have?"

Peire's friend lit up his watch and reflected. "Ten minutes maximum. You're going to have difficulty climbing back up the chimney, and we took longer to get here than I expected. I don't want to worry Jordanne. She must already be getting itchy up there...."

"Fix the lamps, then."

Michel set the four lamps he had brought with him on the ground. The chamber grew progressively brighter, bathed by a frail luminosity.

When his friend was done, Peire set his back against the wall. He parted his legs and extended his arms horizontally, hands open, his skin pressed against the rock.

"Are you sure you know what you're doing?" Michel asked, anxiously. "You know what happened to you in Toulouse."

"I don't have any choice, Michel. I need to verify that the pentagram can communicate with me."

"I don't like it. At the least sign of anything odd, I'll take you back up without asking your opinion."

Peire put his head back against the rock, in the topmost angle of the pentagram. Projections dug into his back, the cold penetrating to his very bones, but he remained stuck there, eyes closed, trying to empty himself out.

He began repeating the troubadour's line about the laurel, like a mantra. Completely absorbed, he concentrated on his bodily responses. The rock behind his back seemed to be getting warmer.

A rumbling sound came up from the ground, then stopped. A long silence followed, and then a new sound resonated between the walls of the chamber: a muffled snigger, and a sentence, "Here you are, then, in my domain."

Peire opened his eyes. He saw two green pupils floating in mid-air on the other side of the grotto.

He saw Michel following his gaze and cried out: "Whatever you do, don't move!"

"What's up?"

"The Drac."

"Bloody hell!" Michel stammered. "That's impossible. It doesn't exist—The Drac is a legend.

As he was speaking, the creature materialized. More than two meters tall, it stood still, its green gaze calmly surveying the two men, examining them from top to toe. It displaced itself in order to move closer to Peire. Its rough hide was covered with what looked like multicolored tattoos.

It arrived a short distance from Peire. He could have touched it by reaching out his arm, but he was still plastered against the rock. The beast pointed a crooked finger at him and spoke.

"Come towards me."

Its voice resonated, deep and dull—but the diction was precise.

Peire observed the creature, surprised by his own sentiments. Although he had felt a visceral terror during his first encounter with the beast, in the Comtesse's house, this time he felt a kind of serenity with regard to the Drac.

"Let's get out of here, quickly!" Michel shouted, retreating towards the exit. "I don't know what this is all about, but I've no interest in rotting here."

The monster turned towards him and roared, displaying its sharpened teeth.

Peire intervened. "No! Don't move, Michel! If it wanted to kill us, it would already have done so."

"How do you know?"

"No idea—I just sense that it has need of me."

The monster stared at Peire, then grimaced. "You're right, I have need of you. Join me."

"Why? You're the Devil! The Devil doesn't need anyone."

"I can reward you. You know how powerful I am...."

"And what will you promise me? Eternal youth, a fortune?"

"Vengeance!"

The word cracked like a whiplash.

"What vengeance? I don't know what you're talking about."

"Think about it, human. What killed your wife?"

Peire was seized by vertigo. Hélène had died in this grotto. She had suffered atrociously. Peire heard her howling, saw her features twisted by agony. He saw her struggling to get

139

away, until she collapsed to the ground, overwhelmed. He tried to deny the evidence, but he had no other explanation.

"They killed her…these filthy pentagrams *killed* her!" he exclaimed, his voice full of hatred.

"Good," sniggered the Drac, satisfied. "You're beginning to understand."

"Don't listen to it!" Michel cried. "It's lying."

The Drac whistled and turned round abruptly. "Silence, human!" it commanded, in a frightful voice. It went to the potholer and took his head between its enormous clawed hands. Then it pressed firmly until Michel collapsed to the ground, unconscious.

"Let him alone!" ordered Peire, in a firm voice. "This is between you and me. Why did the pentagrams kill Hélène?"

"Because they were put here to kill."

"By whom?"

"By the men who preached in this region. They wanted to protect their treasure."

"Why do you need my help?" Peire asked, adding, ironically: "Isn't the Drac all-powerful?"

"The pentagrams are also a trap for me, and I can't get hold of the treasure. Only you can do that."

"Me? I'm nothing special. Why don't you ask someone else to help you? Hundreds of people would take you up on your offer."

"You aren't aware of your own importance?" the Drac retorted. "There are a great many things you still don't know about yourself…."

"What are they? I want to know."

"Only a descendant of Aicart can touch the treasure. Didn't you know that?"

"I don't believe you!"

"You've passed the test of the pentagrams. You're in the middle of one and you're still alive. They won't touch you. Look inside yourself—you'll see that I'm telling the truth."

Peire reflected for a long moment. "And what will you give me in exchange? How many wishes am I entitled to?"

140

"You will have avenged your wife. Isn't that enough?"

Peire thought hard. He had not yet figured out where the Drac was coming from. "I don't understand. You need me, but you're not offering anything except vengeance, even though you possess all the power in the world?"

"Destroy the pentagrams, and then you'll find the treasure," the creature replied.

"The pentagrams are a trap for you...explain why."

"You don't need to know that," the Drac hissed.

"Then I shan't help you," Peire replied, calmly. "And you can't do anything to me. I'm in a pentagram. It's protecting me."

The Drac snarled. Its features were deformed by anger. "The men you call Perfecti placed the pentagrams in a precise formation. They delimit a zone within which I am imprisoned. Destroy them, and you'll set me free."

Peire was startled. "Set you free? But you're the Devil!"

The creature's eyes became brighter. It suddenly disappeared, then reappeared a meter away from Peire. "Don't tell me that you, who have never believed in the Devil, won't help him! You've never followed the precepts of those who name me the God of Evil, even though I'm the bringer of light and knowledge. The world belongs to me—it's my domain!"

Peire listened, his back still lodged against the wall, fixed within the pentagram. Should he yield to the Devil's advances? Surely not. And yet, the Drac was powerful.

"What more do you want?" the creature continued. "Gold. What will you do with it? Immortality? Do you remember one of your songs in which the hero had eternal life? In the end he begged for death, because he didn't want to live any longer after seeing those he loved disappear one by one. Tell me what you want."

Peire would have liked to quit the pentagram, to get out of the situation in which he now found himself, but the stone held him back. He tried to straighten his head, where his thoughts were in turmoil.

"Think about it. Why did your wife die, although dozens of men have explored this cave? Don't you find the coincidence bizarre?"

"Four young men that I didn't know were also killed the other day."

"The pentagrams have awakened because it's the year when the treasure must be revealed. Their mission is to protect it. Have they concealed that from you? Some are aware of it, though…they could have warned you, so that you could have prevented that unfortunate accident. They could have saved your wife."

The blow struck home. Peire felt a sudden intense rage. He tried to tear himself away from the power of the geometrical figure. Behind him, the rock grew warmer, as if in response, but it continued to hold him prisoner.

It was at that moment that Michel got up again, with difficulty.

"Damn it!" he howled, with all his might. "Don't listen to him, Peire! Can't you see that he's manipulating you? Stay in the pentagram!"

The creature half-turned. It looked at the potholer, who stood up straight, facing it, and then it advanced in his direction, its tongue lashing the air. "If you wish to continue to live, vermin, I advise you to depart and leave me with Peire."

"No!" Michel replied, bravely.

The Drac took another step forward. Now it was less than a meter away from Michel, its entire mass looming over him. It lifted its huge hands.

"Stop!" cried Peire.

The pentagram vibrated, and was surrounded by a blue halo. A buzzing sound filled the grotto.

"If you touch him, don't look to me for help any more—ever."

The beast emitted a thin whistle. The color of its scales changed. The Drac drew away from Michel.

"Very well—I'll give you time to think about it," it said. "Think hard about my proposition—I won't renew it. When we next meet, I want an answer."

A greenish mist surrounded the Drac, which evaporated. The cave resumed its normal aspect.

Peire was immediately ejected by the pentagram. He shivered, in a state of shock. His back was aching cruelly. His forehead was covered in sweat and his throat was on fire.

He took two paces forward and slumped into Michel's arms. His friend had come forward to catch him.

"How did you work that trick with the pentagram? The blue light?"

"No idea," Peire murmured. "I was just terribly afraid for you. I didn't want it to touch you."

"At any rate, it made it go away. Tell me that we were dreaming."

"Unfortunately not. The Drac really exists. That was what killed the Comtesse the other evening."

"But the Devil is a myth," Michel insisted.

"I believed that too, before."

Peire went back to the symbol engraved in the rock. He examined it, while Michel gathered up the lamps.

"You won't accept its proposition, then?" Michel asked, illuminating the cave again.

"I don't know."

"Get hold of yourself Peire! You can't get involved in that game!"

"Why? You heard what it said. This thing deliberately killed Hélène. People knew about it, and they didn't warn me. Don't I have the right to claim my vengeance?"

"You said it yourself—it's the Devil. It might be lying. You haven't considered that it might have killed Hélène itself. Why trust it?"

"I have to find out more before making my decision."

Michel sniffed, unconvinced. "Let's go. Jordanne must be worried."

Peire caressed the stone one last time, and then rejoined Michel, who had already inserted himself into the narrow hole that led to the surface.

"Shall we tell her about all this?" Michel asked, during the ascent.

"Yes, we might as well," Peire replied. "She's already encountered the Drac. On the other hand, it would astonish me if anyone else believed us—better to be discreet."

The two men went on slowly, in silence. Peire contemplated the halo of light illuminating Michel's way a meter ahead of him. A diffuse clarity eventually became visible at the end of the tunnel which sloped gently upwards towards daylight. Michel stopped, turned round and put a hand on his friend's arm. He looked him straight in the eyes. Peire," he said, "promise me that you'll think very hard before making your decision."

"First I have to find the people who are in the know. I have a right to an explanation. I need to understand."

Overtaking his friend, Peire marched towards the exit.

Chapter 17

The church bells chimed 2 a.m. A fine rain had begun to fall as midnight approached, veiling the distant village in a moist blur. The temperature was abnormally high for the time of year. The thaw did not usually begin until a month later.

Michel put up the collar of his jacket to protect him from the drizzle. Much given to long walks, he was used to bad weather. Rain did not bother him. He had just spent the evening with Peire, discussing recent events. About midnight, Peire had picked up his guitar to sing old songs. He had then improvised on the various tunes, as he often did on such occasions. Suddenly, chords had come to him, which he had repeated and enriched, then scraps of lyrics—and he had established, with pleasure, that his inspiration had returned: a veritable miracle.

When Michel had left, Peire had gone up to his studio to work, excited by what he had grasped, which he did not want to lose to the forgetfulness of sleep.

Michel crossed the village to his own house, which also served as an antique shop. He had little work to do at present; it was the slow season. He took advantage of the winter to renew his stock, rambling throughout the region in search of interesting items, which he sold to tourists in summer. The rest of the year, numerous regulars from various neighboring towns came in search of rarities.

He went in, hung up his soaking anorak and looked at the three boxes that had been cluttering up the hall for a fortnight. He had not had time to transfer the hermit's belongings to his shop. He had cast a rapid eye over them to make an initial inventory, especially the books, which he had sorted out in order to give those in good condition to Jordanne. There were also several items of craftwork carved in wood, fabricated by local shepherds, which would easily find buyers.

Michel hesitated briefly, uncertain as whether he ought to go to bed or start unpacking the boxes. He felt tired, but curiosity was stronger. He opened the first box, and began by sorting out the books, whose titles he read. He put them on the ground in several heaps, according to subject. Those which were of local interest would go to Jordanne, the rest he would look at later. Then he looked at the utensils. They would surely fetch a decent price from collectors. There was one item in silver, finely wrought, with three turquoises encrusted at the extremity of each of the branches of the cross.

He did not like selling religious objects, because the greater number of them had been stolen from churches. Some buyers did not seem to be very honest. Perhaps he would give it to the parish of Montségur. He was about to put it down in order to open the second box when he heard a scraping sound.

He turned round to look at the entrance door. It was still shut.

Suddenly, a sharp pain caused him to open the hand that was holding the crucifix. It fell on to the tiled floor with a metallic clink, and broke into two pieces. Michel looked at his palm. There was no trace of any wound, and not the slightest cut, but the pain had been quite real. He rubbed his hands together.

While Michel was grimacing, the crucifix seemed to melt and dissolve, while black smoke drifted along the corridor. He observed the strange phenomenon uncomprehendingly. The light-bulb illuminating the hallway began to flicker, then went out.

Michel swore. He had only changed the bulb two weeks earlier, and still it had burned out. That could not be chance. He groped his way towards the kitchen. He pressed the light-switch, but it clicked in the darkness. He swore again. The fuse had blown, and he did not know where his pocket torch was. Naturally, there was no emergency candle-stub. He put his hands out to grope his way to the fuse-box situated at the back of the kitchen, in a cupboard.

As he reached his goal, he heard the sound of breathing coming from the hall. He turned round anxiously.

"Who's there?" he asked.

Michel took a step back, jolting his elbow on a corner of the table. He stopped, uncertain what to do. In the darkness he could not see anything. A piece of furniture creaked. The door of the cloakroom opened and closed again. Something fell to the floor and broke. To judge by the noise it made as it struck the tiles it was the large porcelain vase that stood next to the telephone.

There was no more room for doubt this time; there was definitely someone in the house. He seemed to be looking for something. He was knocked things over, opening and closing doors. He was now in the dining-room. Michel hastily tried to find a weapon in order to defend himself if he were confronted by the thief. He took a step backwards and bumped into the sink. He edged his way to the sideboard and opened the cutlery drawer, soundlessly. His fingers found the hilt of a kitchen knife.

The thief's breathing became louder. He was coming closer. Michel stiffened. He clutched his makeshift weapon harder. A green light had appeared at the kitchen door. A vaguely human silhouette floated a meter above the ground. The light disappeared from time to time, only to reappear in a different part of the room, sometimes to the left and sometimes to the right. A sulfurous odor, accompanied by nauseating undertones, reached Michel's nostrils. The form passed through the table as if it did not exist. Michel made out two large eyes which planted themselves in front of him with a triumphant expression.

The Drac.

Paralyzed, Michel waited, not daring to meet the monster's eyes, prey to panic. The beast whistled. Something sharp dug into his arm. The claws came together, sinking into in his flesh. He groaned and let go of his knife.

Images of his sojourn in the grotto went through Michel's mind at top speed. He attempted a ploy. "If you kill me, Peire will never help you," he articulated, with some difficulty. "Spare me, and I'll try to convince him."

The creature replied with a burst of sarcastic laughter which resounded throughout the room.

"I don't need you, vermin! You're no use to me. Your friend will help me—I've discovered his weak point—and your death will serve my purpose."

An intense burning sensation burst forth in Michel's skull. The Drac had planted a sharp claw right between his eyes. He howled. The echo of his scream echoed within the house, while the creature drew its finger down the length of his face towards his throat, and then ploughed across the torso, the upper and lower abdomen.

Michel was in agony. His pulse beat furiously in his temples. A red mist veiled his vision. He waited for the salutary death that would put an end to the unbearable pain.

Blood spurted from the gash that opened the shopkeeper's body neatly from the forehead to the gap between his legs. The intestines gushed out and fell to the ground in a flaccid and sticky heap.

The beast contemplated the carnage, satisfied. The spectacle always procured it immense pleasure. It kept Michel alive deliberately to feed on his agony. The pain of a human being gave it a joy of which it never tired, and which it loved to prolong.

The Drac whistled when Michel fainted. It placed its hand on his forehead, stuck a finger into the brain, and then stimulated a nervous reflex to wake him up. Michel's turned-up eyes fixed themselves upon it again. With a croak of satisfaction, the Drac slashed his aorta and pulmonary artery with a thrust of its claw. The blood gushed out in a jerky jet. The red flood swept the last vestiges of Michel's strength away. Finally, at the ultimate moment, it withdrew its finger and released the pressure on its victim's skull.

The last thing that Michel saw was two burning eyes positioned a few centimeters from his own.

Chapter 18

19-20-21 September 1980. Peire Aicart sings in Occitan at the Corn Exchange in Toulouse. The photograph showed a view of the city, roseate in the light of the setting sun. The silhouette of a young and happy Peire, guitar in hand, was superimposed upon it.

Sitting in front of the keyboard of his synthesizer, his gaze fixed on the poster stuck to the wall, Peire listened distractedly to the most recent song he had composed. For three weeks, he had felt guilty for being alive. He had devoted himself to one sole task: to finish the music that he intended to dedicate to Michel, his closest friend, the brother he had never had. Michel's death was insupportable, and nothing had succeeded in lessening the pain he felt.

Peire clenched his teeth and his throat tensed. Every time he thought about Michel he was overwhelmed by outrage, mingled with disgust. That death had nothing accidental about it. The Drac had sent him a warning: it now had a means of putting pressure on him—and Michel had paid with his life for the Devil's blackmail.

He heard the main door open; then the steps of the staircase creaked. Peire did not turn around when the studio door closed again. He let himself go when an arm slid around his neck and teeth nipped his earlobe.

"Bonjour, my love."

"Bonjour," he replied.

She sat down in a chair next to his and set a file on the keyboard's side-table, on top of the scores.

"How are you?"

"I still haven't finished. Why did I leave Michel all alone?"

Jordanne took his arm to squeeze it hard. Michel's death had brought them even closer together. During the interment they had remained standing in front of the grave, hand in hand, in a state of shock, ignoring the glances darted at them by the inhabitants of Montségur.

"You couldn't have foreseen what would happen, Peire."

"But I might have been able to prevent it."

Jordanne replied in a reassuring voice. "You're torturing yourself needlessly, and you know that very well. Think about the present instead."

"I can't help it. What will happen? The Drac will come back to demand my help. If I refuse, it will attack those closest to me again—you, for sure."

"Never give in, Peire."

"Jordanne, the Drac will eliminate all the people I hold dear, one by one. It will make life impossible for me. I'll feel responsible for the death of my friends. That guilt will destroy me. Then the police will end up asking themselves why all my acquaintances vanished in mysterious circumstances. I'm risking big trouble. The Drac knows that."

Jordanne let go of Peire's hand in order to walk around the studio. Then she came back to him.

"You mustn't accept its proposition, at any price. You can't make a pact with the Devil."

"Even if your life is in danger?"

Peire stopped the tape and drew Jordanne towards him. He held her very tightly. One of his hands descended along her back while the other passed beneath her blouse to caress her skin delicately. Jordanne let him do it. She lowered her head and planted a long kiss on Peire's lips. Tremulously, she murmured: "Make love to me, Peire!"

He lifted up her skirt, took off her underclothes, sat her upon him and penetrated her with infinite gentleness. He felt her vibrate with pleasure. He abandoned himself and found refuge, yet again, in welcoming arms.

They lost track of time until joy flooded over them. Then they remained entwined, getting their breath back. Jordanne broke the embrace. She got up, dressed herself and kissed Peire lightly on the cheek.

"I've brought you the translation of Rahn's notes. I wouldn't get money for them, but I don't think I've made any howlers. I learned some things about him that his biographers didn't know. I don't know whether he's fantasizing or telling the truth, but it's very interesting."

"Oh yes?"

"Read it first, and we can talk about it afterwards if you wish. Rahn must have had some kind of pocket-book and he sent these pages to the Comtesse. They seem to me to be the last."

"The document isn't complete, then?"

"It's nothing but supposition, mind. If you look closely, you'll see that the leaves must have been torn out of some kind of notebook."

"That's interesting. I'll study them closely."

"One thing: try to set aside your knowledge of the man."

Peire reflected for a few seconds, and then said: "I'll follow your advice."

"One passage ought to interest you. I've underlined it. I've translated it word for word. I've added nothing; it's Rahn who wrote it."

"Thank you."

Jordanne handed him the file. "Read it first. Afterwards you can decide whether you should thank me. Personally, I slept badly last night."

"You too?"

"You're still having nightmares?"

"No, on the contrary—it's as if I no longer dream at all, but I wake up every quarter of an hour."

"Have you read any books that deal with near-death experiences?"

"Yes. I'd like it if you could find me more, even if it distresses me somewhat. Do you know any works in which people have undergone such experiences twice?"

Jordanne thought about it, then shook her head in a sign of negation. "No, I can't think of any. The stories usually only speak of a single journey into the beyond."

"I've finished the book on Rahn. I wanted to form an impression of the individual before reading his notes."

Jordanne got up and kissed him gently on the lips. "I have to go. A party of salesmen is coming to eat at the restaurant this evening; I can't stay for dinner with you. Come over at about eleven. I'll wait up for you, and we'll talk about Otto Rahn."

She headed for the door, but turned back to add; "And don't forget the evening after next. Everybody will be there for Peire Aicart's concert. I'm convinced that there'll be a full house. I've put the news out on local radio."

Peire caught up with her to take her in his arms and hug her. He slid his fingers through her hair. He had not forgotten the evening after his triumph at the Société del Gai Saber, when Michel had pressed him to accept Jordanne's proposition. Peire had agreed, saying that he would dedicate the recital to his friend. If he had known then....

"I hope that you'll be proud of me, even though I haven't sung solo on stage for three years." Jordanne put a finger on his mouth to shut him up. He went on nevertheless, murmuring: "It will be hard, Jordanne."

"You'll be fine, as usual," she replied, stroking his cheek.

Peire made a face, unconvinced. "I might have to do some repeats—I'm afraid that I've forgotten the words to certain songs."

She kissed him one last time before leaving the recording studio.

Night was falling. Peire switched off the computer and rewound the tapes. All that remained was to rework the musical part of the song and the CD would be finished—a month and a half late. Not so bad, after all, for someone who thought it would never be finished.

He went down to the sitting-room, revived the fire by depositing two logs on it and poured himself a vodka, which he downed in one. He installed himself comfortably there, in the armchair, with the Rahn translation on his knees.

He read for more than an hour, absorbed by what he found. When he had finished he remained pensive for a long while, with the final page in his hands. He recalled the books he had read, which had showed him an Otto Rahn quite different from the author of these pages.

He ran through one passage that seemed particularly interesting again. The German researcher mentioned his excavations in a cave close to the village of Ussat, where he had discovered a pentagram. He glimpsed a possibility: that of Otto Rahn hiding his discoveries behind wholly invented stories designed to distract attention. Had the German preferred to pass for a cheerful charlatan in order to avoid anyone looking too closely into his works?

Peire was very excited. This research roused more and more passion in him. He would seek information on the period. Perhaps the old people in the village would remember the excavations made by the Germans…asking questions was not difficult. He was determined to follow through to the end.

The most troubling passage was at the very end of the notes. Rahn recalled an experience that he had had in a cave: his encounter with the Drac. The description matched the creature that Peire knew point for point. The German was in no doubt as to the supernatural character of the beast, but Rahn did not give any details. He specified in two sentences that they had talked for a long time, without even making a start on the substance of the conversation. The notes stopped there, leaving Peire hungry for more.

He inserted the pages in Rahn's book in order to go talk to Jordanne, who must be waiting for him. Raising his eyes to the clock, he started, "Damn!" he muttered.

The hands indicated two o'clock in the morning. Between his work in the studio and his reading he had not noticed the time passing. Jordanne must be asleep by now. He would do well to think of getting a little sleep himself.

He put the book back on the sitting-room table, went to his bedroom, put his hand on the doorknob and opened the door. A dull noise, like a distant clap of thunder, made him jump. He turned round.

Chapter 19

The corridor was dark. All the lights were out. Peire sensed a presence. He moved to the light-switch, which he activated. Dazzled, his eyes required a few seconds to adjust, He started.

The man he had met after coming out of the Comtesse's house was standing in the middle of the corridor. Peire looked at him in astonishment. He had not heard anyone knock or come in. He darted a rapid glance in the direction of the main door; it was still bolted. He took the time to study his mysterious visitor. Dressed in black, short, thin, round-shouldered, he appeared to be so old that his age was indeterminable.

Peire remained mute for some time before he finally decided to speak.

"Who are you?"

"My name is Kyot."

"Kyot...."

He knew the name. He had read it in Otto Rahn's book. The German mentioned the romance *Parsifal*, written around 1210, at the height of the Crusade, by a minnesinger—a German troubadour. This storyteller, whose name was Wolfram von Eschenbach, claimed that his master had been Kyot the Provençal, who had largely inspired his story. Nothing much was known about the man in question. Some authors considered him to be purely and simply an invention of Wolfram's, but the majority of historians thought he was an Occitan troubadour. A few even thought that he was a renowned cabbalist.

"Why choose that pseudonym?"

"Because it's my name, that's all."

Peire sniffed incredulously. He felt ill at ease. "And how old are you? A thousand years?"

"Much older that you imagine," the old man replied.

"What are you doing here?"

"Open your mind. You know the answer. You have all the pieces in hand. You only need to want to believe."

"Peire recalled Rahn's notes. But the man standing before him could not be the veritable Kyot. Impossible. And yet, other improbable things had been happening for several weeks.

Peire cleared his throat, and then said, without much conviction: "Believe in a man who lived in the Middle Ages?"

"Believe in yourself, that's all. You still don't know who you are?"

"I don't understand what you're saying. I'm Peire Aicart, musician, and nothing else. And you can't be 1000 years old."

"Is that so? You've seen the Drac, though. You believe that to be real. But not me?"

Peire felt waves of heat surround him. All around, the room became blurred. The phenomenon only lasted a few seconds, and then the order of things seemed to be restored. In front of him, Kyot waited patiently. He had not moved.

Peire was uneasy. He no longer seemed to be master of himself. His convictions were crumbling. "I no longer understand anything. All the events I've lived through, all the things I've seen...."

"The answers are within you."

"But how can I find them? Everything seems so confused...."

Kyot sighed. He came closer and took Peire by the arm. In a firm tone, he said: "They will come if you listen to them. It's necessary to open yourself up and have confidence. Then you'll know who you are."

Peire shivered at the touch of the icy hand. The old Occitan's fingers clenched around his muscles and a soft warmth climbed up his arm by degrees. He suddenly had a disturbing vision: a ring of mountains, the sun, a clearing. Peire concentrated. He thought that the veil lifted for a moment, but the landscape abruptly grew dark and vanished.

"Tell me who I am, Kyot. You seem to know. Why not give me the answers?"

"I don't have the right."

Peire could not help bursting out into nervous laughter. "What use are you, then? Otto Rahn says that you're the Cathar Errant, who travels through time and sees everything. He claims that you even helped Wolfram von Eschenbach to write his *Parsifal*. But you refuse to enlighten me?"

"No, I'm nothing—merely Memory. I'm here so that people never forget."

"Forget what?"

"The reason that human beings exist."

"Which is?"

"That's one of the answers that you must find within you, Peire. Look hard. Time is pressing...."

Kyot turned round and melted into obscurity. Peire found himself alone again. The more time went by, the more uncertain he became. He, who was proud of his proven rationalism and his pure, hard atheism, now found himself at a loss. He obviously had a role to play in this circus of crackpots, in the midst of monsters and various apparitions—but what? He did not even know any longer who he really was.

A bright stain on the spot where Kyot had been standing attracted Peire's attention. He bent down to pick up a white feather which shuddered in a current of air coming from under the door.

As his fingers touched the dove's feather, he saw the image of the mountain clearing again, still blurred. Then it faded away again.

Chapter 20

A heavy silence, conducive to meditation, reigned within the building. The wooden panels mingled their odor with a discreet scent of laurels and dried lavender. From time to time, the creaking of the parquet signaled the discreet passage of a reader coming into the library. The ambience inside the premises of the Société del Gai Saber was studious.

Seated in a brown leather armchair, Anto riffled through the incunabulum that Jean Rudel had set before him half an hour before. He continued reading it, even though he knew that he would find nothing interesting in the documents that the director of the Société had put at his disposal. He remained stoical, sitting behind a magnificent solid oak desk. Sometimes he dipped into the texts, but in reality he was observing the occasional comings and goings.

In any case, he was not there to extract information from the works he seemed to be reading. His objective was to disturb the members of the Société del Gai Saber. He wanted to force them to make a move, to reveal themselves. In the shadows, the Hounds of God were watching the building and the various members. He was, in fact, privately convinced that the organization was concealing a secret in its bosom.

Anto had been forced to act. Time was against him. At Montségur, the Cathars would celebrate a festival on March 15. In consequence, some event would inevitably occur around that date. The cardinal was certain of it. He did not know what, but he would find out. He still had just over a month to find the cave containing the fifth pentagram.

As he thought about the geometrical figure, Anto had an inspiration. He got up, circled around the desk and left the room that Jean Rudel had placed at his disposal. He reached the hall without encountering anyone. There he stopped to look at the floor. In the middle of the immense entrance, drawn in black on the white flagstcnes, the pentagram displayed itself.

It must have been on this spot, then, that the musician fell ill. Brother Francis had sent him the press cutting relating to the incident. For a moment, he had thought it a mere coincidence. The five pentagrams had, after all, been traced around Montségur by the Cathars in the 12th century. This one, on the other hand, could only date from the era of the building's construction. He had changed his opinion though. On reflection, he had told himself that the symbol surely had not been designed in this location by chance. Then he had asked the Superior of the monastery to obtain information about the musician.

Some little while afterwards, having continued his research in the meantime, he had discovered that the name Aicart was included in the list of the inhabitants of Montségur linked to Catharism. Several members of that family had been among the heretics burned on March 16, 1244. In addition, the archives of the Inquisition revealed that a certain Amiel Aicart had left the citadel on the eve of the surrender, in company with three other Perfecti, carrying the treasure of the Cathars with them.

Anto examined the pentagram meticulously: a very simple design, black lines with no other embellishment. Even the interior was virginal. He took a step forward and drew himself upright in the centre. He waited.

At first he felt nothing. Suddenly, a vibration came from the floorboard on which his legs were set, and he felt himself totter. An intense vertigo seized him, accompanied by a violent nausea.

"Surprising, isn't it?" The voice broke the spell. Jean Rudel was gazing at him ironically. "Are you looking for someone?"

Anto came back to reality. He quit the pentagram and stood in front of the director of the Société del Gai Saber, slightly disconcerted. To mask his disquiet he assumed a haughty manner.

"Simple curiosity on my part. I wanted to see the pentagram at close range. I heard rumor of an incident that took place the other day."

"Regrettable, but the musician is much better. He left the hospital a few days later, in good shape. I received the news. It was a heart attack, but not a serious one. A mere warning."

"You had just given him an award, according to what I read."

"Indeed. A silver flower to reward him for all his work on behalf of our beautiful Occitan language. You should listen to his songs; they have much to say about tolerance."

Anto could not help grimacing. "The Church *is* tolerance," he said, in a dry tone.

Jean Rudel did not repeat the formula. "I hope that the documents we have put at your disposal have given you some answers."

"Let's say that they're very interesting from a historical point of view, but not quite what I'm looking for. I'd rather know what relationship there was between your Société and the Cathar Church."

"I told you the other day—none."

"And this pentagram? You can't deny that there are at least four others in the caves that served for the initiation of heretics!"

"Geometrical figures of this kind can also be found in numerous churches, but it never occurred to me to say that the Catholics were influenced by Catharism."

Anto made a gesture of annoyance in response to the arguments advanced by Jean Rudel. He expected that sort of reaction, but it put his patience to a stern proof. He did not like the idea that his interlocutor took him for an imbecile. If he wanted to achieve his ends, he would need to preserve his calmness.

"You know very well that the pentagram is a Cathar symbol. Why not admit it?"

"But I admit it willingly. It's a historically recognized fact. What I don't understand, on the other hand, is why you want us, at any price, to be the descendants of Catharism...."

"Not the descendants. The Cathars have been dead for a long time. The occasional illuminati who have tried to revive the sect that changed History don't count."

"Why, then, are you obsessed with the hypothesis?"

"The seven founder members of your Société, supposedly dedicated to Literature, were illustrious unknowns who hadn't even written a single poem. They had no fortune. Some highly-placed person must, therefore, have financed that creation."

Jean Rudel stared at him without losing his ironic attitude. Inwardly, he was less sure of himself. The cardinal was raising awkward questions, to which he must not obtain any answers.

"I'd like to know why you're so determined to discover some such link."

"Medieval heresies have always been my passion. I'm interested in the causes of their disappearance. For example, I'm trying to understand why Catharism only lasted for 100 years after the fall of Montségur."

"Are you afraid that your Church will go the same way?"

"Quite the opposite. My Church has survived all the schisms and it is the leading religion in the world, which demonstrates its correctness."

"Look for traces of Catharism in Italy and you'll discover that it survived for much longer than you imagine. Numerous towns in northern Italy were Cathar until the 15th century. Certain great artists even left evidence of it in their works."

"Are you thinking of Michelangelo?" the cardinal asked, immediately.

"Among others...."

"There might be something to be said for certain lucubrations that see a Cathar inspiration in one of his paintings. You see, I'm not as uncultivated as all that. In Italy, the Cathars weren't in hiding. They were even in control of certain regions, but their influence disappeared rapidly."

"If their power hasn't survived, even though they possessed entire cities, how could a modest association like ours have been able to continue the work of the Cathars for 700 years? Your hypothesis is rather audacious, no?"

Anto did not want to yield an inch of ground. "What I understand," he retorted, "is that you refuse to help me. Is it so shameful to recognize that the treasure of the Cathars served to found your Société? On the contrary, you should be proud, you who defend Occitan traditions."

Jean Rudel shook his head, sorrowfully. "Now you're talking about the treasure of the Cathars. The ultimate myth! Why not the Grail, while you're about it?"

"The treasure of the Cathars isn't a myth," the cardinal immediately replied. "It's a well-established fact. Even the most rationalistically inclined historians accept that. Don't forget that the archives of the Inquisition make reference to it."

Jean Rudel's features hardened. "Don't talk to me about the Inquisition: an infernal machine created to exterminate men and women. The worst invention of Catholicism!"

"It had its uses during that troubled period. I don't seek to excuse it, but no more do I condemn it."

"But why afford the least value to testimony extracted under torture?" Rudel demanded, dryly.

"You're mistaken. The three witness statements that mentioned the treasure had not been extracted under torture. The witnesses were even released from prison. That's what leads me to think that the treasure really exists."

"The Cathars had only one veritable treasure: their faith! And you burned it! In the bosom of our Société we've always tried to maintain the memory of that flame."

"You admit, then, that you are Cathars?"

"What would you do about it? You can't any longer send me to the stake by simple denunciation!"

Anto was jubilant. He had succeeded in unsettling his adversary. He excelled at this game—which had paid off once again. He had obtained a very useful item of information.

"No, I can't. But that confirms my theory."

"Think what you will; it's of no importance. What matters, for me, it that the Société del Gai Saber rewards deserving artists every year."

"But you haven't answered my question about the treasure."

"What does it matter whether the gold of the Cathar Church served to found the Société del Gai Saber, or whether the money came from the plunder of one of its founders? In 700 years, in any case, it has disappeared. We exist now on gifts and subscriptions." The two men challenged one another with their gazes for a few seconds, and then Jean Rudel concluded: "That answers your question."

"Better than you imagine. I thank you immeasurably for your precious assistance. It has provided me with many details regarding the subject that interests me."

"Pursue your chimeras, then, since you don't believe me."

"I think that we shall have occasion to meet again," the cardinal said, in a disdainful tone. He turned his back and drew away several paces to savor his victory.

"If you're interested," Jean Rudel said, defiantly, "Peire Aicart is giving a concert at the Leg d'Amor restaurant on Saturday evening."

Anto turned round, unable to hide his surprise at hearing the troubadour's name. He caught a strange glimmer that flickered over Rudel's features.

"That's the musician we rewarded the other day. You know—the one who fell ill while he was standing in the pentagram that you've just quit...it will be a pleasure for me to hear him! Come to the concert—you won't regret it."

Anto left the hall without saying farewell. What he had just heard disturbed him, and led to a new series of questions. Jean Rudel had just intentionally revealed a new element of the story to him: the troubadour. Why? It was up to him to find its place in the puzzle.

Anto remained in the porch for a moment, studying the street. The sun bathed the city in soft light, announcing the imminent end of winter. The sky was clear, the temperature mild. It was one of those beautiful days that encourage a desire to take a stroll, after being shut up indoors for months. The narrow side-street was almost deserted, however.

The cardinal admired the beauty of the historic quarter. The Medieval houses raised their slightly-inclined walls towards the sky. Anto imagined the lives of the generations of human beings which had succeeded one another here. The ancient stones were part of their universe. He felt it keenly. He read them like an open book.

A blast on a horn recalled him to reality. Brother Jean-Michel was waiting in front of the car parked 30 meters from the house of the Gai Saber. The cardinal walked rapidly to the vehicle, opened the door, installed himself in the rear seat and leaned back against the seat. He signaled to his chauffeur to drive off.

"Is the surveillance in place?" he asked.

"Everything's in order. We've made a reconnaissance of the building. Two of our brothers are watching Jean Rudel and two others are watching the entrances with cameras. They'll all be relieved at ten o'clock. I'll bring you their report."

"Very good."

"I've been able to get hold of a complete list of members of the Société, as well as a list sympathizers and one of people who have received awards during the last 15 years. I'll give them to the Superior this evening, so the other brothers can study them. We should be able to make cross-checks."

"You've done the right thing."

"Where are we going, Excellency?" Brother Jean-Michel asked.

The cardinal hesitated momentarily. The troubadour's name was still resonating in his head but he could hardly see himself knocking at his door to discuss Cathars with him. The best time to get close to him would doubtless be after the concert."

"To Fanjeaux. We must hold a conference urgently."

The car left Toulouse. In spite of his apparent calmness, Anto was beginning to sense a certain disquiet. He had thought that he had triumphed over his adversary, but that last remark, launched across the hallway like a challenge, had made him change his mind. He questioned himself. Jean Rudel might perhaps be using him.

"I want to know everything about Peire Aicart. Put him under surveillance. Bring me reports of all his actions and gestures, and the identity of the people he meets."

"I'll give the orders as soon as we arrive," Brother Jean-Michel replied, meekly.

"Have we someone at Montségur who can give us information, and in whom we can have complete confidence?"

"I don't think so. We've never dared to establish ourselves out there. It would undoubtedly be taken amiss...."

The cardinal shook his head. "A pity."

Brother Jean-Michel mistook his superior's meaning. "Don't worry, Excellency. I can take care of the man personally—if you have no need of me, of course."

"I know how devoted you are, Brother Jean-Michel, and I prefer to keep you close to me. The musician is giving a concert on Saturday evening; you'll accompany me to it. Until then, undertake to gather information about him."

The chauffeur nodded his head in acquiescence. "I'm at your disposal, Excellency. By the way, Brother François telephoned me. We've picked up the trail of the Germans. They're occupying a farmhouse not far from Montségur and are under surveillance again."

"Good, very good. I want regular reports, but I prefer that we occupy ourselves with the musician for the moment. And I'd like to visit the four caves with pentagrams to get the feel of the places."

"I'll take you there—but we'll need to go on skis to reach the last one. It isn't easily accessible in winter."

"Ah...that's annoying. I'm no longer young enough for that sort of exercise. It's a pity, but I'll pass on that one."

The chauffeur interrupted them. "A car has been following us for some time, Excellency."

Anto turned round to observe the road.

"It's the black 406 about 100 meters back," the chauffeur went on. "Should I lose it?"

"No, no need. Let them do it if it amuses them. It's also a good way of keeping tabs on our adversaries."

Anto fell silent. He wedged himself into his seat and looked through the window at the passing countryside.

The car took the side road that led to the monastery. The thaw was beginning to make the sap rise in the trees, and the buds suddenly seemed greener. A few weeks hence they would burst under the pressure to let tender young leaves out.

"We're arriving, Excellency," said Brother Jean-Michel.

Anto nodded without replying. The car dropped him off in front of the steps, which he climbed rapidly to reach the East wing. He pushed the heavy oak battens that gave access to the monastery library and pressed a switch. Six lamps lit up in a vast vaulted room, covered with solid wooden beams. The shelves bore dozens of ranks of books and manuscripts.

He began by searching for the word Drac. He finally found it in a book of Occitan folktales. The Drac was nothing but a variant of the Devil. Why had he thought of it while he was standing in the pentagram? He wrote the word *Drac* on a piece of paper with a few instructions. One of the Dominicans was charged with verifying whether the word was to be found in the principal Cathar writings.

The Devil was, in fact, an integral part of the Cathars' belief-system. For them, there was not only one omnipresent and omnipotent God, but two Gods of equal power; they were Manichean dualists. The Good God ruled space and Paradise, while the Evil God reigned without division over the Earth and human beings. They were engaged in a merciless struggle for the souls of human beings, reflected in the perpetual opposition between light and darkness, Good and Evil, God and Satan, truth and falsehood. For the Cathars, Humankind was the heart of that battle. Human beings belonged to the Earth, the kingdom of Evil, and were thus submitted to perpetual terrestrial temptation, but they sought to elevate themselves, to accede to the Kingdom of God. Those who had not attained the state of Perfecti were condemned to Earthly rebirth, over and over again, to continue their progress.

Blasphemy! There was only one life after death: that which delivered Humankind into the arms of the all-powerful Lord—and this Earth, created by God according to the descriptions in the Bible and the holy scriptures, was His Kingdom.

Anto tapped his pen on the wooden table and relaxed against the back of his chair. Abruptly, he sat up straight again and opened one of the heavy volumes set before him, which contained the Inquisition's archives. He searched the pages in sequence before falling upon the passage that interested him, and which he knew by heart. His hands gripped the stout manuscript while he deciphered the characters traced by the application of a quill pen to the thick yellow paper.

As he had said to Jean Rudel, certain witnesses had deposed without being constrained, and being free to leave. Their declarations could therefore by judged worthy of credence. He had before his eyes a proof of the existence of the Cathar treasure. He had not spent 40 years chasing a chimera.

The first testament was the deposition of Guillaume de Bonan:

I heard it said by Bernard Guilhem and Bernard Dovesina, heretics who were with me in the lists where I was on guard, that the heretics Amiel Aicart and Hugo had got out of the castle of Montségur by means of a rope extended to the crag beneath the castle during the night on which the aforesaid castle and the heretics were delivered into the hands of the King and the Church.

Aicart—like the musician. Anto remained thoughtful for a few moments, His hunter's instinct had not let him down. Peire Aicart must have a role to play in the story. He went on to the following text, the deposition made by the commander of the Montségur garrison, Arnaud-Roger de Mirepoix:

When the heretics left the castle of Montségur, which was about to be rendered to the Church and the King, Pierre-Roger de Mirepoix retained in the aforesaid castle Amiel Aicart and his friend Hugo, heretics. During the night after the other heretics were burned on the pyre, he hid the aforesaid heretics and helped them escape. That was accomplished in order that the heretic Church should not lose its treasure, which was hidden in the forest, for these two men knew the hiding-place. I heard it said by Alzeu de Massabrac d'Oracle and by Guillaume-Jean de Lordat that they had previously seen that they could not escape the aforesaid castle in the week before Palm Sunday.

The third testament came from Bérenger de Lavelanet. It was similarly deposited freely before the Inquisitors:

I heard it said by Raymond Monit that Amiel Aicart, Poitevin and two other heretics would be hidden underground when the Castle of Montségur was surrendered. I did not hear and I do not know who let them out of the Castle, or how they got out. I heard it said that these four heretics who left the Castle of Montségur went to the village of Caussou, from there to Prades, and finally to the Castle of So with the heretic Maltheus, whom they met.

The defenders of Montségur were testifying under oath, which guaranteed the veracity of their account. Béranger de Lavelanet was one of the two lords of Montségur. His wife had perished on the pyre because she had refused to abjure her religion. Guilhem de Bonan was a simple soldier whose life had been saved, like so many others, because he had not shared the faith of the heretics.

Anto re-read the testament of Arnaud-Roger de Mirepoix. That one was the most important, because he was the brother of the commander of Montségur. All these declarations had been collected in the months following the capitulation. The events were therefore recent, and nothing could have incited the three men to lie or twist the facts. On the contrary, it was they who had raised the matter the removal of the treasure, as if it were a minor matter. Did the Cathars want to challenge the Catholic Church by announcing that the treasure was in a safe place, and that they would keep it there forever?

For 700 years the Church had been looking for that treasure. To be sure, the Vatican was scarcely bothered about it, but Anto had made it his quest. For years he had put it aside because other missions had been entrusted to him. He had, however, explored numerous trails, with the assistance of certain Dominicans. He had never found the least indication of the exact location or the nature of the treasure—but now, he finally had the elements necessary to discover the truth.

Reassured, he put the heavy manuscripts on a chair, unfolded an Ordnance Survey map on the table, and placed beside it the parchment on which the region was sketched. He marked the locations of the caves with pentagrams and put a cross on Montségur. Then he drew lines between the four caves, hoping to find the location of the fifth by means of the geometrical figure thus formed—but he had to change direction; the idea was too simple. There was nothing conclusive in the design. The cave must be near to the others, though—no more than a day's walk away. He calculated the distances; the shortest straight lines measured less than six kilometers, the longest about 20.

He circled the village of Montréal de Sos. According to the witness-statements, the treasure had been seen there. A design had even been discovered in a cave there in which certain people saw a representation of the Grail. A stupid idea: the Grail was not a symbol of Cathar thought. On the other hand, the treasure that had left the citadel must have had a considerable value in their eyes. Some historians leaned towards gold and silver coins, but Anto thought the hypothesis untenable. Why would the Cathar church have taken such risks for money? They would have been able to get it out of

Montségur long before the siege rather than waiting for the last moment. No, the treasure was much more important. It very probably had a religious value, which might have a decisive influence on the Catholic Church, like the famous Dead Sea scrolls.

He took up Rahn's notebook and re-read it, marking all the places mentioned by the German on the map. When he had finished reading, as he was about to close the booklet, his attention was attracted to a white strip along the margin. He looked at it more closely and realized that some pages had been torn out. He had not been conscious of it before because Rahn's text reached a conclusion and the last page was blank. Even so, the evidence indicated that pages were missing. Perhaps Rahn had torn them out to use them for a rough draft— but the extraction would not have been made so carefully; Anto had had to look very closely to perceive it. The pages had been removed with great care. Obviously, a final section was missing.

Someone had deliberately withheld those pages. He immediately thought of Elke Ströder. She had tried to double-cross him! She had held back the most important information contained in the notebook. That was why she had yielded the "clue" so easily.

Anto roared silently. He would not allow himself to be checked in this manner. He put down the now-useless notebook, left the cell and headed towards Brother François' office. The time had come to unleash the Hounds of God.

Chapter 21

The four spotlights set above the stage were switched on to illuminate the little rostrum installed at the back of the Leg d'Amor. Conversations immediately began to fade away. Silence fell when the room lights went out. The 60 or so people who were present looked at the simple chair and microphone that occupied the stage. The audience waited expectantly.

After 20 seconds Peire appeared with his guitar. Applause broke out. He took his place and set the microphone at the right height. He looked to his left, towards the kitchen—transformed into wings—where Jordanne was standing. She made a gesture of encouragement. He could not remember ever having had such intense stage-fright before. He had refused to eat in the restaurant before the concert He had shut himself up in his house, lying on his bed in the dark, and had not arrived at the Leg d'Amor until the last minute.

His gaze swept the room. Dazzled by the spotlights, he could only make out an indistinct and somber mass. Only the first two rows were at the threshold of visibility. His producer was there. Peire was surprised to see Elke Ströder sitting next to Jacques Desplas. Beside her, he distinguished the presence of an ecclesiastic; a cross on the lapel of his black coat glittered in the gloom.

"Good evening, everyone," he said. "Thank you for coming to this concert. I would like to dedicate it to Michel Viaud, a dear friend who left us recently." His voice began to tremble. He was obliged to pause before being able to continue. "I wrote this first song for him, and I called it *Le Drac*."

He struck a chord on the guitar and began to sing. Absorbed by the music, he did not notice the stupefaction of Anto and Elke. To one side, Jean Rudel smiled.

Peire sang for more than an hour and a half without a break. He found himself back in his element. Nothing else mattered. After each song he paused for a few seconds to explain the meaning to those who did not speak Occitan, then embarked on a new item. Finally, he brought his concert to an end, bowed and left the stage. Applause, which was meat and drink to him, accompanied him into the wings.

Jordanne kissed him on the mouth. "You were magnificent! You had nothing to worry about, you see."

"Thanks," Peire replied, mopping his brow.

The applause in the hall redoubled its intensity. Peire pointed to the stage behind him. "I think I have to go back."

Jordanne burst out laughing. "Don't tell me that you don't want to! I wouldn't believe it."

Peire went gladly back into the glare of the spotlights. He felt a profound exaltation in communicating with his public in this fashion. He took his place and thanked the audience. Then he sang two more songs. When he finished, applause filled the room again. He received a standing ovation. He waited for a few minutes before adding, in an emotional voice: "A man who doesn't know when to quit is ill-mannered."

A murmur of reproof ran through the audience.

"Don't worry," he said. "I won't abandon you yet. I'd like to finish with a song that's particularly dear to my heart. For several days I've never stopped humming it. It will bring back memories to some of you. Before singing it, it remains for me to thank Jordanne for having invited me and you for having gathered in her Leg d'Amor. I ask you to applaud her."

Peire beckoned to her to come to stand beside him. In the wings she shook her head, but in response to the musician's insistence and the appeals of the public she ended up yielding. She set herself at his side, uneasily. She bowed awkwardly and got her feet tangled in the microphone cord. The audience burst into laughter and cheered her as she hurried back to the wings. Peire set his guitar down behind him, came back to the microphone, and finally began his last song:

"*Al cap de set cents ans verdeja lo laurel.*"

He sang the poem *a cappella* for nearly three minutes. The audience listened, utterly captivated. When Peire concluded with the line that had begun the *complainte* there was a moment of silence, then a salvo of applause. Jordanne brought the house-lights up to signal the end of the concert, and Peire left the stage.

"Do you want to eat?" Jordanne asked. "I have a magret."

"Later. I'm too excited to get anything down, whatever it might be. I'll go take a turn outside. I need to stretch my legs."

"Don't stay out there too long. Everyone wants to talk to you or get you to sign their records. Your producer's sold practically all the stock he brought with him."

"I'll be rich, then!"

Peire left the kitchen and found himself in a little garden attached to the restaurant. He buttoned up his coat and walked a little way. Then he paused to contemplate the Pog. The moon was full. By courtesy of its light, Montségur was resplendent on its casket of somber rock.

"A magnificent spectacle, isn't it?"

Peire turned. The ecclesiastic he had noticed at the beginning of the concert was standing a few paces away.

"Excuse me for disturbing your meditation," the unknown man continued, "but I wanted to talk to you. And the sight of the 'dragon's head,' as Queen Blanche of Castille nicknamed it, is always a sublime spectacle." In response to Peire's questioning stance he introduced himself and extended his hand. "I'm Cardinal Anto Sakic."

"The murder always returns to the scene of his crime," Peire could not restrain himself from saying.

"I'm aware that my predecessors in this village left certain memories, and that my presence in this vicinity is not welcome…but seven centuries have gone by. Don't you think the statute of limitations might apply?"

"You're right. Forget what I said."

"I must congratulate you on your concert. Your lyrics are superb. I particularly appreciated the words of your final song."

"You understood all the words?"

"*Per segur*. It happens that I speak Occitan quite well."

173

Peire stared at his interlocutor, surprised.

The cardinal went on: "We're not all inquisitors, you know. Occitan civilization has always fascinated me, as well as the heresies that flourished in the Middle Ages. As I often say, in the form of an aphorism, if one wants to know one's adversaries better, one has to learn their language."

"If you still want to wage war, know that Catharism has been extinct for centuries. The rare individuals who call themselves Cathars of today are merely harmless dreamers drunk on esotericism."

"I used the word adversary, but it was symbolic. In spite of the title of your last song, I agree with you: Catharism, like so many other heresies, belongs to the past. That said, you're *a cappella* performance was sublime. You certainly know how to share your passion."

Peire had listened attentively to his interlocutor. Rumors were abroad in the village regarding the presence of a foreign ecclesiastic who was passing through the region. This cardinal had surely not come to the Leg d'Amor to hear songs in Occitan.

"Isn't it the meaning of the song that actually interests you? I confess that the presence of a member of the Catholic Church—a cardinal, moreover—at my concert surprises me. I find it hard to believe that it's a matter of chance."

Peire had used these words deliberately. He did not want to play cat and mouse.

"Do you think the song might be prophetic?" Anto asked,

"To answer that question, I'd have to know exactly what you're looking for in Montségur."

"The same thing as several other people who are here this evening: the treasure of the Cathars."

"And you think that I know where it is?" Peire's astonishment was not feigned. He had had obviously not expected such an affirmation.

Anto was slightly disconcerted, but he decided to persist with his attack. "You're no mere troubadour. You're the descendant of Amiel Aicart, the man who left that fortress 700 years ago, taking the treasure with him. Don't tell me you didn't know that—I shan't believe you "

"Who told you that he was my ancestor? The name Aicart is common in the region."

"No subterfuge, Monsieur Aicart. What happened to you in the pentagram demonstrates that you're the descendant of Amiel Aicart. You're tied into to the story one way or another. Then again, didn't your wife die in a cave where there's a pentagram?"

Peire tensed. For a moment, he had an urge to punch the ecclesiastic in the face simply for the pleasure of shutting him up. The man was extremely distasteful. Then he controlled himself. His fixed the man with a cold stare before saying: "What do you expect from me?"

"Your help."

"Usually, it's you to whom people come, to obtain the aid of religion. I don't see how can be useful to you."

"And yet we have a common enemy," Anto replied.

"I don't understand what you're talking about."

The cardinal studied the musician briefly. He seemed genuinely ignorant. That seemed scarcely credible, if he really had a part to play in this 700-year-old intrigue. Was Aicart lying? Was he ignorant of his own role? Anto wanted to get to the bottom of the matter.

"You really haven't any enemies? Not even the pentagrams? Not even *Le Drac*?"

Peire went pale as the blow struck home. At that moment, Jordanne came out of the restaurant to summon him back in. He chose to make no reply and head towards the kitchen door.

"The Drac and the pentagrams are our enemies." Anto hurled the words at his back. "We can join forces to fight them. Think hard, Aicart—your choice will be decisive. I'll come back later to discuss the matter with you."

Peire went into the Leg d'Amor without even looking back.

The evening wore on and the reception ran its course. Peire circulated among the crowd, speaking to various people. It was the least he could do for his public. He shook some 20 hands, accepted thanks, and signed numerous autographs. A pregnant young woman, accompanied by her husband, spoke to him for ten minutes. She wanted to know some Occitan forenames for her baby, who was due to be born the following months. Then Jacques Desplas, his producer, congratulated him. He was delighted with the success of the concert. After the release of the compilation he was anticipating a tour that would launch a new album. He would draw up a program to take in the entire South—and afterwards, the new CD.

Peire listened with one ear. Music was the least of his worries, for the immediate future. He kept watch on Anto, who had returned to the restaurant to sit down at a table, a glass of champagne in his hand, in company with a young man whom Peire had already met in Montségur.

The musician felt a hand grip his arm. He turned round. Elke was standing there; she drew him aside.

"Congratulations! That was superb! Extraordinary! I've never experienced such thrills while listening to music. I'm more and more determined to make a record with you."

"Thanks," Peire replied, "but I remain convinced that it's not a good idea from a financial point of view."

"Finances aren't a problem. I'll take care of them—but we'll talk about it later; I don't want to spoil your evening. Let's celebrate your success instead."

She went to a table, plucked a bottle of champagne from an ice-bucket, uncorked it with a decisive gesture, and filled two glasses. She held one out to Peire and raised her own to make a toast.

"To Occitan song!"

"To the treasure of the Cathars!" replied the musician.

Peire waited for the German woman's reaction to his challenge. She did not take it up. She was content to empty her glass and fill it up again.

"To the treasure," she murmured, finally, as she moved closer to him.

Their faces brushed together. Peire stared at the red lips that made contact with his own. The German woman's body pressed against his, and she moved her hips gently. He felt aroused, and let her do it. Behind her, a woman burst out laughing as her companion made a joke. Regaining his presence of mind, Peire shook himself, and then withdrew to a suitable distance.

They were emptying their glasses when Jacques Desplas came to join them. He wanted to introduce Peire to a new group of people. These admirers congratulated him enthusiastically. Elke abandoned them to pour herself another glass of champagne and disappeared into the crowd.

Peire had been talking for five minutes when he noticed the German woman in heated conversation with the cardinal. The ecclesiastic was making exaggerated hand-gestures. Elke remained impassive. Peire tried to escape from his producer, but the latter insisted on continuing to talk about the tour that he was planning to put on. Finally, Peire told him that he would think about it and that they would discuss the project later, with clear heads.

When he returned to Elke, the priest was no longer with her. Peire surveyed the room; the cardinal had obviously left the gathering. Elke was now talking to Jean Rudel. Peire went up to them.

"Ströder," he said, looking her in the eyes. "Are you related to the Nazi who directed the excavations at Montségur in 1943-44?" His conversation with the cardinal a short while before had showed him the advantage of a direct approach. It was useless to proceed with kid gloves; he needed answers now.

"He was my grandfather." She replied. "But he wasn't a Nazi—just an officer in the German army."

"Hold on," Peire continued, "I forgot to mention it to you, but I ran into one of your friends." He paused for effect before adding: "The Drac."

Jean Rude suppressed a start. Elke did not react. She did not seem to understand.

"Where did you see it?" Rudel asked, anxiously.

"In the Buffarnière grotto, at the place where my wife died. It proposed that the two of us should work together to get hold of the treasure."

Jean Rudel went pale. His hand trembled, and he had to put down the glass he was holding.

"What did you reply?"

"I didn't say anything more. I confess that its proposition was enormously tempting."

Peire took delight in seeing Jean Rudel become increasingly distressed as he spoke. He seemed nervous.

"That's not possible. You can't agree to it."

"At least it was frank with me. Not like you, who never stops lying to me."

"Refuse its offer! You don't know what it is."

"But what is the Drac?" Elke put in, obviously at a loss. "Is this that legend concerning the lake again?"

"Yes," Peire replied. "It's the Devil the legend talks about, but the Drac is also a friend of your grandfather and Otto Rahn. A great friend, even." He took the pages torn from Otto Rahn's notebook out of his pocket and held them out to Elke. "You ought to read this. Rahn talk about his encounter with the Drac. Very instructive."

Elke seized the pieces of paper avidly and immediately began to read them, without taking any further notice of the two men.

"We need to have a serious talk," Jean Rudel murmured, taking Peire by the arm to draw him into a corner of the restaurant.

"I'm listening. You've been amusing yourself at my expense, now it's my turn to laugh."

"I never wanted to play games with you. And time's pressing...."

They came to a halt next to an immense fireplace. Jordanne came up to them to fill their champagne-glasses. Before going back to her other guests she winked at Peire.

"Time is your problem," Peire said. "Why should I hurry?"

Jean Rudel looked at Peire compassionately, and then sighed. He put a hand on his shoulder. "You must understand, Peire, I needed to be sure that you were the right person. The pentagram constituted the final proof It symbolizes the New Man—the soul reborn in the body—by means of the five points that represent the head, the two hands and the two feet. When they're reconnected, the star appears." He paused deliberately before spelling it out: "You are that star, because you're the descendant of Amiel Aicart."

"That's what the Drac told me, too. I'm somewhat surrounded. First the Devil, then the Catholic Church, with its Cardinal Inquisitor, then you—and Elke too. I hope I haven't forgotten anyone."

"Exactly—we all have need of you. Each of us is pursuing a goal; without you, none of us can attain it—but the goals are incompatible. The time will come when you have to choose, knowing what is at stake."

Peire sighed. He had had enough of being manipulated. He did not want to assume the responsibilities that everyone in the world wanted to heap upon him. He might as well get to the point. "I'm listening to you, as I listened to the Drac and the priest. It's up to you to convince me."

"I'd prefer to broach the subject later, in more discreet surroundings."

"I need explanations immediately. Otherwise, we have nothing more to say to one another—but the Drac will come looking for his reply."

Peire turned round to signify that the conversation was over. Jean Rudel held him back by the arm. He no longer had a choice. He needed to tell the whole truth. He drew Peire further aside and studied the surroundings intently before proceeding with the revelation.

"Only a descendant of the man who took the treasure away after the fall of Montségur can find it and take it in his hands."

"Has none of my ancestors been capable of achieving that in 700 years? That's odd, isn't it?" As he pronounced these words, Peire experienced a flash of lucidity. *After 700 years*.... "But it's been more than 700 years since the treasure left Montségur...that doesn't work."

"March 16, 1944 wasn't the right year," Rudel explained, having followed Peire's train of thought. "The Perfecti had kept the treasure in the citadel until that date to celebrate an important festival, but the laurel came into flower long afterwards, and it was Amiel Aicart who was there. Now it's your turn. The moment is almost upon us."

"What form does the treasure take?"

"I haven't the slightest idea," Jean Rudel replied. "Nor do I know where it is. All that I know is that on March 16 of this year, the moment will have come. The texts whose guardian I am say: *The descendant of Amiel Aicart must be close by, and he will know what to do.* I am incapable of deciphering that sentence. On the other hand, I think Otto Rahn knew the answer."

"How did he know.?"

"He was the one who was in the plane on that famous March 16, 1944, when your grandfather climbed the Pog. He thought he would discover the treasure that day, but he was mistaken."

"You were kept informed of that, of course."

"My function within the Société del Gai Saber is to watch over and protect Aicart's lineal descendants, like all my predecessors. Before the creation of the society, it was a Cathar Perfectus who had that responsibility, and before him a Bogomil. You know who the Bogomils were, don't you?"

Peire nodded. He had read the history of those dualists, whose name derived from a villager who had called himself Bogomil, a man of God who preached his religion in Macedonia in the tenth century."

180

Jean Rudel explained the origin of the treasure to Peire. Jesus had known about it, thanks to the Essenes, and, long before him, Zoroaster might have been its custodian. It might even have existed at the very beginning of the world's creation.

Peire cut his discourse short, having little interest in such historical considerations. "And my role in all this?"

"It was necessary that you be recognized by Bernard d'En Marti. You had to perish or survive in the pentagram. The patriarch of Montségur recognized you, and sent you back into our midst. You're the one who will discover the treasure in a month's time. I'm supposed to accompany you until the end of your mission. There will be numerous temptations. I have to convince you to resist them."

"Since you mention the pentagrams—why did they kill Hélène? Why didn't you warn me that she was going into mortal danger by entering the Buffarnière grotto? You're responsible for watching over the Aicart family. You should, therefore, have kept watch on my wife, who might logically be expected to bear my children."

Jean Rudel went pale, demonstrating that Peire had just touched a sore point. Since Hélène Aicart's death, the old man had borne the responsibility for her death. He had reproached himself for not having done what was necessary, putting Peire's line of descent in peril. That day, he had judged it unnecessary to have Peire's wife followed when she set off in the direction of the mountain with a party of potholers. But who could have foreseen what would happen?

"A stupid accident, which was not intended—like the recent deaths of the four young men. I don't know how the pentagrams work. I don't have any power over them, believe me." Jean Rudel fell silent. He seemed exhausted. His round-shouldered back was scarcely sustaining him. The burden of the years and the difficulty of his mission were becoming increasingly hard to bear. "I have to show you a document," he finally continued. "You alone can read it, in the capacity of a descendant of Amiel Aicart. It was written by Bernard d'En

Marti himself, but it's only a Latin copy of part of a more ancient text. We've been guarding it closely since the fall of Montségur."

"Did it go with the treasure?"

"No, the parchment left the citadel during the winter of 1243 with the gold and silver that served to found the Société."

"What does the document say?"

"I'll translate it for you; then you'll posses all the elements of the puzzle. I beg you, Peire, at least agree to come and read the text."

"I'll visit the house of the Gai Saber within the week," Peire declared, with an air of finality.

"I'll be waiting for you."

Jean Rudel bowed to him and left the restaurant. Peire could not help feeling sorry for him. He had treated him roughly, although the old man was simply completing a mission defined by the Cathar pope more than 700 years before. His eyes remained fixed on the entrance door for some time, then he finally turned his back on it to mingle with the crowd of guests.

Peire wandered into the middle of the crowd. He went to a table, poured himself a glass of champagne and lifted it to his lips. He had just found out why everything depended on him. In the space of a few minutes, his life had been turned upside down. He did not like the game he had to play at all. He did not have the soul of a hero, and the prospect of offending the Drac, taking into account all that he had learned, seemed even more terrifying than before. How could he prevent it from killing his friends one by one until he gave in?

"It's necessary that you tell me what the Drac said to you." Elke had just rejoined him.

"What do you want to know?" he replied.

"I'd prefer to talk about it somewhere quieter."

"You too? This evening, everyone wants to talk to me in private."

"Are you sure that I only want to talk? Need I be more explicit?"

Peire gaze slid down the slender figure, shown off to full advantage by a close-fitting dress. It rose up again to the plunging neckline, the bare shoulders and the hair, tied back in a chignon from which vaporous wisps escaped. At that moment, he found her more beautiful than ever.

Elke raised her eyebrows, assuming an interrogative expression, and nodded her head. Lifting up her glass of champagne, she dipped a finger in it, and put it to her lips. She sucked it in a sensuous manner.

"Let's go to my place," Peire said, abruptly.

He took her by the arm and drew her toward the exit. When they got to the door, he paused.

"Wait here a minute."

Peire went to the kitchens, where Jordanne was tidying up. She was bent over in front of a cupboard set beneath the work-surface, her arms full of crockery.

"I'm going home, Jordanne. I thought I'd better warn you in case you tried to find me."

The restaurant-owner carefully set her pile of plates down on the shelf in front of her. Then she looked at him. She seemed disappointed.

"You're going? I thought we'd finish off the evening here...."

"I have to talk to Elke. I'd rather discuss things with her in the studio. I'll come back afterwards. Don't worry—I won't be long."

He stepped forwards to deposit a little kiss on Jordanne's lips before rejoining Elke, who was waiting for him outside.

They went through the deserted village without exchanging a word. A greenish light followed them, at a distance....

Chapter 22

The house was dark throughout. The calm contrasted with the animation that reigned over the Leg d'Amor. After the stress of the concert and the excitement of the soirée, Peire felt a sudden relief on finding himself at home. His house had always been a refuge.

Peire closed the main door behind them and pointed Elke in the direction of the sitting-room. His intention was to offer her a cup of coffee and answer her questions. She went in ahead of him, as if to go sit down, and then turned around abruptly. They met one another's eyes, neither of them visibly intent on talking. Peire was seized by a strange sensation of desire, and a mad urge to let himself go.

Suddenly, Elke drew closer and took him by hand. Their fingers rubbed together. Peire was intoxicated by the young woman's perfume. The sensuality of her body, molded within her silk dress, excited him. He drew her to him; she did not resist.

They embraced violently while their hands explored each other's bodies. The kiss was prolonged. They had difficulty getting their breath back. The caresses became more and more savage, as if they were no longer in control of themselves.

Elke tore herself from Peire's grip. She stepped back, and then slipped off her dress with a single sensuous movement. She was not wearing any underclothes. Peire admired her superb body, which swayed in a serpentine fashion. Naked, she advanced towards him. She undressed him slowly and caressed him, her gestures tender, intimate and lewd. She deposited kisses on his body and knelt down.

Peire, immobile, let her have her way. He removed the grip that secured her chignon. Her blonde hair cascaded over her shoulders. Suddenly, he lifted her to her feet and shoved her towards the sofa. He tilted her backwards in order to caresses her and cover her with kisses. Elke began to groan and reared up. Peire lifted her up and took possession of her violently. Then he accelerated his rhythm. She drove him mad. She shivered beneath him, writhed and trembled. He possessed her, and gladly lost himself within her.

A green glow flared up for an instant in the doorway, then faded away. Completely absorbed by the ardor of their frolicking, Elke and Peire did not hear the door open.

Jordanne came into the house and stopped in the sitting-room doorway. First she noticed the dress on the floor, then the two intertwined bodies. Peire could not see her behind him. His body also blocked Elke's view. Neither of them was conscious of being observed.

Jordanne watched them, incapable of movement. Even though she knew that she had no claim on Peire, she believed that a strong sentimental bond had finally developed between them, after many years of delay. She had loved him since childhood, but he had gone away to marry Hélène. After the drama, she had hoped that he might come back; she had imagined that she might even realize her dream.

It all collapsed. At the sight of him making love to the German woman, she felt herself grow weak at the knees. She wanted to run away, but could not tear her eyes away from the spectacle.

Elke began to moan. Peire released a long howl. Jordanne had never heard him cry out like that in her arms. She felt a profound disgust, mingled with anger. Once again, she had lost the man she loved. How many more rivals would it be necessary to tolerate?

She finally tore herself away from the vision of the two lovers and left. She went back along the path, through the garden gate and ran back to her restaurant like a fury. Tears ran down her cheeks. She did not even wipe them away. To think of all that she had given him, to Peire Aicart—and he had betrayed her with the first woman who came along....

"You can't trust anyone, can you?"

The amused voice came from her right. Jordanne stopped short. The Drac was sitting on an embankment. Jordanne remained quite still, unable to react. Then she ran on in the direction of the village. As she reached the first house she stopped, out of breath.

"What a pity. You were so sweet together, the two of you. You made an ideal couple—but the temptation was too strong."

"It was you who shoved that girl, that...straight into his arms!"

The Drac sniffed and replied, with excessive familiarity: "Not at all! Your impetuous *lover* couldn't resist the charms of youth...he's only human, after all. I was merely an audience for the spectacle—like you, my dear."

"I don't believe you! Peire loved me!"

Jordanne would have like to flee, to get back to her bedroom to weep in peace, but the vision of Peire's and Elke's interlaced bodies continued to haunt her. Peire's cry of joy was still echoing in her ears.

"It will soon be time for me to go ask Peire for his answer to my proposal," the Drac added, simply.

"I'll never help you!" Jordanne howled.

The Drac made a whistling sound to make her shut up, and then became unctuous. "Everything depends on who makes the request of him."

"Do you think that I'll incite him to damnation by collaborating with you? It's out of the question."

"Even if I offer you love in exchange? You love Peire, and it's quite easy for me to make that love reciprocal and enduring. Peire would belong to you and remain faithful."

"And for that I have to persuade him to bring you the treasure?"

The Drac emitted a sinister snigger. "The treasure's worthless to him."

"And what is it worth to you?" Jordanne asked.

"Everything I've wanted for millions of years...my ultimate aim, the accomplishment of my destiny," the Drac replied, calmly.

"Which is to eliminate human beings!"

The snigger became louder. "Certainly not—I want them to live."

Jordanne considered the Drac's proposition. Her heart was beating furiously.

"I'm not asking for anything right now," the creature went on, "but think about my offer. I'm not lying when I promise you happiness with Peire."

Jordanne had no time to reply. A green mist enveloped the Drac. When it dissipated, it left behind no trace of its passing.

"I'm sorry about what just happened," Peire said, suddenly embarrassed. "I don't know what came over me."

Elke got up, naked. She did not bother to get dressed again. "I'm not," she said, moving towards the fireplace. "On the contrary, I liked it very much—much more than I would have expected...."

She stretched herself out languidly in front of the flames. "Tell me what the Drac and Jean Rudel told you."

"Why? Do you have a proposition to make to me too? You want the treasure and you have need of me? That was what it was for—your seduction operation and that little sex session just now?"

As he pronounced these words, Peire was conscious of his own hypocrisy. He immediately regretted saying them.

Elke stiffened. She came towards him, measuring him almost menacingly.

"I don't play the *femme fatale,* who uses her body to lure a man. I don't need to. If I made love to you, it's simply because I wanted to. Believe what you want—it's all the same to me."

Peire got dressed, thoughtfully. He was all alone in this adventure, and might need an ally. Curiously, Elke inspired confidence in him. At the thought of their recent frolicking, a blast of emotion surged forth from his innermost depths. He decided to tell her about his encounter with the Drac and his discussions with Jean Rudel and Anto. On the other hand, he would not mention the presence of Kyot or the tenor of his remarks.

"Now that I've told you what I know," he said, finally, "would you like to tell me what you're doing in Montségur?"

"Since my earliest childhood I've lived in the midst of all these legends. My grandfather came back from the war obsessed by the researches he'd supervised. His library overflowed with books on Catharism. As a child I steeped myself in those books."

Elke got dressed, taking her time. "These beliefs were part of my family history, you see. I've always wanted to find this treasure. I've nothing to do with the Drac or the cardinal. It became an obsession for me. I'm ready at last to realize my dream."

She adjusted the shoulder-straps of her dress and went on: "I've spent many months in the region. I've taken part in expeditions and excavations. I've gleaned scraps of information, learning a great deal. Step by step, I deduced that this year would probably produce exceptional events, so I came back to see—but I never expected what just happened between us."

She fell silent. She seemed very emotional. Peire was touched by her fragility. He went to take her in his arms.

"I truly want to help you, Peire. Believe me."

"I believe you," he murmured in her ear. "But I know less than you do about the treasure. I've learned that the Société del Gai Saber is an offshoot of the Cathar Church, and that they have to show me an important document."

Elke pressed herself against him. She felt good, and she felt the need to put him on his guard. "Don't trust the cardinal and his Hounds of God. He's a specialist in Catharism. He's had access to the Vatican archives. He's a fanatic, and dangerous."

"I had an interesting conversation with him this evening, after the concert," Peire replied. "He doesn't seem so threatening…slightly narrow-minded, at most "

"He wouldn't hesitate to kill you—to kill us, all of us, if the treasure threatens the foundations of his Church."

"I'll be careful," Peire promised. He slid his hand through Elke's hair, caressed her neck and kissed her forehead. "Tell me, do you have any idea what the treasure is?"

Elke trembled beneath his kisses, and then assumed a pensive attitude. "I've heard rumor of a legend that might bring part of our beliefs into question."

"Which part?"

"Jesus Christ's tomb. Some people believe that after the crucifixion, his mother and Mary Magdalene took the body away and left Judea in a boat. After their disembarkation, they were said to have come to this region, where they buried him."

Peire had never heard tell of this story, but his knowledge of Catharism was recent and contained lacunae.

"And you think that the Cathars knew the location?"

"No," she replied, without the slightest hesitation. "They didn't consider Jesus to be a person of major significance. I can't see why they would have kept the secret of his tomb. The treasure must be something else."

"The Grail?" Peire suggested. "Otto Rahn explored that trail."

"Perhaps—it's an interesting hypothesis."

"But there's one thing I can't understand, in that case. If the Cathars weren't interested in Jesus, I can't see them conserving the cup that held his blood."

Elke had already thought of that problem. "The Grail is also a magical object. It might have a link to the Drac, in terms of its properties. In Wolfram von Eschenbach's Grail romance, the author claims that the Grail is an emerald dislodged from Lucifer's forehead during his fall."

"That would explain why he wants to recover it at any price. Perhaps it might give him absolute power…."

"The fallen angel who wants to recover his position is a myth as old as the world," Elke agreed.

"Yes, but why would the Cathars have guarded the stone, and why was the Drac unable to take possession of it?"

Elke searched for an answer, then replied: "There's only one way to find that out. Ask it. Me, I always follow my questions to the end."

Peire looked at Elke, and found her incredibly beautiful.

Chapter 23

Brother Bruno lifted up the collar of his overcoat and opened the door. A dog was barking in the distance. A breath of cold air swept through the deserted side-street. The village was still asleep.

The monk left the lodgings where he had spent the last two days, in the very heart of Montségur. He had introduced himself as a simple student of ornithology who had come to spend a week's vacation in the country to take stock of the birds of the local ecosystem, particularly the raptors. He could therefore wander calmly in the surrounding area with a camera and a pair of binoculars without attracting the slightest suspicion.

On the previous day he had strode along several pathways, keeping an eye on Peire Aicart's house all the while. The musician had not made a move all day. He had finally gone to the village at dusk to take something to the Post Office, then he had returned home, where he spent the evening alone. In the absence of any sign of activity, Brother Bruno had left his post at about one o'clock in the morning to write is report and sleep for five hours.

The monk raised his head and studied the sky. One or two stars were still shining feebly; the darkness was turning deep blue. A pale glow in the east marked the imminent sunrise.

Brother Bruno left the village without encountering a living soul. He took a little path that led towards a group of dewy meadows. There was no sound save for the rhythm of his own respiration. He was alone in the midst of nature.

After ten minutes or so, he sat down on a rock from which he had a downward view of Peire Aicart's house. With the binoculars around his neck, he loaded his camera, set it down beside him and commenced his surveillance.

At about midday, a silhouette emerged from one of the side-streets of Montségur and followed a route that led to Aicart's house. Brother Bruno took hold of his binoculars. He immediately recognized Jordanne Sutra, the owner of the restaurant where Peire had dined. She seemed to be in a hurry, and dated rapid glances from side to side. It even seemed to him that she was speaking aloud to an invisible interlocutor. From his observation-point, Brother Bruno could not hear what she was saying.

The visitor went into the house. Brother Bruno took advantage of that to change his position. In a little village like Montségur nothing stayed secret for long. He did not want to be noticed, at all costs.

He continued walking along the path, pretending to be observing the countryside, took a few photographs, and went back down into the valley. He crossed over a little stream, and then went up the other slope, keeping an eye on the house all the while.

Brother Bruno was fervent in his accomplishment of the mission that his superior had entrusted to him. He always obeyed blindly, convinced that the defense of the faith justified any action. He was a worthy successor of the inquisitors who had evangelized the region at the very height of the revolt. He was not afraid of death; it would not have troubled him to deliver himself to it, if the command came from on high.

Cardinal Anto Sakic had unleashed the Hounds of God. That meant that some new peril was threatening the foundations of the Church. At that thought, Brother Bruno stiffened. Today, he had been asked to keep watch on the musician. Tomorrow, perhaps, he would have to take up arms. He would obey without debate, without asking the slightest question. It would not be the first time that he had struck a man down in cold blood.

The Order had sent him to Latin America three years earlier. He had recently gone to one of the countries of the ex-Soviet bloc. Each time he had completed his missions perfectly before returning to Fanjeaux to continue his studies in theology. He was working on antique texts, because he knew several ancient languages. In parallel, he had continued to maintain his physical fitness and his skill in handling weapons.

"I doubt that you'll find any interesting birds in these forests."

Brother Bruno turned round abruptly. On a slightly-elevated embankment, leaning against a tree, stood a man of his own age, just into his 30s. From the height of his little promontory, the man was pointing a hunting-rifle at him.

Brother Bruno did not move. He cursed himself silently. How had he let himself be taken by surprise? He had not suspected for a moment that others might also be keeping watch on the musician—a gross error. He was under no illusion. The man had been waiting for him. He must, therefore, know the true nature of his activities in the vicinity. Brother Bruno did not attempt to justify his presence. He took a deep breath and studied his adversary attentively. The man had taken aim at him, and would not hesitate to fire, perhaps not to kill, but to wound. The hand positioned on the barrel of the rifle was trembling slightly; he was not as sure of himself as he wanted to appear.

"What are you looking for?" Philippe asked.

One good thing, the priest thought, his adversary was nervous. That might be used against him, but while remaining very prudent. It was always necessary to beware of amateurs, because they were capable of anything. Brother Bruno shifted his weight imperceptibly to ensure his stability on the damp ground. He held on very tightly to the camera in his right hand.

"Are you going to answer, then? I asked you a question!"

The priest did not move his lips. He contented himself with staring into the eyes of the man, who was beginning to get agitated. The rifle was not held as firmly, and the barrel was quivering.

"I'll give you three seconds," the other went on. "If you don't tell me who you're working for, I'll put a bullet in your knee!"

The man was losing patience. Brother Bruno envisaged several possible ways of getting out of this awkward situation. He had analyzed all the parameters and several strategies were available. He must choose the best and hold to it. While he asked himself these questions the other counted in a loud voice: "One, two...."

With an abrupt movement, the priest threw his camera at the rifle. Then he leapt into the ravine behind him. He landed on his feet, his legs braced to deaden the shock. Then he raced down the slope at top speed, changing direction occasionally so as not to remain in the line of fire. The shot would not be-long delayed and he was still in the open. Less than 20 meters away, a wood offered him shelter.

Something exploded at his feet. His adversary had fired. Brother Bruno was only a meter away from the trees when the second shot resounded. There was a sharp pain in his thigh. He clenched his teeth and continued running with a limp. He was obsessed by one sole thought: to get back to the monastery to warn the cardinal about this new threat—but first, to get rid of his adversary if he could not outdistance him.

He was finally under cover of the wood, which he tra-versed at top speed, grabbing branches so as not to fall. He stumbled several times. Every stride became increasingly painful. His leg was becoming stiff. He had just caught sight of the edge of the forest when a green mass reared up in front of him.

He did not have time to change course. He ran into the thing at full tilt and found himself laid out on a carpet of damp leaves. Stunned, he did not understand what had happened to him. He got up painfully, and turned toward the obstacle.

First he made out the green eyes looming over him, then the creature as a whole. Leathery wings extended from its back and a roar emerged from its frightful mouth. Brother

Bruno made the sign of the cross. The Drac threw itself upon him.

The two gigantic clawed hands came down on the priest's head with sledgehammer force. The Drac let out raucous cries as it struck with ever-increasing force. Its wings began to vibrate rhythmically. Obviously, it wanted to finish quickly. It dug its claws into his flesh, shredding his muscles and breaking his bones. Brother Bruno did not even have time to howl, nor to pray.

The Drac thrust the dismembered corpse backwards. It turned toward the peak of the mountain. Its features hardened; further prey was on its way. With this one, it could take its time. The Drac headed for the edge of the little wood.

It saw the man who was carefully coming down the steep slope, following the fugitive's tracks. He advanced towards the trees, unconscious of the danger. Prudently, he stopped to study the border of the thicket attentively.

Suddenly, the Drac turned its head. In the distance, it sensed Jordanne's emotions. She was feeling anguish and repentance. She was in doubt; her resolution was weakening.

The Drac reacted instantly. Jordanne was its most powerful piece. She must not weaken. Thanks to her, it would obtain the treasure. Concentrating its will on the young woman, it made haste to meet her.

Philippe glimpsed a brief furtive movement from a distance in the shade of the undergrowth, accompanied by a flash of light. He became aware of the supernatural silence that reigned in the wood just as the birds began singing again.

Chapter 24

The old pendulum clock chimed 11 a.m. The main room of the restaurant, decorated in traditional fashion, was empty of customers. An odor of lavender mingled with effluvia of thyme, garlic and olive oil. Little bouquets of dried flowers distributed on the tables gave the place a characteristic charm.

Jordanne finished laying out the napkins on the plates for the midday meal, knowing all the while that it was unlikely that anyone would come today. The first tourists usually did not arrive until the end of Easter. Out of season, the restaurant was virtually deserted at lunchtime. The restaurant-owner set out the cutlery anyway, and finished preparing the tables.

Three days had gone by, and she had thought long and hard about recent events. Today, having calmed down and stood back, she told herself that in listening to the Drac's proposition she had obeyed a reflexive impulse that was out of character. Everything had been so difficult lately…. Between Peire's attitude, her doubts and anguish, and the things they had lived through since Michel's death, she had ended up momentarily losing her reason.

Without pausing in her work in the restaurant, Jordanne shook her head and released a deep sigh. She was no longer sure where she stood. This morning, she had even gone to see Peire to make that point. She had intended to confess everything and to ask him what he thought about it. When the moment came, though, she had not found the strength to speak. She had confined herself to listening to him talk about his discussions with Anto Sakic and Jean Rudel. He had not even mentioned Elke. Although she knew that there was no formal arrangement between them, Jordanne would have liked it if he had opened up to her—but no….

She had abandoned him them to the book that she had brought him.

She glanced at the clock. One o'clock. Lost in her reverie she had not noticed the time passing. Ideas were jostling in her head. She felt a desire to talk to Peire. She put on her coat and left the restaurant, pausing on the doorstep. The little parking lot in front of her was deserted. There would be no customers. She locked the door and put the bunch of keys in her pocket.

Jordanne went along the street. On due reflection, the confrontation with Peire was unavoidable, but she was afraid. As she emerged into the little village square, she questioned herself. Was it really necessary to go to see Peire, or would she do better to return home?

A ray of sunlight fell through a gap in the clouds upon the water of the fountain and set it alight with a silvery gleam. Spring was approaching at a rapid pace. Soon the leaves would be coming out on the trees. While she walked, Jordanne looked at the signs that announced, for her, the imminent arrival of tourists. She went through the village.

"Elke's coming to see Peire this afternoon. She must have greatly enjoyed that little interval the other night. Her *lover* must have given it just as much thought. I suppose they'll take up where they left off."

Jordanne did not even turn her head. She had recognized the hoarse voice of the Drac.

"You're lying to manipulate me!" she replied, continuing on her way.

"Now, now, Jordanne," mocked the Drac, "have you forgotten what I am?" Confronted with the restaurant-owner's silence, it went on: "She's stolen *your* lover? Will you let the situation with Hélène develop all over again? After waiting for Peire all your life? I thought you'd be more inclined to fight, Jordanne."

"Enough!" she howled, putting her hands over her ears.

"She's coming to get Peire. Afterwards, she'll toy with him, and then she'll leave him. But when she's finished with him, you won't be able to get him back. She'll have destroyed him. He'll never come back to you."

"That's not true, as you know perfectly well! After Hélène, he was crushed. He turned to me."

The Drac burst out laughing. "You're lying to yourself. It was you who pursued him, but he ended up by giving in, because he was worn down. He's never sought your company. He just took what you offered him."

"But we've made love!"

"No, Jordanne. With you, it was to take his pleasure. With her, he's made love. Look...."

The creature made a slight hand gesture, and a green mist formed in front of them. Images materialized in the middle of it, as if on a cinema screen: Peire and Jordanne, during their first embrace, then the second, the third...the scenes succeeded one another, and every time, Peire had the same attitude. He was gentle, taking pleasure but maintaining a certain reserve. Finally, the bodies of Peire and Elke appeared, intertwined. They were literally transfigured, impassioned.

Jordanne watched the spectacle, unable to tear her eyes away. The Drac snapped its fingers again, and the views changed. Now they resembled an artful montage, melting into one another, alternately presenting Peire's face during intercourse with Jordanne and with Elke. The contrast was striking. The truth was cruelly manifest.

The Drac took pleasure in reviving Jordanne's jealousy; then it materialized in front of her.

"Can you really do without my help?"

"Kill her!" Jordanne replied, dryly.

"That's not what I had in mind, for now...if I kill her, you won't have any reason to help me."

"Then I'll get him back on my own."

The Drac disappeared. His voice, a muffled whisper, sounded behind Jordanne: "Keep trying...."

She had responded out of bravado—but the Drac would do everything to thwart her. He had a powerful means of exerting pressure on her: the boundless love that she had for Peire, which he did not reciprocate. He was infatuated with the German woman, and it seemed to be mutual. Perhaps the Drac was nourishing their affection. Without it, she could do nothing. She was ensnared.

Abruptly, she made her decision.

"Wait! What do I have to do?"

"Just convince him to let me have the treasurer when he's found it. Nothing more."

"What proof do I have that you'll keep your promise? Aren't you the Devil, the Father of Lies?"

"Ah...the old beliefs are long-lasting. All the religions represent me thus, but it's false. I bring knowledge. Their God, by contrast, blinds human beings."

Jordanne knew that he was telling the truth. Since her first encounter with him, she had consulted several books about the Devil—or Lucifer, the fallen angel, the master of knowledge, the ultimate accursed one.

"That doesn't answer my question," she persisted.

"I can only give you one answer: you have nothing to lose. You've already lost Peire. As far as I'm concerned, why shouldn't I satisfy your desire once I've obtained the treasure? It won't cost me anything."

Without knowing whence the certainty came, she believed him. She took a deep breath to give herself strength. "All right. I'll try to influence Peire. But if I don't succeed, what will happen to us?"

She waited for a reply that never came. She was alone—quite alone—with her resolve. She resumed walking. From some distance away, two green eyes followed her.

Having arrived at Peire's house she paused to gather her courage, and then went in without knocking. Silently, she made her way to the sitting-room. She saw him from behind, installed on the sofa, reading.

"What are you reading?" she asked, putting her arms around his neck and kissing his ear.

He returned her kiss distractedly, without passion.

"I'm just finishing a book about the legends surrounding Montségur. I'm hoping to find a link between the pentagrams and the location of the treasure."

"Exactly what are you looking for?"

Peire closed the book and got up. He stood in front of the fireplace, extending his hands toward the fire. "A connection with the Devil. It seems to me that the best way to hide a treasure is to deposit it somewhere and then make people believe that the Devil is guarding it. Then people won't go there."

He did not see Jordanne shiver at the mention of the Drac.

"You haven't seen it again?" she enquired.

"No, but it must be observing me, waiting for the propitious moment. Eighteen days still remain before March 16, so it's in no hurry. In my opinion, nothing will happen before then."

Jordanne hesitated, and then took the plunge. "Yesterday evening, I re-read certain passages concerning Lucifer. He might not be the kind of being that has been described to us for millennia. On the contrary, he might well be the one who gave knowledge to human beings."

"A theme dear to witches and other Luciferians. You're forgetting that for the Cathars, the Devil was God's equal and opposite.

Jordanne grew bolder. She responded to what Peire had said, excitedly. "Because they were also Christians, even though their philosophy originated from Zoroaster. They lived under the influence of a Good/Evil duality that has pursued us since time immemorial. God has succeeded in setting the Devil aside, when he might be the future of the human race."

Peire made a slight grimace. Jordanne went on, her voice now full of assurance: "Lucifer is the bringer of light, the most beautiful of the angels, who was punished for his rebellion against God. But was he, too, not inspired by divine transcendence? He's also the accuser, the seducer."

"And the destroyer."

"Granted. Like fire, he brings warmth but also burns."

"It's quite possible…but for the moment, I don't know enough to be confident of one or the other."

"What about me?"

Jordanne's face had straightened, and a tear ran down her cheek. Peire went to her and hugged her forcefully.

"I've got confidence in you. To prove it, I'm taking you to Toulouse. Jean Rudel has to give me a manuscript, which might perhaps enlighten us as to the nature of the treasure."

"You still have no idea?"

No. I've searched hard, but there's nothing precise. I've also thought hard about that song I performed without knowing it. I've asked myself what the story of the laurel might mean to the Cathars. I haven't found anything in the legends."

"It must be a symbol of some sort for them. A plant that flowers in spring. I don't know much about laurel."

"The date isn't a coincidence. Historians think that March 15 or 16 corresponded to a sacred festival. That's what must have made the Cathars ask for a fortnight's delay before surrendering. And the treasure was necessary to its celebration, since it left the castle the following day, in defiance of the treaty signed with the Church and the King."

"What if the treasure consisted of manuscripts?"

"No, they must have known their important texts by heart. They wouldn't have taken such risks to get them out of Montségur, going through the French army's lines under the noses of the Inquisitors."

Jordanne looked at Peire intently. "In any case, the essential thing isn't the contents of the treasure but what you'll do with it."

Peire decided to cut the conversation short. "You're right. It's time to go now."

Philippe headed back towards his car, bewildered. He was having difficulty not vomiting. What a horrible spectacle! Who could possibly have subjected the individual he had been following to such treatment? The scattered remains of the man had smeared the carpet of dead leaves with blood and soiled the bushes.

He had left the corpse where it was, without touching anything and had climbed back up the steep slope. After an interminable march, he finally reached the vehicle, parked by the roadside.

Two green eyes were waiting, hidden behind a tree.

Satisfied, the Drac told itself that it was decidedly lucky. It would finally be able to feast on its second prey, and take its time.

Philippe did not see the attack coming.

Three weeks to go—this was the final sacrifice demanded by his responsibility, Jean Rudel thought. Mechanically, he closed the incunabulum that he had been reading for half an hour, unhooked the telephone placed beside him and dialed the number of Philippe's mobile. No answer. It was the tenth time that day he had tried to reach him. The young man had not called him, as he usually did. Vaguely anxious, Jean Rudel hung up the phone stiffly before going back to his reading.

"Is this what you're looking for?"

The hoarse voice made him raise his head. In front of him, swinging from the end of a clawed finger, was Philippe's decapitated head. A horrible grimace distorted his features, previously so youthful. The Drac let its trophy fall. The head rolled across the desk before coming to rest against the volume. The precious work was blotched with a black liquid.

"I have another one, but it isn't for you. I'm keeping it for your adversary. I'm honest, you see: I'm not taking sides in your ideological conflict."

Nauseated, Jean Rudel gazed at the Drac. "Why? Philippe's death doesn't gain you anything. It's a gratuitous act, which makes no sense."

"A little pleasure that I give myself from time to time. Must a game always make sense?"

"Philippe isn't truly dead. He'll live again, to attain perfection."

"Your disciple wasn't yet a Perfectus. His body will belong to me forever."

"Don't think that you've won. In the final analysis, Philippe will escape you. It's a pity that his first meeting with you had to end in such a tragic fashion. He was very young."

Rudel remembered his first conversation with the Drac, when he was still an adolescent and the director of the Société del Gai Saber had taken him under his protection. The Devil had appeared to him one night. Even though his mentor had prepared him for the encounter, he had experienced intense terror. One single thought came to him: quite simply, he would die. The Drac had contented itself with looking at him for a long moment, holding him at its mercy, and then it had evaporated. After its departure, Jean Rudel had observed that he had wet his bed.

In more than 40 years, he had only seen it three more times, always at Montségur. Today, it was manifesting itself in the premises of the Gai Saber.

The Drac whistled. "You're not saying anything...are you afraid of me?"

"The Devil doesn't frighten me any more—not for a long time. Destroy my body if you want to; my soul belongs to none but the Lord."

The Drac let loose a loud burst of laughter before dematerializing. As it disappeared from the room it pronounced one last sentence: "Don't be so sure."

Jean Rudel lifted up his aged body. The Devil had accompanied him throughout his long life, which he had devoted to becoming good. He had thus accomplished the destiny of a true Cathar. But his predecessor had told him that the Drac could do nothing to him. His enthronement in a cave at Ussat had been a kind of "immunization" against temptation. He could therefore devote himself entirely to his duty. That was part of a vast design, a cycle to which the Drac itself was also submissive.

Jean Rudel sighed. Philippe had just quit the world. A conscientious disciple, shaped for years to succeed him, who had been on the point of ritual enthronement. A devout young man, full of life and spirit…the Société del Gai Saber paid a heavy tribute to the pursuit of tradition.

Rudel shook himself. He had to accomplish his duty. Peire Aicart would be arriving before long. In the first place, he had to acquaint him with the manuscript left by Bernard d'En Marti. Then he had to protect the musician for as long as possible—but a crucial moment would come when Peire must sort things out for himself.

Jean Rudel would have given anything to know what the initiates had found, millennia before. The discovery must have been important, since it had the power to trouble the Master of the world. The old man shrugged his shoulders. Perhaps he would know the truth in a few days. In the meantime, he must not allow himself to be distracted. He left the room, and returned a minute later.

He took the young man's head, wrapped it in the cloth he had brought and cradled it against his bosom, reciting a prayer. He experienced no grief because, like his Cathar spiritual masters, he believed in reincarnation. Human beings would attain Paradise when their souls were pure. To attain that state, one life alone was insufficient—far from it. Philippe would soon be reborn to resume his long journey towards God.

The only regret that Jean Rudel experienced was not having being able to give Philippe the consolamentum, the laying on of hands which transmitted the consolatory Spirit: the message of Christ given to men by love. He similarly regretted that Philippe had had to die so young—but that was part of the cycle. As the sacred date approached, events would become confused. The Drac would strike again.

Holding the head close, Jean Rudel went down to the building's cellars. Beneath the foundations of the house a network of tunnels had been hollowed out. All the grand masters of the Société del Gai Saber were interred in this secret place, along with the bodies of some of their disciples, martyrs to the Cathar cause.

By the wan light of torches attached to the walls, a small silent group was waiting. Under his orders, the Société del Gai Saber had prepared a simple funeral in great haste. A vault was open; Jean Rudel deposited Philippe's head within it. Then he closed the lid. He knelt down to collect himself and recited a few prayers. Each of the group's members then came forward to honor the memory of their companion, with due emotion.

Simon came forward too, his heart aching, to render a final homage to his friend. Raising his head, he exchanged as long glance with Jean Rudel. He understood the mute message. The duty of replacing the director after his death was now incumbent on him. He was prepared for it. He swallowed his grief.

The funeral ceremony ran its course. When it was over, the director returned to his desk. In anticipation of Peire's arrival, the old man brought out *La Croisade contre les Albigeois* from the library, opened it at the page on which the message began, and read one more time.

Yet again, the meaning of the final two pages escaped him. They reproduced a ballad written by a troubadour in honor of Dame Esclarmonde. The name of the poet had been lost and, in spite of his researches, Jean Rudel had been unable to discover his identity. The song was unique and was not found in any other work. The theme, however, was common to numerous troubadours: *Fin Amor*, or Courtly Love. Troubadours always addressed their songs to their Lady—but not to the wife, rather to the beloved. And in this song, Esclarmonde was celebrated. One sole troubadour had spoken to her.

Esclarmonde de Foix: the *grand dame* of Catharism; a person who had always inspired poets and romancers. The daughter of the Comte de Foix, she had been converted to Catharism and had ended up on the pyre at Montségur.

Throughout the years, Jean Rudel had tried to understand the significance of this song, without success. He felt a troubling emotion as he read the lines, though—a sentiment that he could not explain, as if he were close to a truth that would always be concealed from him.

He read the text one more time while waiting for Peire to arrive. All the other details, including those related to his succession, were in order.

Chapter 25

Seated in the rear of the car, Anto watched the entrance door of the Société del Gai Saber. The street was calm and tranquil. Outside the tourist season, this historic quarter was not busy.

Anto fidgeted in his seat. He was prey to an extreme tension. He had not yet rid himself of the anger that had tormented him since the discovery of Brother Bruno's dismembered body. He had summoned Brother Bernard, the community's superior, immediately. Together, they had decided after profound consideration of the situation that there was no longer any question of waiting. It was necessary to act quickly, and above all to strike hard. Their adversaries probably knew the location of the treasure. Every effort must be put into the siege of the Société del Gai Saber.

The Hounds of God had been gathered and then sent to Toulouse. One of the priests had taken over Peire's surveillance. At the end of the morning he had warned the monastery that the musician had left the village in company with the bookseller by the Toulouse road. Anto had immediately taken the decision to join the party on watch. On his order, the chauffeur had raced through the suburbs of the city at top speed. Within five minutes, the car was parked in front of the house in question.

The prelate waited inside the car. He hoped that his analysis was not mistaken. Mechanically he touched the wooden cross which hung over his breast, then recited prayers in a low voice. All around the building, a dozen Hounds of God were awaiting his orders. Four of them were inside, marking out the terrain.

A discreet bell sounded. The chauffeur brought a mobile phone out of his pocket and answered it briefly. Turning to Anto, he announced: "The musician and his companion are here. One of our Brothers has spotted them. They're parking at the end of the street. They're alone—no one's following them."

The cardinal looked at the pavement to his right. After 30 seconds the couple appeared in his field of vision.

"Wait a minute, then occupy the building. Neutralize all those who get in our way. But take care—I don't want any unnecessary violence.

The chauffeur picked up his mobile phone again to transmit the order to the Hounds of God.

Anto frowned when Peire went into the house. He counted down mentally before getting out of the car, escorted by his chauffeur and another priest, who came to join them. They entered in their turn.

The cardinal headed for Jean Rudel's office. He took care not to walk over the pentagram on the way. He pushed the door. Facing him, the old man gave a book to Peire.

"Give me that book!" Anto ordered.

Peire acted as if he had not heard, turning the pages without taking any notice of Anto's interruption.

The cardinal's tone became more menacing. "Give me that book! It belongs to the Catholic Church."

"This book has always belonged to the Cathars; you have no right to it," replied Peire, turning to face him to demonstrate that he was not afraid. He closed the book, then added: "And now it's mine."

"Silence, blasphemer!" exclaimed the cardinal, in a hoarse voice. "That document is returning to us as a matter of right."

"Really? And then what? You want to destroy it just as you've burned thousands of other works in the course of the centuries. You're nothing but a barbarian."

"And, you, the enemies of Christ," Anto snapped, "will be chastised for your opposition to him! Give me the book!"

Jordanne intervened, addressing Peire in a soft voice. "Give him the book. It's not worth fighting…."

"Shut up, Jordanne," Peire cut in. Turning to the cardinal, he went on: "So you're counting on taking possession of it by force? That's why you've come with all your men. The Inquisition has returned."

"I want that document and I'll have it, even if I have to use violence. That won't trouble me in the least. I advise you to give it to me. As you can see, I'm in a position of strength."

None of the participants moved a muscle. They all held their breath. Jean Rudel had taken hold of Jordanne's arm to reassure her.

"The other evening," Peire said, "you talked about an alliance. Let's pool our knowledge and multiply our chances of arriving at the truth."

"You must not ally yourself with him!" Jean Rudel protested, coming round the desk to take the book back.

"Certainly not," Anto said, with a mocking laugh. "He's playing for time, but you have no way out. My men control the building. So I repeat: give me that book!"

Peire looked at the incunabulum one last time before holding it out to the cardinal. "I offer it to you, since you want it so much. But you won't get anything out of it. Without me, it's no use to you."

Anto hesitated.

"Go on, take it! Are you afraid of burning yourself? Be careful, this book may be accursed. I'm not risking anything myself, since I'm already damned by your Christ."

He held out the book. Anto did not move.

"Don't you want it any longer?" the musician asked, ironically.

Anto looked at him without breathing a word. Then he made the sign of the cross, took possession of the book and placed his crucifix on its cover. Nothing happened. He made a visible effort to control the tremor that was agitating his hands.

"The pages in which you're interested are the last two," Peire specified. "Don't bother to read the preceding ones, unless you want to relive the highlights of the Inquisition that ravaged my country."

"Don't worry about me. I'm used to decrypting ancient texts. I'll find what I want."

Jean Rudel advanced towards the cardinal, interposing himself between Anto and Peire. "Don't think that you can get what you want in this fashion, Sakic. We're no longer in the Middle Ages!"

"So what?" Anto sneered. "How do you intend to resist me? The two men guarding your building have been neutralized. You're in no shape to face up to me."

The cardinal caressed the book with his hand. He nodded his head in Peire's direction. Then he looked at Jean Rudel and Jordanne.

"On that note, dear friends," he said, "I'll leave you. I would have taken advantage of your hospitality for longer, but I have some reading to do. I leave you to your Cathar memories."

Slowly, the ecclesiastic backed away from the desk. Just as the prelate's tall silhouette crossed the threshold, Jean Rudel took a step in his direction. Peire retained him by the arm.

"You're letting him go without making any attempt to stop him? You haven't even read the text. Without it, you'll never find the treasure!"

Peire did not reply. He beckoned to his companions to follow him. He left the desk and walked as far as the entrance to the hallway, where he leaned on the door-frame. Jean Rudel and Jordanne came to a halt next to him. "Have a safe journey!" he called. "And thank you for your lovely visit!"

The cardinal turned abruptly. His expression, as he looked at Peire, was full of hatred. He hugged the book to his bosom. The two men challenged one another with their gazes. Anto did not see the blue light that sprang up from the ground behind him. At that moment, one of the priests stepped over the pentagram.

A flash of light sprang from the geometrical figure, which was transformed into an immense ball of fire. A muffled explosion shook the building. Anto and several of his men were hurled against the walls. The windows shattered.

Before their eyes the Brother was transformed into a human torch. In less than 20 seconds he was no more than a charred corpse shriveled up on the flagstones. The immense flame burst into several spheres, which fell upon each of the priests. The victims collapsed to the ground one after the other.

Anto found himself lying full length on the flagstones. He stood up, avoiding a ball of fire that passed over his head. He was still holding tight to the precious work.

"Lord!" he moaned, looking at his men.

To his left, a young priest was writhing convulsively in the midst of flames. To his right, another of the Hounds of God received the ruddy ball head on. He tottered, clung to a tapestry mounted on one of the wall-panels, then fell backwards, brought down by the fire.

The cardinal watched, powerless, as his men were transformed one after another into heaps of cinders. He looked at Peire, who was surrounded by a blue halo and whose face seemed transfigured.

Anto collected himself and turned to flee. Jean Rudel immediately launched himself in pursuit while Peire observed the scene calmly. By his side, Jordanne was biting her fist in order to prevent herself from screaming.

The director caught up with Anto on the threshold of the building. He seized him by the collar and drew him violently backwards. Rudel's hands gripped the book and pulled, without success. The cardinal clung to the incunabulum, unwilling to let it go. Jean Rudel began striking the cardinal's arms and breast. Anto remained impassive beneath the avalanche of blows. Still clinging to his booty, he staggered but remained upright.

Finally, Jean Rudel decided to attack his enemy's face. He punched him one the nose with all the violence of which he was capable. A crack resounded. Momentarily blinded by the shock, Anto screamed in pain. He let go, and Jean Rudel took advantage of it to seize the book.

Realizing that he had just been deprived of the volume, Anto became mad with rage. He threw himself on Jean Rudel, who had no time to protect himself. Both the cardinal's hands had already closed around his neck.

Jordanne screamed as she watched the old man suffocate, incapable of getting free. That brought a reaction from Peire, who shook off his torpor. He ran along the hallway, closed in on the two men and launched a mighty blow of his fist into the ecclesiastic's face. Anto did not relax his grip.

Jean Rudel was beginning to lose his color. His gaze flickered. He finished up letting go of the incunabulum, which fell to the floor with a dull sound. Before the cardinal had time to react, Peire bent down, gathered it up and retraced his steps. He took Jordanne by the hand to pull her towards the exit.

Anto was furious. With an abrupt gesture he broke the neck of the old man, who slumped to the ground. Then he stepped over the body and raced in pursuit of the couple. He paid no attention to the trajectory that he was following. Running like a madman, he crossed over the pentagram. He was thrown to the ground as if he had run into an invisible wall.

Anto got to his feet. He trembled with fury in the face of the obstacle raised in front of him.

Peire turned to face him. He was holding the book.

The cardinal threw himself in Peire's direction, howling. His body encountered a resistance that yielded immediately. He fell forward on the flagstones.

He got up. As if in slow motion, his eyes registered Peire's reaction. The latter had raised his hand and was pointing in the direction of the centre of the room. A blue light surrounded his head first, then his entire body. Anto did not see the ball of fire emerge from the pentagram. Abruptly cut down, he collapsed. His clothes caught fire. While he was consumed, his twisted mouth babbled a Pater Noster. The jerky voice echoed briefly in the now-deserted hallway.

Peire stepped over the charred bodies strewn on the flagstones. Very calm, he felt prodigiously indifferent to the sight of the spectacle. The pentagrams had protected the treasure and he had recovered the book. That was all that mattered.

By his side, Jordanne seemed to be in a parlous state. She followed him without resistance, confiding herself entirely to him. Peire took her by the hand and headed for the exit. When they reached the entrance door, an enormous gale of laughter resounded around them. Peire paused and looked in every direction, but did not see the Drac. The laughter died away.

Leaving Jordanne briefly, Peire went back along the hall to kneel beside Jean Rudel's corpse. He stretched the old man out and crossed his arms over his breast. Jean Rudel would no longer be there to help or advise him. Now, he must sort things out himself.

At that moment, Peire realized that through all the important phases of his life, the old man had been present, in a discreet fashion. The Société del Gai Saber had protected him without his being aware of it. He collected himself before the old Cathar's mortal remains, murmuring a prayer, and then he got up again.

He surveyed the devastated hallway one last time. It was important to get rid of all proof of any supernatural phenomenon in these premises. Without knowing how knew it, he was sure that the secrets of Catharism were safe, well-hidden, in the cellars of the building. Before going out, clutching the manuscript to him, Peire made a gesture in the direction of the pentagram.

The couple left the building without running into anyone. Once outside, Peire examined the surroundings. He could not see any of the cardinal's men. He drew Jordanne with him along the street. Behind them, plumes of black smoke rose up from the house.

Peire turned to look back at the burning building. A dove, emerging from nowhere, took flight from a part of the roof that was still intact and passed over his head. He watched it fly away. It seemed to him that he glimpsed some significance in the bird's passage, but the precise sense of it escaped him.

The siren of a fire-engine sounded in the distance. Gawkers were beginning to come running. Peire helped his companion into the car and drove off. They went through the suburbs of Toulouse, then out into the country.

The road was clear. Peire drove without saying a word. From time to time he darted a rapid glance in the direction of his passenger. Jordanne remained silent and distant. Peire did not dare speak to her: she had just undergone a traumatic experience and seemed to be at breaking-point. He took mental stock of recent events. One group of protagonists of the search for the treasure had just been exterminated. That simplified one aspect of the situation. Most important of all, though, he was progressively discovering his own role. With the manuscript, he would know even more.

He put his foot on the accelerator. Montségur was waiting for him.

Chapter 26

The studio was cluttered with papers and empty beer-bottles. The room was weakly illuminated by the dial of the recording equipment. The shutters had not even been opened.

Peire switched off the radio that had controlled the rhythm of his life for a week. He listened to all the news bulletins, on the lookout for the slightest clue. Hardly any journalists were talking any longer about the fire that had destroyed one of the most beautiful monuments in Toulouse and caused the death of some 15 people, several of whom were monks who had come to view an exhibition.

He went down to the kitchen to make a coffee. He started as someone knocked on the window: a man dressed in black. Peire immediately identified him as a priest. He signaled that he would let him in at the door.

"Bonjour, Monsieur Aicart," the man said, when Peire opened the door. "I'm Brother Bernard, Superior of the monastery at Fanjeaux. I'd like to talk to you. I was a friend of Anto Sakic. I knocked several times but you didn't answer, then I made a tour of the house."

Peire let him enter without replying. He pointed to the sitting-room, then to an armchair beside the fireplace. "I hope you're not afraid of getting burned?" he murmured.

"I shan't stay long," Brother Bernard replied, in a neutral voice. "I wanted to give you this."

He held out a little package to Peire, who opened it. It contained a parchment on which a map was drawn. Peire unfolded it carefully. He went to the fireplace to read it by the light of the flames.

"Why?" he asked, raising his eyes again.

"That map was confiscated by the Inquisition from Bélibaste, the last Cathar, in 1321. I thought that it should return to you by right."

"Thanks," Peire stammered, trying to work out what the ecclesiastic was doing.

"Now you're alone in confrontation with your destiny. Anto's gamble failed. Personally, I'll be content to observe you."

"You won't intervene? Your superior was very keen to involve himself in my affairs...."

Brother Bernard did not respond to the quip. "I don't know; everything depends on you...and on the treasure. I simply want to warn you that we will be behind you all the way."

"Thank you. I'll take it under advisement. I won't see you out—you know the way...."

Once again Brother Bernard ignored the irony of the riposte. The priest bowed, turned on his heel, and left the house. Peire examined the map. It would not be of any great us to him. His knowledge of the region was too superficial, even though he had been born in Ariège and had always lived there.

He put down the parchment in order to pick up the manuscript again. He re-read the poem several times, without the lines evoking anything. Jean Rudel was not there to advise him. He could not see the connection between these Occitan verses and the discovery of the treasure.

He had an urge to call Jordanne to ask for her help, but he suppressed it. He had had no further contact with her since the massacre at the Société del Gai Saber. He had called at the restaurant on the day after those terrible events but had found the door closed. A notice on the door announced the closure of the establishment for an indefinite period. Possessed by doubt, he had knocked several times without obtaining any reply. Finally, he had returned home and had telephoned from there. On the tenth ring Jordanne had answered to tell him that she needed to be alone for a while. She would call him back when she felt better.

Since then, Peire had had no further news. After several days he had given up on her. He had devoted himself to studying the parchment, whose significance he had not succeeded in discovering. What had the anonymous troubadour been trying to say? What was the connection between Esclarmonde and the Cathar treasure?

He had researched the Lady in question, learning that she had been burned with 200 other Perfecti on the eve of the day on which the treasure had left the citadel of Montségur. She could not, therefore, have known the location of the treasure.

Peire found himself back at his point of departure. He read the poem again. He hoped to find some detail therein that had escaped him, but in vain. No inspiration came into his mind. There were ten more days until March 16 and he had no way to track down the treasure, no viable clue. He closed the incunabulum again and picked up the map that the priest had just given to him. He tried to interpret it, to set names he knew to the castles, caves and mountains, but he did not get anywhere.

Abruptly, he thrust the map and the incunabulum into a bag, picked up Rahn's journal and put on his coat. Since Jordanne did not wish to help him, Elke would accept without any hesitation. She had telephoned him several times in the last few days but he had preferred to wait before seeing her again. His sentiments regarding Jordanne were ambivalent. He would have liked to establish where he stood with her before finding himself face-to-face with Elke again, but he no longer had time to be patient. Jordanne refused to call him. She had taken the decision for him.

He swept away his last scruples, closed the door of his house and got into his car. An hour later he arrived at the lodgings where Elke was staying. He parked in front of the door. Two men immediately rushed out, pistols in hand. Peire took a step backwards. Elke appeared on the threshold and spoke to them in German.

"Wolfgang and Kurt, my friends," said, introducing the two men to him. "It hardly constitutes a warm welcome, but I'm wary after what happened to the priests in Toulouse."

She kissed him on the mouth: a real kiss. The two Germans faded away discreetly.

Peire went into the sitting-room. Elke gave him a cup of hot coffee while he summarized some of the recent events. Then he told her about the priest's visit. He unfolded the map, showed her the poem and told her that he had reached an impasse. Elke listened attentively. When he had finished she went to the table, where she studied the map more carefully. She held it up to examine it before putting it down again carefully.

"We know four caves that possess pentagrams. This map testifies to the existence of a fifth. That's where the treasure must be.

"But I've checked the ordnance survey maps and I can't figure out where it might be found."

"What if this map is useless?" Elke asked, abruptly.

Peire looked at her uncomprehendingly.

"You've just told me that it belonged to the Catholic Church," she continued. "A trophy of war, since it was in the possession of Bélibaste, who was undoubtedly the last veritable Cathar. Do you really think that he needed a document to tell him where the cave was?"

"So it's a decoy, abandoned by the Perfecti to set the Catholics on a false trail!"

"Why not? In my opinion, it's worthless, except to inflame the imagination of the Inquisitors. On the other hand, the poem seems to me to be very important."

"Was it Anto who told you that?"

For a moment, Elke lost control of her emotions, but she pulled herself together immediately.

"I know that you were in contact with the cardinal at one time," Peire continued.

"That hasn't prevented you from coming to tell me everything, and showing that you trust me by bringing the documents."

"I'm here, it's true. I suppose you had your reasons for associating with Anto Sakic."

"I can explain them to you, if you wish."

"You can tell me some day if you want to, but it's not necessary. It's all the same to me."

"Yes, but you ought to know if you're to take me fully into your confidence," Elke persisted.

Peire set the problem aside with a small hand gesture. Elke abandoned the subject and returned to the manuscript. "Have you heard of the massacre of Avignonet?"

"I've read something about it in a book," Peire replied. "It was because of the assassination of the Papal legates that the second crusade took place. The event was obviously the origin of the fall of Catharism."

Elke pointed to the poem and said: "It was to recover this document that Bernard d'En Marti organized the massacre of Avignonet and took all those risks."

"Impossible! He was perfectly well aware that the murder would have disastrous consequences for the entire region. The Pope could not leave it unpunished. It was the ideal excuse for eradicating Catharism."

"And yet it was done. The document had fallen into the hands of the Inquisitors—I don't know how—but Bernard d'En Marti ensured its recovery, signing his own death-warrant in the process."

"You're sure that it was definitely this manuscript?"

"Yes, I'm certain of it. Anto told me that. The Cathar church left the map in the hands of the Inquisition to put them on a false trail."

"That doesn't explain the importance of the poem. I've looked at it from every angle, but haven't found anything. The Cathars surely didn't employ a secret code—Jean Rudel would have told me. I'm blocked. In the end, I gave up."

"There ought to be a list of names with the poem."

"I don't have anything else. Do you know what it was?"

"According to Anto, it might have been a sort of genealogy, rather like the one included the Bible to prove that Jesus was descended from Adam and Eve. It must concern the guardians of the treasure, or those who can touch it. You must be the last on the list, since Jean Rudel was very precise about your being the only one able to get near it."

Elke took the manuscript and sat down beside Peire. "I'd love you to sing this poem. That might give us a clue."

"But I don't have the least idea of the melody!"

"Don't tell me that you're incapable of improvising. Do you remember the song you performed during the award of the silver Laurel?"

Peire concentrated for a few minutes. He memorized the first stanzas in order not to forget the words. Mentally, he searched for chords. Then he launched himself into it. His voice filled the room. From the first note the words came naturally. The song spoke of Esclarmonde's last day, when she had left Montségur with the long line of Perfecti marching towards the pyres installed at the foot of the citadel. Then she arrived at the foot of the Pog, flanked by two Inquisitors. Esclarmonde sang. She was then transformed into a dove and flew to a mountain, which opened up. The poet concluded by suggesting that his Lady had vanished into the bowels of the Earth.

When he had finished, Elke said: "The dove...sing me the last verse again, please."

Peire sang the requested passage again. Elke listened to it attentively; then a broad smile lit up her face.

"The dove!" she said, leaping to her feet. Then she threw herself around Peire's neck to kiss him.

"If a mere dove can put you in that state, I wish Esclarmonde had turned into a golden eagle!" Peire said, laughing.

"The dove is a clue! Do you know that several engravings of doves have been found in the caves? Historians think that it's a matter of Cathar symbolism. We only have to find one of those caves."

Peire tempered her enthusiasm. "I don't think that can be the solution, Elke. It seems too simple to me to draw a dove on the wall of a cave to say *the treasure's here—help yourself*! The symbol must have another meaning. We have to think about it."

"There's no hurry," Elke said, insinuating her arms beneath Peire's pullover to caress his bare skin.

"He's making love right now."

The words had come out of her mouth without her being aware of it. Jordanne turned round in the restaurant kitchen, which she had closed a week before. Her reflection in the glass showed her an exhausted face. She turned away, unable to bear seeing herself like that any longer. She did not even notice the presence of two green eyes, which were watching her from the other side of the window.

In spite of the pills she took every evening, she had not succeeded in forgetting the frightful experience she had undergone in the hallway of the Gai Saber's house. Every right she dreamed about fire, pentagrams and charred bodies…and Peire had abandoned her for another woman.

That morning, she had wanted to apologize for having ignored him in recent days. She had arrived at his home just in time to see his car disappear round a bend. She knew where he was going. It was obvious.

During the short return journey she had been preoccupied by dark thoughts. Since then, she had been alone in a cold and empty room, incapable of ridding herself of the images crowding her head.

"I'll kill her!" she exclaimed.

She took hold of a large kitchen knife, which she had violently embedded several times over in the underside of a cork mat set in her work-surface. Every time the point sank in, Jordanne imagined that she was striking her rival.

She planted the knife one last time, and then went into the bookshop. Peire belonged to her; she must win him back. But the Drac had not yet appeared, and without its help she was lost.

It was five o'clock in the afternoon when Peire drew up in front of his house. The atmosphere surrounding him was strange: not the slightest sound, no wind, no birdsong. Even the murmurs of the village, which often reached this far, were stifled. He turned to look up at Montségur. A few patches of snow around the Pog testified that winter was reluctant to end.

Peire's gaze lingered on the castle, as if the old stones might send him a message, but no sign came from the mountain. The location of the treasure remained an enigma. Peire had left the manuscript and the map at Elke's house so that she could continue to study them. She had invited him to stay overnight, but he had refused without knowing why. He had a vague need to be alone, at peace, in his home.

He finally abandoned his contemplation, locked the car and turned to the house to go in. Stopping short, he caught his breath.

Chapter 27

Motionless, posed in front of the door, the dove cooed. It was as white as snow. A light breeze coming from the south lifted the soft down on its crop.

Peire stared at it, fascinated. This was the dove he had seen on several occasions in recent weeks. Each time, he had asked himself where it came from. One cn or two occasions he had attempted to follow it. In a flash of inspiration, he made the connection with the poem about Esclarmonde. He knew that the dove was here for him.

Suddenly, the world around him underwent a metamorphosis. Peire froze, and his body seemed to become lighter. Darkness enveloped him, as in the pentagram, and for a moment he thought that he was about to die—but he would not depart in that fashion. He had not yet found the treasure. He heard his heart beating and felt his blood coursing throughout his body. Abruptly, the sensation ebbed away.

He looked around before realizing where he was: in the middle of Montségur, in the immense courtyard. Completely disorientated, he could not understand how he had got there. Kyot appeared in the doorway that gave access to the keep. The old man came towards him, walking unsteadily.

"We're beginning the final act. Wagner would have loved to set this libretto to music."

Peire felt a flash of annoyance. The old man's cryptic speech seemed to him a trifle overcomplicated.

"I still haven't figured out your role in the play."

Kyot gestured vaguely, taking in the fortress and the surrounding countryside. "Seven hundred years ago, a drama was played out here: a crucial episode in the history of humankind. Like others before it, since the appearance of human beings—and who remembers it?"

"Get to the point, Kyot!" Peire said, impatiently.

"I'm the Memory of these places. I remain here so that no one will forget, because there's always one man who has to remember, and—above all—has to be there at the fateful moment.

Peire raised his eyebrows. "And I'm that man?"

"You've known that since the beginning. You've always known it, even if you took no account of it."

Peire was surprised by his own reaction. Curiously, Kyot's words found an echo in him. Another part of his memory had just revealed itself. He looked at the old man gravely.

"Tell me what I have to do, Kyot. I don't even know where to find the treasure. If I do discover it, what am I supposed to do with it? Help me."

"It's not my role to reveal your mission to you. I'm content to perpetuate the memory. The signs you're waiting for are to be found within you."

"And if I fail, what will become of you? What will you do if I ally myself with the Drac and give the treasure to it?"

"You're free to choose. The course of events is a matter of indifference to me. I'm only Memory."

Peire turned aside to hide his disappointment. "Then you too will abandon me?"

"That's in the nature of things. You must confront your destiny alone. Search hard for the answers. Now I have to go; we shall never see one another again."

Kyot addressed one last smile to Peire. Then he marched off in the direction of the citadel's main gate. As he drew away, a dazzling radiance illuminated the courtyard. Peire shielded his eyes. When he took his hand away, he was in front of his house again.

The dove was no longer there.

In its place was the Drac.

"Bonjour, Peire. The hour draws near."

Peire did not react. He was still suffering the shock of Kyot's revelations.

"Have you chosen your side, then?" the Drac asked, with a broad smile.

Peire felt unready for a confrontation, or even a discussion. He still had not made his choice, and had no precise idea of what he was supposed to do. He simply shrugged his shoulders and went past the creature without replying.

"Think of Jordanne...you could be happy together. Give me the treasure and you'll have everything you want."

Peire continued walking calmly toward his house, turning his back on the Drac.

"Is it Elke you want, then? I've seen how much you desire her. You can have her. I can arrange a glorious future for you. You know what I expect in exchange."

Peire took a key out of his coat pocket and inserted it in the lock.

"Ask and you will be served. All that you could wish, even if your wildest dreams. I can give you everything. *Everything.* I only want one thing—a very small thing."

Peire slammed the door behind him.

Chapter 28

The Sun was unable to penetrate the layer of thick grey cloud. The first drops of rain were falling, soon replaced by hailstones. The garden was covered by a sheet of little white grains. The shower continued a little while longer, then stopped.

Peire went out to get some air. He could no longer bear inaction. He walked down the street in front his house, his hand in his pockets. Perhaps he would see the dove. He had not yet seen it again.

Three days had gone by, Three long days of going round in circles, fruitlessly. He had read and re-read the poem. He had sung it over and over again, without getting anything out of it. No clue, no new idea...nothing. Today was March 16. Up above, lost in the clouds, Montségur was on watch.

Peire looked in the direction of the fortress one last time, and then went back in. He began wandering aimlessly between the sitting-room, the bedroom and the studio, unable to settle down to any task. The enigma obsessed him. He had thought long and hard about all the elements comprising it, but he still did not know where the treasure was. He had hope that Kyot's presence might help him, but the old man had not returned. Peire was definitely alone.

He went out of the house again to contemplate the Pog. The weather was clearing slightly. Up above, the walls stood firm under the assault of the tormented skies. Peire shook his head at the thought of the road he had traveled in recent months. A year earlier, he had taken the followers of Catharism for harmless visionaries. For him, the movement was more of a tourist-trap than a genuine religion. Today, though, he would not abandon his quest for anything in the world. Whatever happened, he would do everything he could to discover the secret that his ancestor had protected.

He was increasingly nervous. He was waiting for a sign. What if it did not come? Impossible. Peire was sure of that; something would emerge, entirely naturally, to set him on his way. It was afterwards that everything would become complicated.

"What are you thinking about?"

The somnolent voice drew him out of his mediation. Elke was standing in the doorway. She stretched, and then rubbed her eyes. To hide her nudity she had put on a long woolen pullover, which reached down to her thighs. A fugitive ray of sunlight came through the clouds, illuminating her sleepy face momentarily. With her hair tousled and her gestures nonchalant she seemed to him more beautiful than ever.

She had spent the three preceding days with him, helping him in his research. They had analyzed all the hypotheses, studied all the clues and unpacked every word in the poem before finding themselves back in bed, making love.

"I was thinking about what might happen today."

"Are you ready?"

"Yes. Even though I don't know what's in store for me. I feel like a marionette that everyone's been manipulating since the beginning.

Elke reflected momentarily. "I don't see it that way. Since the beginning you've always had your free will."

"But I've never been able to exercise it. I've been used. How do you know that they're not still toying with me? I feel vulnerable."

"No one can do anything against you—not even the Drac. You know that very well."

Peire was far from sharing his companion's confidence. Elke placed her hand on his and he felt anxiety surge through him. He drew the young woman to him and hugged her very tightly before kissing her tenderly. Then he sat down on a boulder that served as a bench in front of the house. They remained still, looking at the Pog.

Elke finally broke the silence. She got up and said, laughing: "I'm going to get dressed. This isn't the right outfit for searching for the Cathar treasure."

"Wait," Peire murmured.

Peire held her back by the hips and maneuvered her until she was in front of him. Then he slid his hands along the curves of her thighs. He lifted up the pullover and began kissing Elke's soft belly. His mouth approached her blonde fleece.

"I, on the other hand, find you very seductive," he said.

"Peire!" Elke exclaimed, with a little laugh. "If anyone were to see us...."

"They'd think that I'm a lucky man."

With both hands he bent her backwards slightly, then resumed his intimate kisses.

Elke moaned. Her hands gripped Peire's hair. Her body trembled and her breathing accelerated. She stiffened as pleasure arrived.

Elke's cry of joy brought forth an echo. Peire reacted immediately. He raised his head and searched for the origin of the sound.

"The sign...." he murmured.

The dove was cooing a few meters away from them, perched on one of the lower branches of a cherry-tree.

Elke made the link with Esclarmonde de Foix. "You're right. It will guide us."

"It's been coming to see me for weeks. I've wanted to follow it several times. How could I have been so blind?"

Elke smiled at her companion. "Blind? I don't think so. You weren't ready."

"It's waiting for me. Will you come with me?"

"Certainly. But I have to get dressed. I'll hurry, I promise."

Elke went into the house while Peire watched the dove, motionless on its branch. She came out again three minutes later, having hastily put on jeans and sandals. She had retained the large pullover.

Peire turned to the cherry-tree. "Go, we'll follow you," he said to the dove, simply.

The bird immediately took flight.

Crouching behind a rock on the hill overlooking Peire's house, Jordanne put down the pair of binoculars she had been using to spy on the musician and his German whore. She sat back against the rock. Tears poured down her cheeks.

For three long days she had been spying relentlessly. She watched out for their comings and goings and had caught the couple several times kissing outside the house, holding hands, and exchanging complicit glances. By night, she watched the ballet of lights switching off and on in the somber façade. Once, through a ground floor window, she had even seen them snuggle up together, kiss and get undressed. She could not distinguish their bodies clearly, but they had caressed one another, naked, in the lighted bedroom, until Peire had come to close the shutters to protect their intimacy.

The evenings were even harder. Jordanne had spent three days picturing the German woman in Peire's bed, as he made her groan with pleasure. She tortured herself by imagining their amorous play—but what she had just seen was the worst of all. Peire's comportment with his whore, in broad daylight, on the terrace of his house, was a veritable insult to her.

Jordanne had clenched her teeth while she had watched Peire's hands sliding over Elke's body. She had shivered while his mouth was set upon her rival's groin. She had been forced to retain a howl of anguish when Elke found delight beneath the lips of the man who, a few days earlier, had still been her lover.

Jordanne shut her eyes. For three days she had been hoping for a word, a gesture or a summons from Peire. Nothing. It had not come. She no longer existed. The German woman had turned his head, had put a spell on him.

Tears were still running down Jordanne's cheeks. That diabolical woman had stolen the love of her life. At that thought, she wiped her face and tried to pull herself together.

229

She had difficulty suppressing the tremor that shook her hands. After a minute or so, she calmed down.

The restaurant-owner came to her feet. The terrace was deserted. She studied the surrounding area for a moment before catching sight of the couple going into the forest. Jordanne felt a surge of hatred. Today, a symbolic date, Peire had left to meet his destiny. He had chosen to abandon her, who had always loved him, preferring that schemer who only wanted the treasure.

It was time to act if she wanted to win back Peire's love. She went back to her restaurant, put on her mountaineering boots and collected a large knife, which she slipped into a small knapsack. She no longer had any other choice than conflict. Peire belonged to her; she would fight tooth and claw to get him back. She closed the door, took a walking-stick and marched toward Peire's house. When she reached the edge of the village she took a side-path that headed towards the woods. Higher up the slope, she turned on to the hunting-path that the couple had taken.

Behind her, a mocking laugh resounded. The Drac had been keeping her company for three days. She had not even noticed its presence. She scarcely paid attention to its comments regarding Peire and his whore. It had returned to the subject incessantly since she had found it in her restaurant, waiting for her, after the fire at the house of the Gai Saber. As time had gone by, she had become more and more inclined to take up its offer, although she had not given it her word.

The Drac was triumphant It had her in its power. Furious, she kicked a pebble, which rebounded along the road. There was no question of going back. She would lose her soul, but, with the Drac's help, she would get Peire back. In exchange, the Devil might take what it wanted. That was no longer of any importance to her.

Chapter 29

As Peire and Elke went further up the valley the summits of the Pyrenees seemed to draw closer. Fatigue was creasing their faces, for they had been walking for four hours along ancient pathways overgrown with vegetation. They had crossed fords, climbed steep slopes, stumbled on ancient moraines, following a narrow path with a sheer drop to one side along the flank of the mountain. They had also encountered a quagmire into which they had sunk knee-deep, obliging them to make a detour. For a moment they had been afraid that the dove might outdistance them, but every time they paused it waited for them, perched on a branch or a rock.

The path was now winding through the bottom of a steep-sided gorge. After a particularly difficult passage, they had called a brief halt to recover.

Elke seemed exhausted. "Do you have any idea where it's taking us?" she asked, breathlessly.

"None. The summit to our right is the Pic de Saint-Barthélémy. It overlooks the valleys of Montségur and Ussat.

"Ussat...that's where the caves used by the Cathars for initiations were, with the pentagram and dove designs. Do you think it might be taking us to those caves?"

"I don't know. There are numerous caves a little higher up. I once explored one of them. My ancestor might have hidden the treasure in one of them...but that's pure conjecture."

"We're not heading towards the famous legendary lake?"

Peire studied the path before replying. "No, that's further to the right. It seems to me that this path is taking us towards the peak."

In front of them, the dove took off. It fluttered its wings briefly before coming to rest in a tree a little further away, where it waited for the couple before resuming its flight.

The path ran beside the turbulent waters of a torrent. Behind them, in the distance, on the other side of the valley, the castle of Montségur was watching over them, but it disappeared around a bend, leaving them alone. A little higher up the path plunged into the forest again.

They marched on for some time beneath the conifers, breathing in the odor of their resin. They were treading on a thick carpet of fallen needles. The dove took flight yet again to perch on a branch at the edge of a clearing. In the midst of the thickly-clustered tree-trunks it was hard to make out. Peire instinctively hastened his steps. Every time that he saw it fly off, he had but one dread: that of losing it. It was their only guide. But it always waited for him.

After walking for 20 minutes up an increasingly steep slope, the silence of the forest was suddenly broken by a noise in the foliage 30 meters lower down. Peire turned his head, his pulse accelerating violently. A capercaillie flew over their heads. Elke stopped beside him, hands on hips, short of breath.

"I can't go on any longer," she murmured.

"We're entitled to a rest," Peire said.

He studied the surroundings, trying to get his bearings. He had no idea where they might be going. He would have liked to see Kyot or Bernard d'En Marti appear, but he was under no illusion. He must entrust himself entirely to the dove.

Peire turned towards Elke, who had sat down on a rock, and held his hand out to her.

"Shall we go on?"

Elke got up, with a sigh. The dove resumed its flight towards the summit.

They resumed their interminable march. They did not exchange a single word. They put one foot in front of the other like two well-oiled machines. Sometimes, one of them stumbled, but immediately continued to make progress.

Peire and Elke had left the forest. Having left the trees behind them, they were now in a region of arid scrub. Stunted bushes huddled around scattered rocks. The soil was dry, and the cracked ground was strewn with stones.

The couple advanced mechanically. They had passed beyond fatigue. They could have marched for days in that rhythm.

In the middle of a clearing the dove landed on a dead tree. They overtook it without noticing that the bird had not quit its perch. After a few meters, Peire realized that the dove was behind them. He frowned. Elke stopped in her turn.

"I'm not tired, you know. We can go on."

"Look!" Peire said, sharply. "The dove isn't taking off."

Elke did not understand right away. She stared at the tree. The bird did not move.

"Do you think this is the location of the treasure?" she asked.

"If the dove has stopped, it's doubtless because we've arrived—but I can't see the entrance of a cave. Look in that direction, and I'll explore this way.

After ten minutes of searching they met up again in the clearing. There was not the least trace of a cave, no fissure in the rocks. The place seemed perfectly ordinary.

"Your ancestor must have buried the treasure here. I don't see any alternative."

"You're right. I'm an idiot—I made absolutely no provision for that eventuality. I haven't brought a spade. How are we going to dig?"

"With our hands."

"But we don't even know where it is! Are we supposed to get down on all fours? It will take hours."

Elke reflected momentarily. "And what if the treasure isn't here?"

Peire immediately rejected that possibility. The treasure had to be here, close by. He did not know why or how, but he was sure of it—absolutely sure.

He studied the clearing. The dove was still perched on the dead tree. By degrees, he became aware of a peculiar ambience surrounding the tree. It was as if the humus radiated an intense serenity, which impregnated the whole place.

Suddenly, he had a feeling of foreboding: a violent sensation of irrational fear that only lasted a fraction of a second. He regained control of himself and examined the surrounding terrain. Everything was calm. There was no apparent reason to panic, but Peire remained prey to a profound malaise. The dove had not budged. When he looked at it more attentively, its attitude seemed bizarre.

Peire drew closer to the dead tree. The bird remained quite still. He came close enough to reach out his hand to touch the white plumage. The dove was cold and rigid. It resembled a stuffed animal. Peire withdrew his hand.

"What time is it?" Elke asked, unconscious of the anxiety afflicting her companion.

"2:20 p.m. Why?"

"We still have time to search. Perhaps the entrance to the cave is a little further away."

Mechanically, Peire put his hand on the tree. He shivered. His fingers had contracted about a branch, as if by some reflex. A black veil covered his eyes for several seconds, while the muscles of his face were paralyzed. Then he relaxed his grip, shook his hand and took a step backwards.

Elke looked at him in surprise.

"What kind of tree is this?" he asked her.

Elke raised her eyebrows. She had not expected any such question. She came closer, in her turn, and examined the tree. "I'm not an expert gardener. Why?"

Peire ignored Elke's reply. He walked around the tree, examining it minutely. He caressed it several times. All of a sudden, it became obvious to him.

"The laurel!" he exclaimed. "A laurel...." The words of the song came quite naturally to his lips: "*Al cap del set cents ans, verdeja lo laurel.*"

Elke immediately understood what he meant. "Do you think this tree is the laurel in the song?"

He reflected for a few seconds. He had simply been reminded of the song, but she had just voiced a possibility that he had not glimpsed before."

"I'm convinced that this laurel has a connection with the treasure."

"Your ancestor presumably buried the treasure here and planted the tree so that it could easily be found again," Elke concluded.

Peire remained unconvinced. He examined the bush without any clear idea of what he was looking for. He still felt a slight anxiety deep inside. Elke had picked up a large stone and knelt down to scratch around the roots.

"I don't think that can be the right answer," he said.

"The treasure's here, that's certain," Elke replied, digging harder. "It's March 16, and the dove led us here. This is the laurel in the song. What more do you need?"

"Stop—you might ruin everything…."

"What are you saying? On the contrary, it's necessary to uproot it to get deeper down."

"The tree *is* the treasure," Peire said, gravely.

Elke stopped abruptly. She raised her head to look at her companion.

"How can a tree be the treasure? That doesn't make sense. You're talking nonsense."

She went back to work frenetically, grunting with effort.

"Stop!"

"Why stop? We're so close! The treasure's there, waiting for us!"

"There's nothing underneath it by soil and rocks."

"How do you know that?"

"Think about it, "Peire said. "It's obvious."

Elke got up. She touched the tree. Her fingers were instantly immobilized. A flood of warmth flowed up her arm. She calmed down. She withdrew her hand, and then advanced it again, towards the tree. She felt the same sensations.

"If the tree is the treasure, then it wasn't hidden by your ancestor and I don't understand the purpose of your presence." Elke's voice was slightly tremulous.

"*Verdeja lo laurel*," Peire repeated. "It will flower today—you'll see."

Peire began to sing.

Elke interrupted him "No, not that song! Try the poem instead. Do you remember the words?"

"Yes," he replied, without hesitation.

Elke came towards Peire, took him in her arms and kissed him on the lips. "Go on, then," she said.

Holding Elke against him, he began to perform the poem. He had closed his eyes in concentration. His deep voice filled the clearing.

Elke trembled with emotion. Peire had never sung as well. Suddenly, she held her breath: the dead tree had put out a bud. Then another appeared. She dared not interrupt Peire, who was in mid-song. Astonished, she watched the metamorphosis of the laurel that was returning to life. It was now covered in little pale green shoots. Little by little, there were opening up to form elongated leaves of a deeper shade.

As Peire began the final verse, a voice sounded in the silence of the woods.

"Get away from him!"

Jordanne was standing three meters away from them, a knife in her hand. She had the appearance of a madwoman.

"He loves me. You stole him from me with your honeyed words. Now it's finished—you're going to die."

"You don't know what you're saying, Jordanne," said Peire, searching for words to calm her down. "We'll talk about it, straighten it all out—but first put down the knife."

"Yes, my love, it will all be straightened out. When I've killed her, we'll be together again, and we'll talk, just like before."

Peire shuddered. A wild hatred was burning in Jordanne's eyes. "I love her," he said, softly. "You can't do anything to change that."

"That's what you think, my angel. She's bewitched you. She's amusing herself with you, and only wants to get her hands on the treasure. Think about it, and you'll see that I'm right. The treasure is for the two of us, and no one else."

Peire detached himself from Elke and went to stand beside the tree.

"Here's the treasure! A simple laurel-bush...nothing to do with the Grail, gold coins or an emerald, is it?"

Jordanne approached in her turn, without he eyes ever leaving Elke. She examined the bush at close range. She placed her hand on a leaf.

Jordanne was seized by a violent vertigo, and an electrical discharge climbed up her arm. She recoiled. Tremulously, she pointed her finger at Elke. "Even this tree refuses to let me touch it! It's your fault!"

"You're delirious," Elke replied, disdainfully. "I haven't done anything."

"You've taken him from me," Jordanne roared. "You've slept with all the men in the region, and as that wasn't enough for you, you wanted him. Because he was mine. You're nothing but a filthy German whore. He's fucked you like a prostitute."

Elke looked daggers at Jordanne, who had just wounded her deeply. She had already had to suffer so many insulting speeches in the past, because of her nationality, or rather because of her grandfather. She had promised herself never to allow herself to be treated in that fashion again. She experienced a cold rage. She hurled herself at her rival.

Peire was quicker. He grabbed the arm that was holding the knife and forced it backwards. She resisted, and the blade embedded itself in Peire's forearm. He released Jordanne and stepped back. He put his hand over the wound to stem the flow of blood.

Elke took advantage of the opportunity to attack. She disarmed Jordanne with a single whirling kick. The knife fell to the ground a meter from the laurel. Then she threw herself into hand-to-hand combat.

Although Elke was trained in combat techniques she was surprised by Jordanne's determination. Blinded by jealousy, the latter acquired an uncommon strength.

Elke concentrated in order to making her assault scientif-
ically. She weathered the blows as best she could, attempting
to parry them. Jordanne lashed out, scratched and bit. Elke
applied a hold designed to destabilize her adversary, but Jordanne grabbed her by the hair, dragging her down with her.
The two women rolled on the ground.

Wounded and powerless, Peire watched the scene unfold.
The two combatants were punching one another ferociously.

After a long struggle Elke ended up sitting astride her rival. She immobilized her by trapping her arms beneath her
knees. She put both hands around her neck, and squeezed her
carotid arteries with her thumbs. Jordanne was about to faint.
Elke savored her triumph momentarily.

A cracking sound reverberated in the depths of the wood
with such violence that the tree-branches bent. A green mist
materialized at the edge of the clearing. The Drac appeared,
and subsequent events seemed to occur in slow motion.

It simply lifted a finger. Elke felt a burning pain in her
chest, and was hurled backwards. Her head collided with a
large stone. A trickle of blood stained her blonde hair.

Jordanne coughed. Still dazed, she got up on her knees,
rubbing her aching throat.

"Kill her!" growled the creature, addressing itself to Jordanne.

Jordanne crawled in the direction of the knife, which was
lying on the ground two meters away. She grabbed it and
moved towards Elke, who was rising to her feet with difficulty. She raised her arm to strike with all her strength.

Peire had also precipitated himself towards them, with
the intention of disarming Jordanne. His foot tripped over a
root. He fell forwards, into the knife's trajectory. Jordanne did
not have time to react. The blade plunged into his breast.

Releasing a scream, Jordanne let go of the weapon's hilt,
and covered her face with both hands.

Peire looked at the protruding hilt in astonishment. He
felt nothing. He seized the knife and withdrew it abruptly from

the wound. He felt the warmth of the blood impregnating his shirt. Suddenly, his legs gave way under him and he collapsed.

Everything became clear to him.

Elke ran to his side. She knelt down. A single glance established the seriousness of the situation. At the sight of the blood flowing from the wound she howled, and seized the knife. With a neat and well-aimed throw, she hurled it in Jordanne's direction. The latter remained motionless, stuck by stupor. The blade embedded itself in her throat. Jordanne collapsed to the ground.

The Drac burst into gales of laughter. It had enjoyed the spectacle.

Elke learned over the man she loved tenderly. Until that moment, she had not realized the strength of the sentiments she harbored. She caressed his hair gently. He was breathing with difficulty. His eyes seemed to be fixed on a point directly behind her. He nodded his head in the direction of the bush and managed to articulate a few words that she did not catch. She put her ear to the wounded man's lips.

"The laurel.... Get me closer...to the laurel," he murmured. "I have to finish the song."

Elke knew that it was important. She positioned herself at the level of his head and passed her arms beneath his armpits. Bracing herself, she began to drag him over the ground.

A bestial cry went up from the edge of the trees. "No!" The Drac's terrible voice echoed in the clearing. Elke looked up.

It became wheedling. "Don't do that, Elke. Don't move his body. You might kill him."

"He'll die anyway."

"I can bring him back to life...."

"You're lying! Only God has the power to give life."

"Ah, life...I can't restore life, that's true. But what is life, actually? I know how to create the illusion of life. You'll never even know that he's dead. You'll have him to yourself—entirely to yourself. Bring him to me and I'll revive him."

239

Elke hesitated. The idea of saving Peire was tempting. She recalled the last three days they had spent together: their joy, their laughter, their kisses. She imagined spending her whole life with him....

A discreet groan from Peire attracted her attention. He opened his mouth in one final effort. "No, Elke...the laurel," he murmured, in a single breath.

Painfully, he lifted his arm and succeeded in taking her hand. He squeezed it. Elke shivered. As in the moment when she had touched the bush, she felt secure and calm. She understood what Peire expected of her. Taking hold of her companion's body again, she resumed dragging it.

"Stop!" shouted the Devil.

The Drac groaned. It lifted a finger. Elke felt a pressure on her back, which impeded her progress. For a second, she was overwhelmed by discouragement. She burst into sobs.

Peire moaned. Elke mobilized all her strength and composure. "No! I won't give up!" she cried, bracing herself to push back the invisible wall.

She gained about a meter.

"STOP!"

The Drac moved its hand. Elke felt as if all her limbs were paralyzed. She fought with all her might to continue her progress, centimeter by centimeter.

"STOP!"

The Drac snarled and extended its arms in Elke's direction. She was hurled backwards. She landed on her back. The fall knocked the breath out of her. She stood up, set her feet under Peire's armpits, bent her knees, and picked him up again. She held him in her arms, hugging him to her bosom, and continued her painful advance.

The Devil howled. She was jostled and shaken, but Elke continued to gain ground. It scarcely mattered to her that she was being maltreated. She no longer had anything to lose. She had decided to sacrifice herself for Peire. Blows rained down upon her, but she always got up again.

As she came closer to the laurel, Elke felt the creature's power diminish. The tree was protecting her. She was now dragging Peire's body without difficulty.

"If you want him, come and get him," she said, challenging the Drac.

The Devil howled. It advanced towards the couple. A flash of lightning rose up from the ground and struck it, obliging it to retreat.

"I can't penetrate this clearing!" it raged.

"Get away!" Elke exclaimed.

The Drac released a terrible howl. It lifted its fists toward the sky. A muffled rumbling sound climbed the mountain by degrees. Grey clouds formed and there was a crash of thunder. A violent wind blew over the forest. The trees were bent, leaves were torn away, branches snapped. The tormented clouds opened up to release enormous hailstones. Lightning striped the sky, hurtling toward the ground. Loud explosions reverberated in the valley as the thunderbolts touched down. In the midst of the unchained elements, the Devil gave voice.

From the shelter of the clearing, the impassive Elke ignored it, her hair barely stirred by a faint breeze. With one last effort, she finished dragging her companion and set him down by her side, at the foot of the laurel. She remained bent over him, prostrate, on the lookout for the slightest sign of life.

Peire no longer felt anything. He made out the tree in a red blur, and then lowered his eyes to look at his wound. His blood was running on to the exposed roots of the tree and was absorbed by the soil.

Peire opened his mouth to finish the song. It was no more than a murmur, but he finally sang the last couplet of the poem. A long tunnel of light appeared in front of him. He had already visited that place. He was not afraid He went forward, his mind at peace, knowing what awaited him at the far end. Bernard d'En Marti came to meet him and welcome him with open arms.

Elke moaned. Peire's face had taken on an ochreous hue. His breast was rising and falling weakly. His last reserves of strength were ebbing away. A flicker of lucidity showed in his gaze, which then clouded over again. She leaned over, and collected his last breath in her mouth.

Raising her tearful eyes again, she could not help marveling. Rays of warm spring sunlight were falling into the clearing. Haloed by a soft light, the laurel was covered with delicate pink flowers.

The Drac lowered its arms. In spite of its power, the tempest had been calmed instantaneously.

"You've won, but I still have eternity before me," it said, spitefully. "Human beings aren't yet ready to attain perfection. I'll have other opportunities."

A blue light rose from the ground. The earth began to tremble. The creature's body exploded, struck by a thunderbolt emitted from the clearing. The echo of its strident voice continued to sound momentarily, before being lost amid the trees. The green mist had dissipated,

Elke finally noticed the geometrical form of the clearing: an immense pentagram.

For a little while, the forest was silent, as if struck by a stupor. Then, little by little, birdsong increased.

Kyot approached Peire's corpse and leaned over to stroke his forehead.

"Why?" Elke asked, her face covered in tears and her body shaken by sobs.

The old man lifted her up and caressed one of the laurel-flowers, emotionally. "He had to give his life to save those of all human beings," he replied. "Every 700 years the laurel must flower, and for that it needs a human sacrifice."

"Why Peire?"

"Because he's the descendant of a very long line, which extends back into the mists of time. Only an Aicart can revive the laurel."

Elke bent over Peire's corpse, took his hand and squeezed it hard.

"The laurel gives life to human beings," Kyot went on, with conviction. "The Earth belongs to the Devil, but it does not possess human beings. They have a chance of attaining Paradise, on condition that they become good. And as they cannot achieve that in one life alone, the soul is reincarnated from generation to generation until it is perfect."

"I still don't understand why Peire had to die."

"As his ancestors have done before him, he came to save the world for seven centuries. The sole condition of human reincarnation is that the laurel comes into flower. An Aicart must give his life and sing the poem. Peire's blood and voice allowed it to flourish."

"What if he hadn't come? Or if he'd died—what would have happened?"

"Then the Devil would have won. Souls, no longer able to reincarnate, would belong to it for all eternity."

"Why hasn't the Drac destroyed the laurel?"

"It doesn't have the power to do so. Inside this pentagram it can do nothing. These geometrical figures are linked to the Tree of Life. They exist in order to keep the Drac prisoner in the bowels of the Earth, within a narrow perimeter. Most of the time, it's asleep. Every 700 years, it wakes up, and its powers increase until the laurel flowers again, precipitating it into limbo again." Kyot drew a dove's feather out of his pocket and stroked it delicately. "Only the man designated by the dove may choose to sacrifice himself to save humankind," he concluded.

Elke wiped away her tears and rose to her feet. "You mean that Peire has made a gift of his body, like Christ?"

"He also, by his sacrifice, permitted humans to have a chance of attaining Paradise," he agreed.

"Why did he have to die? He might have lived. You said that it's his blood that made the laurel flower."

"No, it was his death. But Peire's soul still lives. It will be reincarnated after passing through a place of purification, where the images of those he has loved await him—Michel, Hélène and others. That's how the cycle is always completed.

243

The descendancy has never been interrupted. The Société del Gai Saber is there to attest to it; for centuries it has watched over the Aicarts. Before that, other organizations watched over the line."

"But Peire has no child. What will happen now?"

Kyot shook his head. "That's a veritable problem. I suppose it will find its solution. Doubtless another family, designated by Bernard d'En Marti, will take up the torch. I have no knowledge of the future; I can testify only to the past. But I know one thing: the cycle will continue."

"You seem very sure of yourself...."

"I was there when the first man was sacrificed and I'll be present when the last dies and all humankind will become Perfecti—if the Devil doesn't triumph before then."

Kyot turned his back and crossed the clearing. He disappeared into the foliage.

Elke remained standing for a long time, turned towards the direction he had taken, staring into infinity. She did not notice that one of the laurel's petals had fallen into her open hand, which was posed over Peire's body.

Chapter 30

On the other side of the window the leafless trees trembled in the cold. The sky was grey. Surrounded by sinister buildings, the lot where a bare dozen cars were parked formed a blank and lugubrious space. The bitumen was covered in snow. A few flakes were still falling.

Elke caught sight of her reflection in the glass. She seemed exhausted, and there were dark circles under her eyes. She had lost her arrogant demeanor and no longer put on make-up. She bore the stigmata of ordeals undergone.

Since Peire's death time had been drawn out in a melancholy fashion. She had lived through a terrible spring, during which she had thought that she would never get over her pain. A long summer, hot and toilsome, had exhausted her physically. Autumn had come in its turn, more depressing still. With the arrival of winter, she hardly went out any more. Three long seasons had dulled the grief somewhat, but not the memories.

In two weeks time the Christians would be celebrating the birth of their Christ. Elke recalled another savior, who had given his life that a tree might flourish, thus winning a respite for humankind, without anyone knowing. Her heart constricted. People everywhere were looking forward to the holiday and to enjoying themselves. Millions of children would go into ecstasy at the sight of toys placed at the feet of fir-trees. In spite of the approach of that period of general rejoicing, though, she found herself alone in this white room, with a simple bed, a television and a bag containing a few clothes.

She had always detested hospitals.

A diffuse pain gripped her abdomen, a brutal reminder of the reason for her presence in this place. Elke doubled up, stifling a small scream. She was reluctant to call for a nurse.

A few seconds later, the pain diminished. Elke took a deep breath and straightened herself out again.

Elke walked to the bed, lifted the coverlet and sat down on the white sheet. She pivoted to install herself in a semi-recumbent position, with her back supported by the pillow. She took an old incunabulum out of the handbag set on her bedside table. Since Peire's death the work had never been out of her custody. They had been reading it together on that last day, just before seeing the dove. Like the few other personal items of his that she had kept, it was a souvenir of the man she loved.

She put the book close by, under the pillow. She took up her Walkman, into which Peire's cassette was permanently loaded, put the earphones on and pressed the PLAY button. Then she went to sleep, lulled by the music.

A pressure on her hand made her jump. She opened her eyes abruptly. A young man was standing next to the bed. He was tall, dark, a trifle awkward, and his chestnut-brown eyes were full of compassion.

"You startled me, Simon," she said, removing the headset.

"How are you, Elke? We were told that you had been admitted to hospital and were worried."

"I'm all right, thanks," Elke replied, nodding her head. "As well as can be expected in my condition, at any rate."

Simon studied her for a few moments. In spite of the fatigue, she seemed to be in good shape. Her beauty had not faded away; it was now a simple, natural beauty. These last months had been very hard, though. She had recovered slowly from the ordeal she had undergone. She seemed calmer now, more at peace, having learned to live with the burden of the past.

"Will you allow me to keep you company until the end?" Simon asked, timidly.

"Certainly—but that might take time, and you must have other things to do."

Simon sat down next to the bed. "I'll stay as long as necessary. You need help, and someone to be with you. I'm here to watch out for you, don't forget that."

Elke stared at him briefly, without saying anything. "I owe you so much—you and your friends...." she said, finally. "You've already done so much for me. What would have become of me without you?"

"Your place is here, among us," Simon affirmed. "The Société del Gai Saber will always watch over you."

Mechanically, Elke lifted her hand to the medallion that she wore around her neck: a Cathar cross. She placed her other hand on her distended belly and caressed it. Life was in there. A slight kick responded to the gentle pressure she exerted.

Suddenly, Elke grimaced. A new pain afflicted her kidneys and spread to her hips. She stiffened as the wave gripped her uterus and began to breathe in the manner she had learned in ante-natal classes.

The contractions were becoming more rapid and increasingly powerful. The birth was expected that evening, if all went well. The baby she had been carrying for nine months would finally see the light of day. Peire's baby.

"The baby's coming, Simon," she said. "Will you be able to take care of the birth-certificate?"

"No problem. I'll do that for you. I hoped you'd ask."

"I regret that the child can't bear his father's name."

That thought brought tears to Elke's eyes. Since the second sonogram she had known that she was expecting a son. He would resemble his father. But he would not be called Aicart.

"Elke I need to talk to you. We have a proposition to put to you."

"I'm listening."

Simon cleared his throat and continued: "It's important to both of us that this child should be officially recognized as Peire's legitimate son. Traditionally, the name of Aicart has always been attached to the laurel. The line has never been interrupted."

"And how do you expect to accomplish that?"

"One of the members of the Société del Gai Saber works in the civil service, at the Mairie. We've explained the situation to him. He's prepared to inscribe in the registers, under the date of March 1, an anticipated recognition of paternity made by Peire before his death. It's the only way to ensure the paternal affiliation, so that the child can bear his father's name. We need your agreement, in order that the marginal legality of the operation is never revealed."

"You're talking about producing a forgery."

"Elke, it's a matter of the survival of the human race."

"I suppose you know what you're doing."

"You've nothing to fear. I've been working on the problem since I took over the direction of the Société. I have all the necessary support. Will you authorize me to register the baby as Peire's legitimate son? What are you going to call him?"

"I'd like him to be named Michel," she said, smiling. "Michel Aicart."

Simon sighed with relief. Elke had given him her approval.

Elke hesitated, then took out the book that she had placed under her pillow. "This should return to you. Simon. I thought of keeping it in memory of Peire, but after the inestimable gift that you've just made me, I have to give it back to you."

Simon took the volume and examined it religiously. "*La Croisade des Albigeois*!" he exclaimed. "We thought it had been lost."

"Cherish it, carefully. The poem about Esclarmonde de Foix will bring the dove back one day…."

For the infant stirring within her, she softly hummed the song of Montségur. The cycle would not be broken. In 700 years, the laurel would flower again."

THE END

SF & FANTASY

Guy d'Armen. *Doc Ardan: The City of Gold and Lepers*
G.-J. Arnaud. *The Ice Company*
Aloysius Bertrand. *Gaspard de la Nuit*
Félix Bodin. *The Novel of the Future*
André Caroff. *The Terror of Madame Atomos*
Didier de Chousy. *Ignis*
C. I. Defontenay. *Star (Psi Cassiopeia)*
Charles Derennes. *The People of the Pole*
Harry Dickson. *The Heir of Dracula*
Sâr Dubnotal *vs. Jack the Ripper*
Alexandre Dumas. *The Return of Lord Ruthven*
J.-C. Dunyach. *The Night Orchid. The Thieves of Silence*
Henri Duvernois. *The Man Who Found Himself*
Henri Falk. *The Age of Lead*
Paul Féval. *Anne of the Isles. Knightshade. Revenants. Vampire City. The Vampire Countess. The Wandering Jew's Daughter*
Paul Féval, *fils. Felifax, the Tiger-Man*
Arnould Galopin. *Doctor Omega*
V. Hugo, Foucher & Meurice. *The Hunchback of Notre-Dame*
Michel Jeury. *Chronolysis*
O. Joncquel & Theo Varlet. *The Martian Epic*
Jean de La Hire. *Enter the Nyctalope. The Nyctalope on Mars. The Nyctalope vs. Lucifer*
G. Le Faure & H. de Graffigny. *The Extraordinary Adventures of a Russian Scientist Across the Solar System* (2 vols.)
Gustave Le Rouge. *The Vampires of Mars*
Jules Lermina. *Mysteryville. Panic in Paris. To-Ho and the Gold Destroyers*
Jean-Marc & Randy Lofficier. *Edgar Allan Poe on Mars. The Katrina Protocol. Pacifica. Robonocchio. Tales of the Shadowmen* (anthos.; 6 vols.)
Xavier Mauméjean. *The League of Heroes*
Marie Nizet. *Captain Vampire*
C. Nodier, Beraud & Toussaint-Merle. *Frankenstein*

Henri de Parville. *An Inhabitant of the Planet Mars*
Polidori, C. Nodier, E. Scribe. *Lord Ruthven the Vampire*
P.-A. Ponson du Terrail. *The Vampire and the Devil's Son*
Maurice Renard. *The Blue Peril. Doctor Lerne. The Doctored Man . A Man Among the Microbes. The Master of Light*
Albert Robida. *The Adventures of Saturnin Farandoul. The Clock of the Centuries.*
J.-H. Rosny Aîné. *Helgvor of the Blue River. The Givreuse Enigma. The Mysterious Force. The Navigators of Space. Vamireh. The World of the Variants. The Young Vampire*
Brian Stableford. *The New Faust at the Tragicomique. Frankenstein and the Vampire Countess. The Shadow of Frankenstein. Sherlock Holmes & The Vampires of Eternity. The Stones of Camelot. The Wayward Muse.* (anthologist) *The Germans on Venus. News from the Moon*
Kurt Steiner. *Ortog*
Villiers de l'Isle-Adam. *The Scaffold. The Vampire Soul*
Philippe Ward. *Artahe*
Philippe Ward & Sylvie Miller. *The Song of Montségur*

MYSTERIES & THRILLERS

M. Allain & P. Souvestre. *The Daughter of Fantômas*
Anicet-Bourgeois, Lucien Dabril. *Rocambole*
A. Bisson & G. Livet. *Nick Carter vs. Fantômas*
V. Darlay & H. de Gorsse. *Lupin vs. Holmes: The Stage Play*
Paul Féval. *Gentlemen of the Night. John Devil. The Black Coats: The Cadet Gang. The Companions of the Treasure. Heart of Steel. The Invisible Weapon. The Parisian Jungle. 'Salem Street*
Emile Gaboriau. *Monsieur Lecoq*
Steve Leadley. *Sherlock Holmes: The Circle of Blood*
Maurice Leblanc. *Arsène Lupin vs. Countess Cagliostro. Lupin vs. Holmes: The Blonde Phantom. The Hollow Needle.*
Gaston Leroux. *Chéri-Bibi. The Phantom of the Opera. Rouletabille & the Mystery of the Yellow Room*
William Patrick Maynard. *The Terror of Fu Manchu*

Frank J. Morlock. *Sherlock Holmes: The Grand Horizontals*
P. de Wattyne & Y. Walter. *Sherlock Holmes vs. Fantômas*
David White. *Fantômas in America*

SCREENPLAYS

Mike Baron. *The Iron Triangle*
Emma Bull & Will Shetterly. *Nightspeeder. War for the Oaks*
Gerry Conway & Roy Thomas. *Doc Dynamo*
Steve Englehart. *Majorca*
James Hudnall. *The Devastator*
Jean-Marc & Randy Lofficier. *Royal Flush*
J.-M. & R. Lofficier & Marc Agapit. *Despair*
Andrew Paquette. *Peripheral Vision*
R. Thomas, J. Hendler & L. Sprague de Camp. *Rivers of Time*

NON-FICTION

Stephen R. Bissette. *Blur 1-5. Green Mountain Cinema 1*
Win Scott Eckert. *Crossovers* (2 vols.)
Jean-Marc & Randy Lofficier. *Shadowmen* (2 vols.)
Randy Lofficier. *Over Here*

HEXAGON COMICS

Franco Frescura & Luciano Bernasconi. *Wampus 1*
Franco Frescura & Giorgio Trevisan. *CLASH*
 Luciano Bernasconi, Jean-Marc Lofficier & Juan Roncagliolo
Berger. *Phenix 1*
Claude Legrand, Jean-Marc Lofficier & Luciano Bernasconi.
Kabur 1
Franco Oneta. *Zembla 1*
Lina Buffolente, Jean-Marc Lofficier & Jean-Jacques Dzia-
lowski. *Stangers 1: Homicron*
Danilo Grossi. *Strangers 2: Jaydee*
Claude Legrand & Luciano Bernasconi. *Strangers 3: Starlock*